SO-AIP-686

Lori Copeland
Catherine Creel
Kay McMahon
Bobbi Smith

Loves so rapturous, passions so strong, they transcend the boundaries of the ages. Here is a breathtaking quartet of timeless tales from four of the most accomplished authors in the realm of romantic fiction—stories of rebirth and renewal, of lovers magically united across the centuries. Share the wonder, the exhilarating ecstasy, the exquisite glory of love eternal and true—that neither time nor destiny can deny.

Avon Books Presents

Timeless Love

*Don't Miss These Romantic Holiday Anthologies
from Avon Books*

AVON BOOKS PRESENTS:
BEWITCHING LOVE STORIES

AVON BOOKS PRESENTS:
A CHRISTMAS COLLECTION

AVON BOOKS PRESENTS:
CHRISTMAS LOVE STORIES

AVON BOOKS PRESENTS:
CHRISTMAS ROMANCE

AVON BOOKS PRESENTS:
HAUNTING LOVE STORIES

Avon Books are available at special quantity discounts for bulk purchases for sales promotions, premiums, fund raising or educational use. Special books, or book excerpts, can also be created to fit specific needs.

For details write or telephone the office of the Director of Special Markets, Avon Books, Dept. FP, 1350 Avenue of the Americas, New York, New York 10019, 1-800-238-0658.

Avon Books Presents

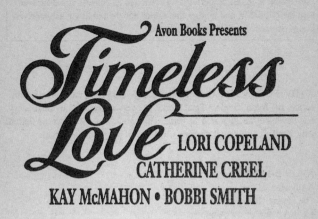

Timeless Love

LORI COPELAND
CATHERINE CREEL
KAY McMAHON • BOBBI SMITH

"A Sutton Press Book"

AVON BOOKS • NEW YORK

If you purchased this book without a cover, you should be aware that this book is stolen property. It was reported as "unsold and destroyed" to the publisher, and neither the author nor the publisher has received any payment for this "stripped book."

AVON BOOKS PRESENTS: TIMELESS LOVE is an original publication of Avon Books. This work, as well as each individual story, has never before appeared in print. This work is a collection of fiction. Any similarity to actual persons or events is purely coincidental.

AVON BOOKS
A division of
The Hearst Corporation
1350 Avenue of the Americas
New York, New York 10019

For All Time copyright © 1993 by Sutton Press and Lori Copeland
Timeswept Love copyright © 1993 by Sutton Press and Catherine Creel
Destiny's Spell copyright © 1993 by Sutton Press and Kay McMahon
Eden's Gate copyright © 1993 by Sutton Press and Bobbi Smith

Published by arrangement with Sutton Press, Inc.
Library of Congress Catalog Card Number: 92-90421
ISBN: 0-380-76853-4

All rights reserved, which includes the right to reproduce this book or portions thereof in any form whatsoever except as provided by the U.S. Copyright Law. For information address Sutton Press, Inc., 288 Watchung Avenue, Upper Montclair, New Jersey 07043-2426.

First Avon Books Printing: February 1993

AVON TRADEMARK REG. U.S. PAT. OFF. AND IN OTHER COUNTRIES, MARCA REGISTRADA, HECHO EN U.S.A.

Printed in the U.S.A.

RA   10 9 8 7 6 5 4 3 2 1

Contents

Lori Copeland
FOR ALL TIME
1

Catherine Creel
TIMESWEPT LOVE
107

Kay McMahon
DESTINY'S SPELL
189

Bobbi Smith
EDEN'S GATE
281

For All Time

Lori Copeland

Justice while she winks at crimes,
stumbles on innocence sometimes.
                    —SAMUEL BUTLER

Prologue

BREATHLESS as she entered the tiny cave, Rosita Feliz fell to her knees before a crude altar. The young woman's fingers trembled as she lit a candle and a flame sprang to life, an insignificant flicker in the dank chamber.

She reached up to lower her black *mantilla*, and her hair spilled over her shoulders in a silken mantle. Her skin was still feverish from her lover's touch, but her heart was still cold with fear.

Closing her eyes with weariness, she whispered, "Please, *el Salvador*, my beloved Joaquin Murieta dares much and fears not at all. His heart is filled with bitterness, and he can find no peace until he has vindicated his enemies' sins.

"You must protect him, for his mortality is fragile," she implored, her voice intensely passionate. "Though he vows his undying love, he will not listen to me! Each morning I awaken filled with dismay, for I know that surely this

3

will be the hour he is taken from me, and this I cannot bear."

Outside the cave, the wind moaned through the bare tree branches.

Her voice softened and grew humble. "Joaquin is not as they say. He is good, not evil, caring more for the safety of his followers than for himself. And should death seize him from me, I will be unable to endure the pain. I beg of You, send someone who will make him listen—someone who will take him from this dangerous path, someone who will save him from himself."

The candle flame flickered, threatening to plunge the cave into total darkness.

For over an hour she knelt on the hard ground, her voice growing raspy from her heartfelt petitions.

Finally, when her strength ebbed, she rose, covered her hair, and extinguished the candle.

A moment later, she slipped from the cave and ran back to camp through the darkness.

1

"A WHAT?"

The clerk at the flea market smiled. "A Gypsy box. Got it in a few days ago. Left over from an estate sale last week."

Lifting the colorful box closer to the light, Corky frowned. "Interesting."

"Yes, that it is," the clerk mused.

At his tone, Corky glanced up. When he noted her quizzical look, he added, "It's nothing. Just a knickknack that seems to turn up from time to time."

"You've sold this box before?"

"Well, yes," he admitted. "I've been here five years, and I've seen it . . . oh, I'd say, this is the third time."

"Ooohhh," Corky's friend Dalia exclaimed. "How interesting!"

"It is an interesting piece, and a bargain if you're in the market—"

"No." Corky handed the box back to him. "Not today, thank you."

5

"Oh, pooh, Corky, where's your sense of adventure?" Dalia scoffed as she picked through an assortment of old laces and buttons.

"Back in the classroom where thirty kids trampled it to death, I guess. Whoever said teaching young minds is a gift from God doesn't have my kids."

Captivated by another antique, Dalia moved toward a distressed-oak pie safe. "If you ask me, your lack of enthusiasm is a terminal case of the blahs."

Silently admitting that Dalia was right, Corky held up a thirties-style dress that had somehow survived time in someone's attic. Lately, her life seemed as dull as airline food.

"You don't know anything about the box?" Corky directed her question to the clerk, deliberately keeping her tone nonchalant.

"No. It originally came inside a crate of assorted relics from the attic of a local estate." The clerk paused, glancing at the box again. "I wish I did have some history on it. I have a feeling it would be intriguing."

He set the box back on the shelf and dusted its garishly painted surface with paternal care.

Dalia dropped the ostrich fan she was looking at and joined Corky at the counter. "It is unusual, isn't it?"

"Well, it's a little—"

"It is not! It's charming. I like it. Maybe some Gypsies did own it."

"Gypsies, my foot. I don't believe in all that stuff—do you?"

"Well . . ." Dalia studied the box. "Maybe I do."

"No, you don't."

"Oh, come on, Corky." Dalia's impulsive side kicked in. "Let's buy it."

Corky realized that the more she argued against buying the box, the more Dalia would be determined to have it. "Dalia, I can't afford it! It's the end of the month!"

Dalia shrugged. "We'll split the cost. You can keep it six months, then I'll take it home for six months." She smiled at the clerk. "We'll take it."

The clerk hurried to wrap the old box in layers of brown tissue paper before the two women could change their minds.

Corky felt a twinge in her purse strings as she realized that she could have had the red blouse in Martindale's window, the one with the white stitching around the collar, for what her share of ownership in this Gypsy box would cost her.

The clerk's fingers caressed the painted wood lovingly, and Corky wondered why, if he liked the box so much, he didn't keep it for himself. When Dalia paid him, Corky noticed that he turned and intentionally handed the box to her.

"I hope the box serves you well," he said with a pleasant twinkle in his eye.

"That was a strange thing for him to say, wasn't it?" Corky commented as they stepped outside a moment later.

"Oh, I don't know. It beats the standard 'Have a nice day, little ladies.' "

* * *

"How about a frozen yogurt?" Corky asked as they started for the car.

"Might as well. I guess you don't have a date, either?"

"No."

Of course neither one of them had a date, Corky thought. She knew that Darrell, the man Dalia was dating, was a traditionalist in the extreme. Saturday night only was his motto. And her own love life wasn't exactly booming. She couldn't remember the last time she'd gone out, except to that teachers' convention last month, and that could hardly be considered a social event.

Her mother was right. Her expectations were too high when it came to men. She had her share of opportunities for dates, but most of the men she met at school functions were less interested in romance and more concerned about getting a paper published, or earning a higher salary.

Where was the man who could romance a woman in the tradition of Valentino or Errol Flynn, or even Patrick Swayze? If she spent one more evening discussing faculty meetings, problem kids, and lunchroom gossip, she would scream.

"How about coffee and dessert at my place instead? I've got cheesecake," Corky offered, suddenly in a mood to indulge herself.

The look on Dalia's face mirrored her weakness. "Cheesecake?"

"Strawberry cheesecake."

"Think of the pounds." Dalia groaned.

"Sorry, you're talking to someone who can't gain weight if she tried."

"Oh, yeah," Dalia mocked. "I forgot, you're cursed."

"Darn it, the light's out again," Corky complained a few minutes later, as she flipped the switch in the downstairs entrance to her apartment.

"You really should think about moving. I wouldn't like living over a business in the middle of town."

"It's not so bad. Since Sam has decided to retire, he's put the flower shop up for sale. I'm hoping the new owner will keep the place up better."

Corky loved the old apartment, despite its imperfections, and it suited her tastes perfectly. The high ceilings with carved wood trim and matching wainscoting on plastered cream-and-peach walls were reminiscent of the old forties' movies she adored. Dalia had accused her of having "Casablanca Syndrome," and she supposed she did, but this apartment had been quite a find when she'd stumbled across the classified ad two years ago.

A teacher's salary wasn't much, so her dreams of owning a vine-covered cottage in the country would probably never come true, but for now she was comfortable. And for all she knew, perhaps someday she would find a man who was looking for a relationship that would last longer than the time it took to mold Jell-O.

"I'll start the coffee."

The tiny kitchen was, of necessity, efficient, and Corky was by nature a neat, organized person; it took only a few minutes for her to make coffee and cut the dessert.

She opened a can of cat food, dumped it on a paper plate, and set it on the floor for her cat, Cleo. When she returned to the living room, Dalia had unwrapped the Gypsy box and was looking at it closely.

"This must be, by far, our most worthless purchase," Dalia admitted.

Corky gave her a really-now look as she set the tray on the coffee table.

"Look! It has a secret drawer." Dalia slid the small compartment open and peered inside. "Geez, will you look at this?"

"What is it?"

"Something wrapped in a black cloth."

Corky leaned forward as Dalia carefully removed the cloth to reveal a worn deck of cards and a thick square of paper yellowed with age.

Corky's eyes widened. "What is it?"

"I don't know. Some kind of . . . Turn on that lamp, will you? I can hardly see—"

Corky snapped on the lamp, then perched on the arm of the sofa, looking over Dalia's shoulder at the strange cards she was spreading on the table.

Corky shook her head. "Those are the strangest cards I've ever seen."

"They're Tarot cards," Dalia marveled.

"Tarot? Aren't they . . . Isn't that kind of like witchcraft?"

"Oh, pooh, I don't believe in witchcraft. I wonder who they belonged to?"

"What's the piece of paper for?"

"I don't know." Dalia carefully unfolded the yellowed paper. "It looks like . . . directions for reading the cards, maybe. I'm not sure."

Leaning closer, Corky studied the piece of paper. "What does it say?"

"Let's see. Wands equal diamonds, that must be like diamonds in a regular deck of cards. Anyway, it says that diamonds are associated with enterprise and glory and identified with fire."

"What's that one?"

"Cups. It says here, cups equal hearts. According to this, readings depend on the way the cards fall, in combination with other cards, plus the frequency with which cards of a given suit re-occur."

The two women exchanged looks of confusion.

Dalia shrugged, putting the paper down and picking up her plate. "Oh, well. You lay out the cards in stacks while I try to read them." Savoring the cheesecake, she eyed Corky expectantly.

"Me! Why me? I don't like to mess with these kinds of things, Dalia." Corky wasn't one to take chances; even reading her Leo horoscope in the morning paper made her uneasy.

"Oh, come on, Corky. We're not 'reading' the cards, we're just looking at them. We don't know anything about this kind of stuff. What could it possibly hurt?" Dalia held the paper again as she ate.

"I don't know, but all this hocus-pocus makes me nervous." Corky took a bite of her dessert.

Undaunted, Dalia glanced back at the cards. "Cups equal hearts, associated with love and happiness and identified with water. Swords equal clubs, associated with strife and misfortune, identified with air. Pentacles equal spades, associated with money and interest, identified with earth. Wow, weird. I wonder if it really works?" Leaning over, she placed her empty dish on the table.

"Dalia—" Corky warned, trying not to let her imagination run wild.

"Oh, look! The first step, it says, is to select the court card—"

"Dalia—"

But it was too late; Dalia was on a roll. "You choose a wand card, Corky, because you have blonde hair and blue eyes. I must choose a cup card because I have light brown hair and hazel eyes. And then, since we're women, we each choose a queen card."

"How about another piece of cheesecake?" Corky offered, hoping to distract her friend.

"No, thanks." As Dalia spread the cards wider, a second piece of paper fell out from between two cards located near the middle of the deck.

Corky drew back as if she had been singed. This whole thing gave her the creeps. "What's that?"

Dalia, not the least bit intimidated, unfolded the paper and read it aloud. "Beware the magic of the cards. Read with care, and your future will be revealed. Handle with scurrility and—"

"Handle with scurrility?" Corky prompted when Dalia seemed hesitant to go on.

"Yeah, you know, handle with disrespect or abuse—"

"I know what scurrility means, go on!"

"Oh . . . the rest of it is missing, torn off."

Corky shivered involuntarily.

Dalia tossed the paper aside and picked up the other sheet. "It doesn't matter. Look, this page tells how to lay out the cards."

"Forget it."

"Come on. What's the harm? Look, you're always dreaming about Mr. Right. Let's see if he's in the cards—"

"This is foolish—"

"So, be foolish for once. What's the big deal?"

"All right, let's just get this over with." Corky knew when she was beaten.

"Shuffle the cards."

Corky picked up the deck gingerly, certain they were about to be cursed.

"Oooee," Dalia teased with a grin, drawing out the sound to make it sound scary. "Ooooeee."

"Very funny."

"Now, concentrate on a question we most want answered," Dalia instructed.

"Pertaining to what?"

"Oh, what kind of man we'll marry, or what type of man is good for us. We'll each picture a particular hero in our minds."

"Easier said than done. I can't think of a single man I've met lately whom I'd have on a bet."

"That's the point. Think of your *dream* man. Maybe someone from the pages of history, a dashing, wickedly handsome sort."

Corky thought for a moment, and the only name that flashed into her mind was Joaquin Murieta, but only because his name had come up that day.

"Have you thought of anyone?"

"Joaquin Murieta, I guess. We studied about him in class today."

"Who's Joaquin Murieta?"

"A Robin-Hood type of Mexican bandit who lived back in the 1850s during the California gold rush days. He was bitterly resentful of the way Americans treated the Mexican miners and other minorities." She paused, recalling part of the lesson that day. "Legend says that he carried a string of human ears around his saddle horn."

"A man like that turns you on?"

"Good grief, Dalia, you act as if I'm actually going to get him," Corky grumbled. "It is also said that Joaquin Murieta was a lineal descendant of Spanish kings," she added.

"Sorry," Dalia said with a shrug. "Never heard of him."

"Perhaps that's because you teach French," Corky replied.

Dalia's eyes returned to the sheet of instructions. "Okay, I'll try for the real Robin Hood, whom I fervently hope really looks like Costner—or maybe I'll just try for Darrell."

"Robin Hood or *Darrell*?" Darrell was okay, but Corky didn't see how she could connect the two men in the same breath.

Dalia glanced up. "What's wrong with Darrell?"

"Nothing. Darrell's okay."

"All right, lay out the cards while I try to read them, and remember to concentrate on finding a man like Joaquin Murieta."

"Really, Dalia." The disbelief was clear in Corky's eyes.

"Just lay the cards out. Draw a card and place it next to the top of the card you've already drawn, like this." Dalia drew the first card to get them rolling. "Now, you draw one."

Corky drew a card.

"Let's see, that's the court card." Dalia picked up the yellowed page and read for a moment.

"And what does the court card mean?"

"It indicates the conditions in which the seeker, that's you, lived in a previous life. That's good, since we've picked men from the past to pattern our heroes after."

"Right." Though she felt like a complete fool, Corky waited, looking at Dalia. "Now what?"

"I'm not sure. Do you feel any different, have any sudden intuition about any particular man you might know?"

"Not one single intuition. How about you?"

"No, nothing. Draw four more cards and lay them in a square around your card, first one on the left, the next above, then one on the right, and one below."

Corky felt as if someone were running an icy finger down her spine, and she suddenly tired of the foolish game. Pushing the stack of cards aside, she reached for the empty cheesecake plates to carry them into the kitchen.

"Oh, come on! It was just getting good," Dalia complained.

"Sorry. I'm an old party pooper!"

Defeated, Dalia sighed, then glancing at the clock, she grimaced. "Oh, geez, look at the time! And I've still got papers to grade."

"Not me. I'm having seventh-grade finals tomorrow," Corky called above the sound of the garbage disposal.

"Tomorrow? Why so early?"

"So I'll have time to get my grades finished early."

"Cheater." Dalia yawned and stretched languidly. "Well, see you in the morning, kiddo. Coffee, seven-thirty as usual?"

"Unless Joaquin comes in the night and whisks me away to a life of breathtaking excitement," Corky teased.

Dalia swished dramatically toward the door, humming a tune that sounded to Corky like "Some Enchanted Evening."

Reaching for the kitchen light switch, Corky spotted the deck of cards spread out on the coffee table and decided to tidy up before she showered.

Although she had told herself that she wasn't at all curious, she sat down and stared at the cards. She selected another card from the top of the deck and turned it over slowly.

The Lovers. She picked up the yellowed paper and read that this card signified a choice between sacred and profane love. Reversed, it signified parental interference, danger of a marriage breaking up, or quarrels over children. The possibility of a wrong choice also existed.

She frowned, tossing the card aside. She didn't need any help in making wrong choices. She was good at that.

Outside, the moon began to slide behind a cloud, and a breeze sprang up to tease the otherwise sultry air.

She turned over another card and stared at it. The Nine of Cups. The picture depicted a well-fed, well-satisfied man who looked like a rich merchant or maybe a man of property.

The night grew darker, and the wind increased, banging the French door against the wall.

Hesitantly, she turned the Nine of Cups over, wishing *she* could find a man who looked that good.

Turning the third card over, she saw the Chariot. "Guess I'm going somewhere," she muttered as she got up to close the French door as a rumble of thunder sounded in the distance.

Stepping onto the small balcony, she glanced up at the churning clouds and shivered from the peculiar reversal of weather. A moment ago the night had been filled with stars and balmy breezes.

Another clap of thunder added to her anxiety, and she turned and hurried back inside.

Bending over the coffee table, she quickly began to gather the cards. The Chariot card slipped through her fingers and fluttered lightly to the floor.

Grumbling, and holding firmly onto the deck of cards, she picked it up, but it slipped from her grasp and fell to the floor once again.

Crouching on her knees beside the table, she grunted as she reached for it, but the card slid farther away.

"Butterfingers," she muttered to herself, trapping the card between the table leg and the wall.

Stretching full length on the floor, she fumbled beneath the table. Her fingers were almost on the card when she felt her foot tangle in the lamp cord.

Muttering beneath her breath, she jerked her foot, and the room went pitch-black.

2

JOAQUIN Murieta de Castillo lay spread-eagled on his back, snoring, his slender chest rising and falling with each resonant breath.

Snorting, he grimaced and rolled to his side, one hand searching the feminine curves beneath the blanket. Snuggling closer to her shapely warmth, he smiled as his other hand explored the nicely rounded buttocks molded against his loins.

Hearing an indignant gasp, he stirred and muttered, "Did you say something, *amante*?"

"Move the *hand* or lose it, buddy!"

"*Sí*?" Cracking one eye open sleepily, Joaquin squinted.

The sound of a hand meeting flesh exploded inside the tent, jolting Joaquin to full awareness. Rubbing his smarting cheek, he sat up and groped for the lantern. A moment later, the tent was flooded with light.

"*Qué diablos*! What the hell's the matter with you, Rosita—?" He broke off as he came face to

19

face with a pair of feminine eyes he'd never seen before.

For a moment they stared at each other; then they both bolted backward on the pallet as if they had been shot.

"*Who* are you?" they shouted.

"Who am *I*?" they parroted.

"*Yes*, who are *you*?" they demanded in unison.

"*Wait* a minute!" Joaquin sprang to his feet, his hands dropping low to shield his nakedness from the woman's astonished eyes.

Corky looked away as he hurriedly grabbed for his pants.

"What are you doing here?" he demanded, hopping around as he shoved one slim leg into the trousers, then another.

"What am I doing here?" She stared at him, totally confused. What was *he* doing under her coffee table? Was he a burglar? Her heart raced. "You tell me, Mister! If you don't get out of here, and right now, I'm going to scream the rafters down!"

"Tell you *what*?" Fumbling with the buttons on his fly, he glared at her, then glanced uneasily through the partially opened flap of the tent. "You must leave!" Lowering his voice, he added harshly, "*Inmediatamente*! If this is Guerra's idea of a joke, I . . ."

Corky's eyes shot up to demand his silence. "Wait a minute." A knot the size of Gibraltar was beginning to form in the pit of her stomach as she realized she was no longer in her apartment but in some sort of tent. Oh, my Lord. She'd seen this man before, today, in class, in a history book! Glancing down, she saw the deck of Tarot cards still in her hand. She stifled a scream.

Joaquin Murieta.

"If Rosita hears of this—"

Groaning, Corky felt herself grow lightheaded as Joaquin's hand came out to steady her, his tone becoming infinitely more cajoling. "*Señorita*, please, I mean no disrespect to your beauty, but I beg your understanding. My heart belongs to another—my Rosita." His voice dropped to a hushed whisper. "She does not share ... she does not forgive a man ... *her* man for wandering." His features sobered. "You must believe me, most lovely one—my Rosita would not find another woman in my bed a cause for merriment."

Wide-eyed, Corky stared back at the image who had stepped out of the annals of history, who was standing here *talking* to her. She could *see* his lips moving. Was it possible that Joaquin Murieta was actually here? *Joaquin Murieta*, the reckless deviant who had killed and marauded his way through the 1850s? It couldn't be. This was *insane*.

"You must go," Joaquin insisted in flawless English when he realized that she didn't appear to understand what he was saying. Dragging her to her feet, he guided Corky to the opening of the tent. Peeking around the flap, he was assured that his exit would be undetected, and he pulled her outside.

"Where are you taking me?" she demanded as she stumbled to match his long-legged pace. This is not happening, she thought wildly. She was dreaming!

Muttering in Spanish, he tugged her along behind him, oblivious to her question.

A moment later, they entered a second tent, where she was unceremoniously handed over to a man who was rudely awakened from a sound sleep when Joaquin curtly declared, "Mateo. Get rid of her."

The man called Mateo sat up, trying to focus his eyes on the source of this sudden fracas.

Corky stood in the doorway, trying not to stare at the glorious black hair covering the man's incredibly broad chest. He had the most unbelievably long lashes over the darkest eyes she'd ever seen. The man before her was an impressive representation of the *criollos*, or native born Spanish dons, of the nineteenth century. Yes, it was a dream she decided; no man in today's society could compare with the utter *machismo* of this man. As Corky and Mateo continued to stare at each other, Joaquin turned on his heel and abruptly left the tent.

"*Madre de Diós*," Mateo muttered. "What is the trouble?"

"The cards. They have foretold this."

Whirling, Corky tried to make out a stooped form silhouetted against the doorway.

"Now you have frightened yourself," a voice coming from the obscured form scolded. "I can see it in your eyes. One who is not a reader should not be laying out the cards." Sighing, the shadowy form entered the tent. "But you need not fear. I have been sent to protect you."

Mateo, trying to locate his pants, was at a loss as to what was going on. Finding his trousers, he slipped into them, then he reached for a match and lit the lantern.

"What is happening to me?" Corky exclaimed as she tried to make sense of what was occuring. As the darkly cloaked form drew closer to the light, Corky could see that it was a very old woman. Her face was lined with age, her hands gnarled and veined.

Moving slowly and with great effort, she brushed Mateo aside and knelt on the floor of the tent. She grasped the deck of cards from Corky's hand and spread them out before her.

Corky fought back hysteria as she repeated her inquiry. "What is happening, and where am I?"

The old woman glanced up, puzzled. "Why, where did you wish to be?"

"I didn't wish to be anywhere. . . ." Corky paused, her eyes focusing on the Tarot cards as the meaning of the old woman's words washed over her. "Oh, my gosh." She looked up, and all the color drained from her face. "This is Joaquin Murieta's camp."

"Is this not your wish?"

"Oh, my *gosh!*" Groaning, Corky buried her face in her hands. What had she done? *What had she done?*

"You have a most curious reading," the old woman commented, poking at the cards as if she expected them to speak back to her.

"I don't know anything about those cards," Corky said defensively. Dalia! Where was that blasted Dalia? This was all her fault! That's why she was having this nightmare—because of the conversation with Dalia earlier, and all this nonsense over the cards.

"One should not tamper with the unknown, *el desconocido.*" Leaning closer, the old woman studied one card closely. "Ah, the Lovers. You are, perhaps, concerned about someone you love? A man, perhaps?"

Corky glanced at the man, who was watching them in silence. He was so ruggedly handsome that it was hard not to stare. "I'm not in love with anyone."

"Ah, then you are seeking a lover."

"No—I'm neither in love nor seeking anyone."

"Then the fates have chosen you for a different reason," she decided.

"Fates?" the man finally said.

"*Sí,* it is here, in the cards." She stabbed at the cards, and the lines around her eyes deepened. "Our guest has much to learn, some good, some not so good." She straightened, releasing a weary sigh. "And much is laid upon my shoulders."

How could this have happened? Corky wondered. Why had she ever touched those cards?

Mateo's features darkened. "What do you speak of, *Vieja?*"

"There is no need for worry, *mi hijo.*" The old woman's voice was gentle, but adamant. "No harm is to come to her." She looked up and met his gaze. "No harm, *mi hijo*. You will see to that."

The man stood behind Corky, his height towering over her insignificant five feet two.

Cringing, Corky closed her eyes and waited for the worst. This man was magnificent, yet intimidating. She could feel the heat of his eyes boring into her, and suddenly there was not enough air to breathe in the close confines of the tent.

"Who is she, *Vieja*?" His voice was deep and resonant, sending a chill of anticipation up Corky's spine.

"It matters not. Take her to the fire in the morning and see that she is nourished."

The man's dark gaze moved back to Corky, then returned to the old woman. "Would it not be more suitable to summon one of the women?"

"Nay. You are the one," she said matter-of-factly.

"But Joaquin is wary of strangers—"

"This *extranjera* will bring us no harm. The assurance is here." She gestured toward the cards.

Yielding to the old woman's wishes, Mateo bowed his head respectfully. "It shall be as you say, *Vieja*."

The inertia Corky had felt ever since she had suddenly found herself in Joaquin Murieta's bed began to fade.

"Listen, I don't know how I got here, but I want to go home. This is all a huge mistake." The old woman appeared to be knowledgeable about the cards, and by now, Corky was grabbing for straws. "Please, you've got to help me—"

"It is not within my power," the old woman said. "The power now lies within you."

She disappeared through the opening in the tent before Corky could stop her.

Stunned, Corky turned and was once again presented with the formidable sight of Mateo's stalwart chest.

Their eyes met, then dropped away uncertainly. For a while silence hovered between them, and Corky could see he mistrusted her with every fiber in his body.

Finally, he reached for a blanket and handed it to her. A moment later, he blew out the lantern, and she stood in the dark, wondering what to do now.

She heard the man lay down on his pallet once again and soon soft snores broke the silence. Although she was terrified and confused, she also remembered that the old woman had said she would come to no harm. And this man would protect her. She had to be content with that as she, too, slowly sank to the floor of the tent, wrapped in the blanket which still retained his pleasant masculine odor.

Corky looked up from the fire as the sound of hoofbeats filled the air. Lowering the meat she was about to eat, she watched as a horse and rider burst into the camp.

A rousing cheer went up as the magnificent white horse reared on its hind legs and pawed the air with its hooves. As soon as his horse had settled all four feet on the ground again, Joaquin Murieta gave a shout of jubilation.

Corky wilted with relief when she saw that his saddle horn did not hold a chain of ears—human or otherwise. However, she couldn't deny that her choice of heroes had been appropriate. A wicked smile crinkled the corners of his memorable face as his laughter rang out over the hillsides.

As she watched Joaquin, she frantically sought answers to her dilemma. What had she been doing before she ended up in Joaquin's bed? She frowned, trying to remember. She had been crawling under the coffee table trying to pick up a card—the Chariot card. Did that signify something? Through some insane quirk of fate, was the Chariot card responsible for her being here?

Her attention returned to the horseman and she thought that the pictures in history textbooks had treated him unfairly. Joaquin Murieta was a formidable man.

"Joaquin!" The shout reverberated through the crowd. "Joaquin!"

Corky leaned closer to Mateo, who had barely spoken to her since being appointed her protector. She had the feeling that he didn't particularly relish his assignment, but that nineteenth-century Spanish superstition would make him honor it.

"Where is Rosita?" she whispered, recalling the history book's claim that Joaquin and his lover were inseparable.

"You should pray she does not return soon," Mateo returned coldly.

It was clear to Corky that he found her suspect, even though the Old One had said no harm was to befall her. Corky couldn't imagine what her role in all of this was, and she wasn't sure she wanted to know. "Where is she?" she inquired of Mateo.

"You do not know?" His voice mocked her.

She chose to ignore it. "No."

He weighed his answer for a moment, then replied, "She is at the border between Mexico and what the *gringos* call California. That is the land of my people."

"And today's date?"

"July 1853."

"Oh, Lordy." Corky felt sick. "That's what I was afraid of."

He turned to look at her, puzzled.

Corky's mind whirled with a myriad of thoughts as she watched the charismatic Joaquin ride through camp, greeting his followers. According to history, there had been five Joaquins—surnamed Carrillo, Valenzuela, Ocomorenia, Botellier, and Murieta. Murieta was the most noted among the *banditti*. Legend told that the young, adventurous Murieta had turned to a life of crime to avenge the atrocities he had suffered at the hands of the American miners. With his eyes flashing and his knife ever ready for a *gringo's* ribs, he'd become known as a ruthless, low-down character, a cutthroat, and a thief at heart. And now, through her reckless use of a deck of cards, Corky found herself in the devil's own camp.

"Something is wrong with your food, no?" Mateo glanced sternly at her half-eaten meal. "You do not eat."

"I'm not hungry."

"As you wish, but you will be."

Corky didn't like the ominous sound of that, so she forced the fork back to her mouth. They ate in strained silence, Corky trying to ignore the pair of curious eyes that refused to leave her.

"Tell me your name." Mateo's voice was low but commanding.

She swallowed against a dry throat. "Corky McBride."

He looked up.

She met his cynical gaze calmly. "Cordilla, actually, but they call me Corky. I heard Joaquin call you Mateo, but I'd like to know your full name."

"Mateo Armandez Rivas."

His eyes moved over her slowly, and Corky was surprised at the ripple of excitement that again swept through her. Few men in her life had aroused such an immediate awareness.

"Your clothes. They are not what a woman wears."

Corky glanced down at the jeans and football jersey she'd worn to the flea market, and at the slippers she'd put on once she and Dalia had arrived at her apartment. Suddenly she wanted to curl up inside her fluffy scuffs and die.

"What is this Chicago Bulls?" he asked as he resumed eating. Apparently he could read English because he recognized the lettering on the jersey.

"Oh . . . a basketball team—Michael Jordan—Air Jordan?"

He stared at her again.

"It's a game."

Selecting a morsel from his plate, he asked quietly, "Do you suffer an illness of some sort?"

"An illness? No. Why?"

His gaze skimmed over her head lightly. "Your hair."

"What's wrong with my hair?" Her fingers ruffled the ends of her short locks. She'd just paid twenty-seven dollars for this haircut.

"It is short, like a man's."

"It's the latest style," she returned crisply.

"Where?"

"In—oh, never mind." It was useless to try to explain that she was from Muncie, Indiana, when he obviously didn't know that such a place even existed.

He suddenly set his plate aside and stood up. "The Old One has placed you under my protection, so no harm will come to you, but I wish to know *what* has brought you to Joaquin's camp."

"Well, I'm not a spy, if that's what you're thinking."

"I make no assumptions. I am asking who you are, and why you are here."

Corky sighed, tearing off a piece of bread. "You want the truth?"

"I do not ask for *decepción*."

She drew in a deep breath, then released it slowly. "I think I've been caught in some kind of time warp."

His cool composure suddenly wavered. Lifting his head, Mateo looked around to see if anyone was listening. Then his gaze returned to her. "I do not know why I am asked to watch the *loca*."

"You think I'm crazy." She glanced away. "That's just great. You don't believe me."

"I don't believe you."

"Mateo, *mi amigo*!"

At the sound of the commanding voice, Corky turned to see Joaquin Murieta striding toward them. He passed through the throng, greeting each man and woman as he made his way to the communal fire.

"And who have we here, Mateo?" The color of his eyes deepened when he recognized her. Whirling, he had started at a fast clip in the opposite direction when the old woman, who had been sitting quietly by the fire, stood up.

"That Joaquin, he runs like a spring jackal." The old woman's mockery slowed Joaquin's footsteps. "Come, you need not fear. She will bring you no harm."

Joaquin turned, glancing nervously around the crowd. "Has Rosita returned to camp?"

"No, she still journeys with her brother, Luis."

Relieved, Joaquin grinned and approached Corky, exuding charm. "Ah, my lovely one. Welcome to my humble camp." Bending from the waist, he brushed his lips across the back of her hand. "What might one so fortunate call you?"

"Corky—or Cordilla. Whichever you choose."

Mateo and Joaquin exchanged pained looks at the mention of Corky's avowed name. They obviously found it peculiar.

"A lovely name for one so lovely. And how is it that we have not met before, Cordilla?" Joaquin turned to look uneasily over his shoulder.

"I just got into camp," she said wryly.

"Ah, and I see you have chosen a most appropriate *protector*."

Corky saw the muscle in Mateo's jaw tighten. "The *Vieja* has chosen me to see that no harm comes to her."

"Ah." Joaquin's grin was nothing short of ornery. Turning to the old woman, he inquired pleasantly, "A relative, *Vieja?*"

"No."

When Joaquin appeared momentarily confused, she added, "It is in the cards."

"Ah, *sí*. The cards." He smiled as he faced Corky again, and the old woman faded into the shadows.

Corky watched him studying her, his eyes missing nothing.

"The Old One has been our friend for many years," he said. "She has warned me she will not always be with us, but neither will she leave until another comes to take her place. She is our talisman, our good luck charm, and she serves us well. I do not question her wisdom. If the Old One asks that no harm befall you, then you have my word that you will have the protection of the camp. Mateo will follow her wishes."

As Murieta strode off, Mateo looked at Corky, his eyes dark with resentment. She could see that he was still not convinced that the old woman knew what she was doing.

"No more lies, Cordilla. What is your purpose here?" he demanded.

"You do not trust my words?" The old woman stepped from the shadows, wrapping her shawl tighter around her bent shoulders.

"I trust only what I see and know."

"Then see and know this. This woman will make a mark upon your life. A deep mark."

She laughed, almost a maniacal sound, and Corky shivered with apprehension. She wished the Old One hadn't said that.

Turning on his heel, Mateo walked off, his long strides filled with agitation.

With a sinking heart, Corky watched him go. Joaquin was slim and graceful, and he clearly commanded the respect of his followers; but, Mateo Armandez was taller, broader of shoulder, and more imposing.

"If you are to complete your mission, you must be cooperative," the old woman warned. "Mateo is not a man to aggravate."

Corky planned to be cooperative, the old woman could bank on that. The way she had it figured, the old woman was her only hope of reversing this bizarre situation.

The *Vieja* patted her shoulder reassuringly before she walked away. "Do not concern yourself. Mateo is the man in the cards."

Corky turned. "What?"

"Mateo, the *amante*, the Lover. The other half of your heart."

3

THIS simply could not be happening. She was caught up in some sort of crazy fantasy, Corky told herself as she sat in Mateo's tent later, staring into the darkness.

Never, in her most imaginative dreams, had she experienced anything remotely close to this situation. Joaquin Murieta was a configuration from history, a man she'd taught in her class, a man whom she probably wouldn't have given another thought if it hadn't been for Dalia's urging. Now, by some incredible quirk of fate, she found herself in his camp of followers.

A figure darkened the doorway of the tent, and her heartbeat quickened at the sound of Mateo's voice.

"You do not sleep."

"I can't," she admitted, aware that she was exhausted but afraid to close her eyes.

After entering the tent, Mateo lit the lantern. He removed his *sombrero* and tossed it onto one of the several pallets scattered about the large abode.

"Is there something I can do to make you more comfortable?"

"Zap me back home."

"This word 'zap.' What does it mean?"

"Nothing."

Corky glanced away as he began unbuttoning his shirt. She had to admit that his physique was overpowering and that the sight of his broad chest, molded by ridges of tight muscle, unnerved her.

As he tossed his shirt aside, she saw a pattern of scars across his back, graphic evidence that he had once been brutally beaten.

He stretched out on the pallet and closed his eyes. "Did you arrive here by horseback or private conveyance?"

So, he was back to interrogating her again. Corky had been afraid he would eventually get around to asking that specific question, and she didn't have an answer.

"I don't remember."

"The *Vieja* says you have been sent to help us. How do you mean to do this?"

Sighing, Corky stared at the lantern. "I haven't the slightest idea."

Her gaze moved to him and she knew, despite his relaxed pose, that the slightest unusual movement would have him on his feet, ready to strike. The lamplight gleamed on his coal-black hair and made his features seem even more patrician. If she'd been asked to describe her idea of a classically handsome man, she would have described someone much like this man, Mateo Armandez.

"You don't trust me, do you?" she asked.

"I don't know what to believe of you, Cordilla. You would agree that your sudden appearance is curious, as well as your clothes?"

"I'm not an enemy."

"How can I know this, when, in your own words, you cannot explain your presence here?"

It was a logical question, but she knew—somehow she just knew—that she couldn't lie to this man; and frankly, she didn't have the answers just this minute. "Well, you don't have to worry about me," she supplemented lamely.

"Ah, but I must. It is my responsibility to see that no harm comes to you, and if I were to discover that you were an enemy, that would make my job all the more unpleasant."

"Then I suppose you'll just have to ask the old woman what I'm doing here. She's the only one who seems to know what's going on."

"Yes, the *Vieja* is your champion, but be assured that you will seldom leave my sight, and you will have no opportunity to escape."

Corky lay back on her pallet, her eyes drooping with weariness. "Who is the Old One? A relative? A mentor to Joaquin?"

"The Old One came to us years ago when her home was destroyed by winds."

"Is she some sort of psychic?"

"I do not know this word."

"Does she know the future? Do you believe that's possible?"

"I do not know about the mystery in the cards, but on many occasions the Old One has warned us of impending trouble. We have learned to listen to her words, however strange they might seem."

"And you accept what she says without reservation?"

"It would be wise if you slept." He rolled onto his side, drawing a blanket over him as he dismissed her. "The others will be joining us soon."

Her eyes opened slowly as the meaning of his words sank in. "Others will be sleeping here?"

"Yes—you, me, and others."

"You must be kidding."

"Does this concern you?"

"Well, yes . . . I'm accustomed to sleeping alone."

"In Joaquin's camp, no one sleeps alone."

"Is there a shortage of tents?" It seemed to her that if they were *banditos*, they'd steal enough tents for each one to have his own sleeping quarters.

"No, it is Joaquin's way."

Brother, I hope this doesn't mean they're all a bunch of kinky weirdos, she thought. She sat up. "If you don't mind, I'll take my blanket and roll up somewhere outside—"

A hand on her leg stopped her. "That is not necessary. There is ample room for you."

She surveyed the interior of the tent, which would soon be filled to capacity. "Where?"

His lips curved in a half-smile. "Here, beside me."

So, this was how it was to be.

"I don't think so." She started to leave again.

"Do I cause you concern?"

She was beginning to resent the almost taunting pitch in his voice. With a sigh, she realized that it didn't matter if he caused her concern or not. She wasn't going to sleep out in the open where anything could crawl on or over her.

"Come. Sleep," he invited.

"Don't try anything funny," she warned.

"I have no ambition to be a court jester," he assured her.

Judging from the impatience in his voice now, she was reasonably sure he would leave her alone. As if in a dream, she found herself lying beside him as the lantern slowly flickered, then went out.

Corky came awake slowly, listening to the breathing of the others who occupied the tent. Though the men were peacefully snoring, something different had stirred her from a sound sleep.

Easing up on one elbow, she saw Mateo asleep, facing her, the moonlight illuminating his handsome features.

His skin was not dark or light, but the color of toast. He truly was an unforgettable man. She recoiled at her own forbidden attraction. This man, she reminded herself, was also a dangerous, bloodthirsty outlaw, willing to kill at the drop of a hat.

Outside, the muted night sounds came to her—horses stamping, coyotes howling, the music of a soft guitar being strummed by someone who stood guard around the campfire.

The two pallets opposite her were occupied by Carmelita and Guerra. She recognized the couple as having quarreled during dinner that night, causing quite a scene. From what she had overheard, Carmelita and Guerra's relationship was volatile, and Carmelita's hot temper was legendary among the group.

Apparently, whatever was bothering the lovers had been settled before they'd come to bed, because now they lay closely entwined in each other's arms.

Rolling onto her other side, Corky drew the blanket up closer. How very strange this all was. Corky McBride, lying beside a Mexican outlaw who was hunted by American authorities.

How long would she be here? Was her stay permanent, or could she expect to be whisked back to her apartment at any moment?

A rustling sound came from Guerra's pallet, and Corky shut her eyes, praying that they were not going to . . . well, just that they were *not*.

Beside her, she sensed, rather than heard, Mateo's breathing change.

Holding her breath as the rustling grew more pronounced, she was wondering if he was thinking what she was thinking. The answer wasn't long in coming. He suddenly said, with unquestionable authority, "Carmelita, if Guerra is found dead in the morning, I will personally hold you responsible."

In that instant a knife flew through the air and struck the tent pole directly above Corky's head. The wood quivered with the force of the throw. She froze.

A woman's voice uttered a stream of Spanish in a low and vehement voice.

"My *madre* has nothing to do with this, and I will speak of this matter no more," Mateo warned as he rolled back onto his side, irritably doubling his pillow under his head. Apparently Carmelita's furious reference to his parentage had not offended him, Corky realized.

Carmelita jerked the blanket back in place, then lay back down beside her sleeping husband.

Aware that Corky was still frozen in place, Mateo said quietly, "She will cool down by morning."

"She was going to stab her husband!" Corky whispered vehemently.

"But she did not. She is only angry."

"But she threw a *knife*—"

"She will do nothing more, this I promise you. Go back to sleep."

And for some completely illogical reason, Corky did.

* * *

When Corky next awoke, sunlight was streaming through the tent. Bolting upright, she was relieved to see that they were alone. Mateo was already up, pulling on his boots.

"Where are the others?"

"They rose earlier."

Pushing her hair out of her face, Corky yawned. "You should have awakened me."

"You were resting very soundly."

She glanced up, wincing. "I wasn't snoring, was I?" Lord, she hoped she hadn't been *snoring*.

Smiling, Mateo stood up and tucked his shirttail into his trousers.

Ohhh! She'd like to slap that smug look off his face! Crawling off the pallet, she tried to brush the wrinkles from her jeans, wishing she had a bath and clean clothes.

"I will ask one of the women to see to your needs," he said as if reading her mind. "You will need proper shoes and clothing."

"You don't like my scuffs?" she mocked, determined to be as snotty to him as he was to her.

"They do not appear serviceable in a hard rain."

Smart ass, Corky thought as she knelt to straighten the bedding. "What did you do before you joined Joaquin?"

"I am trained in the law."

She glanced up, shocked. "You're a lawyer?"

"I am."

"Then how can you ride with men who have been branded outlaws?"

She could see he was hesitant to discuss his personal life with her, but he finally answered, "Because I resent the wrong that has been dealt to me and my people." He paused in the doorway of the tent, his eyes meeting hers evenly. "Exactly what do you know of Joaquin and his cause?"

Corky thought for a moment about the history lesson she had recently given. "That his gold mine was taken from him by unscrupulous American miners. In the process, he was brutally beaten and Rosita was violated before his very eyes."

Mateo's brows lifted with interest.

She continued, "I know that Joaquin tried to overcome his bitterness by moving deeper into the valley, where he staked yet another claim, only to be shamed publicly and forced to witness his brother's hanging when the horse he had borrowed from his brother turned out to be stolen."

"You seem to know my leader well."

"I only know what I have read in history books."

"These 'history' books you speak of? Perhaps you have one with you?"

She saw cynicism cloud his eyes again, and she resented it. Turning away, she plumped a pillow. "No, I don't have any history books with me."

"A pity."

"The scars on your back—do they have anything to do with why you're here?" she asked.

"I, too, have had my property taken from me by the *Norteamericanos*. They came like thieves in the night, with torches and whips, and burned my home and my office. I was more fortunate than some. I was found by a friend, and my life was saved."

"So that is why you follow Joaquin," she murmured, aware of the pain and degradation this man must have suffered.

"No, that is not why I follow Joaquin Murieta."

Turning, he walked away, leaving her to try to figure out what it was that compelled him to follow a notorious bandit.

DURING the next few days, life quickly settled into a routine for Corky. Joaquin Murieta exercised his revenge much as a hungry man devoured his meal. If a claim was seized unfairly, Joaquin's band of followers dealt the proper vengeance; if a brother was treated unjustly, the perpetrator was swiftly and suitably made to pay for his crime. They ran off his cattle and stole his horses. They held up lonely travelers to relieve them of their valuables, and they robbed saloons and stores.

It was a horrible way to live, yet Corky quickly decided that Joaquin wasn't nearly as heartless as history had branded him. In fact, at times he seemed caring, almost benevolent. He appeared to be a man dedicated to justice, not evil, for he preyed only on Americans who refused him the right to search for gold.

While the nightly pep rally was going on, Corky wandered away. She was permitted to come and go as she wished, provided she didn't stray far from Mateo's discerning eye.

Perched on a large rock, she gazed about until she spotted her protector sitting near the fire with Joaquin. Oh, Mateo was a handsome devil, all right. Dark, brooding, yet with just enough old-world charm to make him irresistible.

As if he felt her scrutiny, his dark eyes lifted to meet hers, and she looked away, once again struck by the directness of his gaze.

Was she out of her mind? She should be scared witless by the situation she was in, but instead she reacted to his glances like a teenager. And what had the old woman meant when she'd said that Mateo was the other half of the Lovers card? Exactly what was that supposed to mean?

Her thoughts drifted to her previous life. Was anyone feeding her cat, Cleo? And her mother— her mother must be sick with worry by now, not to mention Dalia. Dalia would be beside herself trying to find out what had happened to her.

And her students? Who was in charge of her class now that she had mysteriously vanished without a trace?

Frustrated at having no answers, she focused again on the camp followers who sat close to their leader, listening with rapt attention to Joaquin's tales of adventures. Rosita sat by Joaquin's side, attentive to his every word.

There were a few women in camp, but they had failed to warm up to Corky and she didn't kid herself as to the reason. While she would have welcomed a friendly ally, she knew she was being tolerated by Mateo and the others in camp only because the old woman had said she should be.

Her eyes traveled slowly over the assembled men as she tried to decide whom she could trust. Young Reyes Feliz, Rosita's sixteen-year-old brother, had taken an instant liking to her, although Rosita—who had returned the previous evening—had not been as quick to reciprocate. Corky was aware that she had been the object of Rosita's distrustful eyes more than once. Especially when Joaquin was near.

Claudio Merendez appeared to be about thirty-five, considerably older than the others. Corky didn't trust him at all. He had a savage look about him that matched that of Three-Fingered Jack, whom she knew she couldn't trust. Like Joaquin, Claudio was a commanding figure with a calculating mind that made him as wily as a serpent.

The man they called Valenzuela took great pride in his work, pretending to be Murieta, and performed his duty well. She had heard the men laughing and telling about how unsuspecting citizens would scratch their head in bewilderment, wondering how Murieta could steal a herd of horses one moment and be two hundred miles away robbing a bank the next.

Pedro Gonzalez, another of Joaquin's devoted followers, was a skillful spy and an expert horse thief, who, with Mateo, kept the others well-supplied with mounts.

"You are very quiet tonight."

Corky started at the sound of the deep voice. While she'd been daydreaming, Mateo had left the fire to join her.

"I was just thinking. He's very commanding, isn't he?"

Mateo's eyes moved to his leader. "Joaquin Murieta is a born leader."

"There are those who say he is ruthless and evil."

"Then they are fools."

She looked up, puzzled by his part in all this. She knew his immediate purpose, the feeding and tending of the large herd of horses that such an operation demanded, but she wondered about his inner motive. He appeared to be well-educated, levelheaded, and passionate about his cause, not unlike many of the men who followed Joaquin, yet there was something about him that made him seem more intense, more committed.

"What will become of you and the others when Joaquin's revenge is finished?" she asked, for she knew that day would eventually arrive. She knew everything that would happen to Joaquin Murieta, including the way the young twenty-two-year-old zealot would supposedly meet his death.

"We will return to our lives."

"What is your life, Mateo?"

"This is my life." The look in his eyes told her not to overstep her bounds. He might protect her, but he did not trust her.

"And later, once the bitterness ends?"

"When the retribution against the *Norteamericanos* is complete, then I will seek my peace."

Corky studied his face in the moonlight, a face resolutely carved by the rigorous life of espionage and crime. He was standing so near that she could detect the soft rise and fall of his chest. *Mateo*. His name whispered to her on the breeze. Why did she feel safe with him? Because he was her protector, or was it something more elementary? She wasn't sure. Yet, as safe as she felt with him, it was difficult for her to conceal her contempt for his cause.

"It is not as you think," he returned curtly, again seeming to read her thoughts. "I ride with Joaquin not only to avenge my transgressors, but because of a vow I made to his grandmother."

"His grandmother?"

"She was good to me when I had no one else and I was very young. If it had not been for her, I would not have had anything to eat many nights, and the cold would have seeped through my bones until I wept. When events turned Joaquin to the wrong side of the law, it was I Ricio came in search of, with tears in her eyes, asking that I do whatever I could to protect her grandson's life."

Mateo turned slightly at the sound of Joaquin's voice speaking to the group.

"We live our lives as we see fit, and we will exact our revenge against those who hate us simply because we are *Mexicanos*! We have outwitted the enemy, despite the cost of loved ones. We have sat around fires and shared whiskey with the ghosts of those who no longer sit with us. There were times when as many as twenty of us perished, but still we were not beaten."

"Joaquin! Joaquin!" the men cheered.

Corky shivered as she listened to the tales of harrowing escapes.

"How can you live like this?" she whispered after a while.

"We do so because we have a cause."

And when the cause is gone? she wondered again. What would the outlaws do then?

"Where is your home, Mateo?" There was suddenly so much she wanted to know about this man.

He hesitated, then admitted soberly, "I have none, but I will make one when the time arrives. There are many things I desire."

Her eyes met his with a silent challenge. "Tell me about these things you desire."

His dark eyes searched her face, and for a moment she thought he might refuse to answer. "I desire the love of a woman. I desire what Joaquin shares with Rosita," he said slowly.

Corky's eyes drifted back to the circle of men and women, where Rosita watched Joaquin with adoring eyes. She nodded. "Yes, I think most of us want the kind of relationship Joaquin and Rosita share."

"I have not found my Rosita, but I will . . . one day," Mateo vowed.

He was so close that she could feel the heat from his body and see the fine line of his sensual lips. His eyes were as black as obsidian and as mysterious as the night.

Dragging her gaze from his, she studied the group and counted nearly a hundred of Joaquin's fighting men. Some of them, she knew, had only recently joined his cause.

"No matter what the *Norteamericanos* do, we are greater and stronger," Joaquin was declaring. "I lead two thousand men who are in Sonora and Lower California. I have money deposited in safe places, and I will yet arm and equip fifteen hundred to two thousand men to make a clean sweep of the southern counties." His eyes burned with passion. "I will make them remember what they have done to me, to us, by burning their *ranchos*, and driving them from their property so rapidly that they won't have time to build an army! By the time they regroup, I will be in the mountains where they will never find me! Our wrongs will at last be avenged! We will divide the riches and spend the rest of our days in peace. This I promise you."

A cheer rose from the crowd, and the men's eyes burned with enthusiasm at the magnificent plan he presented. Even Corky had to admit that she felt his energy, the drive and power he exuded in order to hold such a large band together with undivided loyalty.

"They would follow him anywhere," she marveled.

"We *have* followed him—everywhere."

She glanced up and found that Mateo had moved closer. Her lips parted to speak, but her words faltered as he lowered his mouth slowly to hers. "Ah, that you would tell me the secrets you possess, lovely one," he whispered as his lips brushed hers.

She tensed, recognizing his ploy. He was using his male magnetism to wring the truth out of her—only there was no truth to wring. She didn't know why she was here any more than he did. But, for some reason, it didn't matter. Nothing mattered except this vibrant man and his dynamic cause.

His lips were firm and warm, and when they lingered searchingly over hers, she found herself responding. Her fingers drifted to rest against his chest, and she allowed herself to enjoy the moment even though she knew his tactic.

Groaning, he pulled her hard against him, his mouth taking hers hungrily.

"You are an intriguing woman, Cordilla," he murmured. "It would make me sad to find that you were my enemy."

"It makes me sadder to know you are patronizing me, you conceited, overbearing jerk," she breathed.

He withdrew, and she could see a smile forming at the corners of his mouth. "This word, 'jerk.' I am to assume it is not one of praise?"

"You could say that."

Again, he pulled her to him roughly. "Tell me who you are, Cordilla. I do not believe the cards have sent you."

A gruff voice suddenly rang out. "Mateo!"

Mateo's hands dropped from her waist as Three-Fingered Jack called out again. Gazing down at her, she detected a challenge shining in his dark eyes. "I will join you in the tent . . . soon."

As he strode away, she leaned against a tree, her knees suddenly trembling.

Her gaze followed Mateo as he joined Three Fingers at the fire.

"You are troubled, *niña*." The old woman had approached while Corky was still lost in thought.

"I don't know what to say or think," Corky admitted.

"Much has happened to confuse you."

Corky wished she could see the old woman's face better, but it was hidden by the darkness.

"Why have you given me protection?"

"The cards have protected you. They tell of your wish to bring no harm. Quite the contrary, you will be of help to Joaquin."

"I can't possibly see how. I don't know why I'm here, or what my purpose is for being here."

"Do not despair. In time the purpose will be revealed. All in good time," she promised.

"I'm sorry, but I don't believe in the cards."

The old woman smiled wanly. "It is not necessary for you believe, only that you fulfill your mission. There is a power that none can control. That power can be challenged, but it cannot be altered." She turned stiffly and started to shuffle away.

"Old One . . ."

Turning, the old woman looked over her shoulder. "*Sí*?"

"About Mateo?" The man both terrified and fascinated her.

Her smile was veiled now. "He will be with you in whatever happens, if that is what you wish."

"I don't know what I wish. How will I know?"

"You will know. It is inside you. All you must do is search for it."

5

IT'S not like me, Corky thought, as she made her way to the small bend in the stream where she took her early-morning baths before the others awoke. For her, the previous evening had been one of wonder and confusion. Mateo had kissed her and the feelings he stirred were new and powerful, too powerful to contemplate on this warm summer morning.

Her thoughts returned to the previous night, and she blushed at the memory of the moment when, lying near Mateo, she realized that he, too, was remembering the stolen kiss in the firelight. His uneven breathing had been proof of that. However, nothing further had happened, and Corky had felt a sense of inexplicable loss. She had never felt this way about a man, and the thought that she was becoming more and more attracted to a ruthless outlaw confused her even more. Her musings ended abruptly when she found herself standing with her bare feet on the bank of the river.

Looking around cautiously, she noticed that all was quiet. In fact, the whole world seemed to be waiting, but waiting for what? Shrugging, she slipped her arms out of her Mexican blouse. A breeze wafted in from the river, and she realized that if she stayed out on the bank too long she would get a chill. After hurriedly stepping out of the full peasant skirt, she waded into the stream toward the center where the current was swift. She had to swim strongly against its pull.

Suddenly she felt something tugging at her ankle and panic seized her when she realized her foot had been snared by a submerged tree branch. Overwhelming fear assailed her as she struggled to free it, but hysteria rose in her throat when she realized that she could not. Is this what the old woman meant? she agonized as she inhaled yet another mouthful of river water. Is this to be my fate? Am I never to know what it is to live and to love?

Without warning, she felt a warm hand grasp her ankle and gently release her foot from the entanglement. Though she was free, she was too weak to swim back to the bank and slowly she allowed herself to sink down once again into the water's depths.

Again the hand was there, raising and cradling her head so that her face turned toward the bright, warm rays of the sun. She could now see the arm that held her as her savior made his way to the bank. She instantly recognized the golden-brown arm as the same one that had held her the night before. And as she drifted into blackness, she remembered the old woman's prophecy.

Laboriously, Mateo made his way to the bank. When his feet touched the sandy bottom, he turned and drew Corky against his chest. With a mighty surge, he stood and walked the rest of the way, carrying the now almost unconscious woman in his arms. Gently, he lay her on the grassy bank and thanked God that he had arrived in time to save her. He had seen her leave the tent earlier and had decided to follow her and demand that she reveal her purpose for being in Joaquin's camp. But now, as he gazed at her nude body, all thoughts of interrogation and mistrust disappeared. Now all that existed was this woman and this moment.

Corky slowly opened her eyes to find herself gazing into the dark onyx ones which had haunted her thoughts before her swim. These couldn't be Mateo's. These eyes registered concern and . . .

"Are you all right?" Mateo anxiously leaned over her prone body. Corky felt the rivulets of river water trickling down on her breasts and his muscular arm cradling her like a child.

"Yes. My gosh, I almost drowned! Thank you," she gasped.

"The pleasure was all mine," he whispered.

His seductive tone of voice made her realize that she was naked and that he was enjoying that fact. Struggling to sit up, she pushed his hand aside as he tried to help her.

"What are you doing here?" she demanded as she struggled to regain her composure.

"Rescuing you."

"No, I mean, what are you *doing* here?"

"Looking for you," he breathed.

"Why?"

"Ah, *señorita*, must we always be at sword's point?" he asked as his eyes once again caressed her body.

Avoiding his gaze, she stood up and hurried to where she had taken off her clothes. His eyes darkened as he watched her gracefully pull on the garments which were too big for her slim form.

When she was finished, she turned to him, her face registering her unease with this most private moment.

"You do not answer me," he said.

"I have nothing to say to you."

His hand shot out to catch her arm as she turned and started up the path toward the camp. "No, *chica*, I am not finished."

Before she could escape, Mateo pulled her into his arms. His wet garments soaked her thin cotton dress. She felt his heat and her own, and unexpectedly the fire which he had ignited before burst into flame again. Without thinking, Corky wrapped her arms around his neck and the world ceased to exist. Only his lips on hers mattered; only the driving force of this man mattered. Not the fate which had brought her here, not the old woman's ramblings, not the Tarot cards. Only this man and this moment mattered.

Without warning, Mateo quickly raised his head and the spell was shattered. Before he could speak, Corky broke from his grasp and fled up the path, more confused than ever.

"We ride into town this morning."

Corky looked up the next day to see Mateo standing in the doorway. As always his presence, her pulse quickened and her cheeks flushed.

"Why do I have to go?"

"You are not to leave my sight."

"Oh, right. For a minute there, I forgot." As if she could forget.

"There is no need for animosity," he reminded her as she brushed past him.

"Still don't trust me, do you?" she admonished.

"No."

Grinning, he followed her.

When they arrived in town, Corky noticed that Joaquin and Mateo caught every woman's eye. They were exceptionally striking men. Joaquin, his long, black hair falling to his shoulders and his black eyes dancing wickedly at the young ladies, made a splendid sight. His fine black suit, in sharp contrast to his prancing white horse, made him appear the epitome of manhood.

Mateo was equally resplendent in a close-fitting *charro* suit made from the finest materials purchased in Spain. In sharp contrast to Joaquin, his coal-black hair was cut in the Spanish style of the times, close cropped with curls forming at his nape. He presented a most dashing figure, and Corky blushed as she remembered that magnificent form pressed against her nearly naked one and her own response as she threaded her fingers through his thick locks. Yes, both were splendid men, but only one, the man on the black stallion, held her gaze and her thoughts.

Several of the young women cast an eye in Mateo's direction, and Corky wondered how long it would take him to reciprocate. When she nosed her mount closer to his, he turned to look at her with a grin.

"Does something trouble you, *señorita*?" he inquired pleasantly.

Her eyes drifted to the two young women who gazed adoringly up at him. "They're lovely, aren't they?"

"Perhaps, but none so lovely as the one who rides at my side," he returned, his eyes dancing with amusement.

She returned his gaze, wondering if he were serious or just playing a game with her emotions. Nothing had been said or had passed between them since the encounter by the riverbank. It was as if they had left it unspoken in order for it to be savored and therefore to be treasured for a later time.

Corky saw him bend down to accept a rose from one of the women, and suddenly she felt as if someone had stepped on her heart. The pain was acute and unexpected. Since when did she care what this man did? She abruptly averted her gaze so that he could not read her thoughts.

Reining her horse away, she rode beside Guerra the rest of the time.

They bought their supplies, and Mateo bought a white blouse and a blue skirt for her while they waited for his river-soaked boots to be repaired. Surprised by his gesture, she thanked him, then tucked the new purchases away in her saddlebag. He didn't fool her. He was still trying to wheedle the truth out of her, but the blouse and skirt were too lovely for her not to accept; it was his loss, not hers.

As they were preparing to leave town, Joaquin, ignoring the curious crowd, reined his horse close to a building and paused to study several posters tacked to the weathered boards.

Corky and Mateo rode up beside him to get a closer look at what had captured his attention. There were signs, one for a boat for "sail," another to hire a cook, one for the loss of a brown mule, and a fourth that was written in a fair English hand.

Five Thousand Dollars Reward For Joaquin Murieta, Dead Or Alive.

The poster went on to state that the citizens of San Joaquin County were offering the reward for the "noted robber."

Expecting Joaquin to tear down the notice, she was surprised when he dismounted his horse and dug a pencil stub out of his pocket. Kneeing her horse closer, Corky watched him print an additional line at the bottom of the notice.

I will give $10,000! Joaquin.

Spinning on his heel, he caught the expression on her face and chuckled with pleasure. "I am worth it, no?"

With that now familiar laugh, he swung onto his horse and kicked it into a gallop, leading the way out of town.

It was the rainy season, and because of the dampness in the air, it seemed to Corky that she spent most of her nights by the campfire.

As she felt the warm cloak around her shoulders, she shifted, remembering that Mateo had provided her with the *serape* to ward off the evening chill.

She had seen little of him since they had returned to camp. He had been secluded with Joaquin and their most trusted men, planning new courses of action. However, at dinner that evening she had overheard him saying that in a few days, Three-Fingered Jack and Valenzuela would return from Sonora. When they did, Joaquin would have the money needed for his new ventures.

With a hot cup of coffee in her hand, she sat by the fire, listening to the night sounds. Soon she and Mateo would retire to their tent. Since the night Carmelita had tried to slit her husband's throat, Mateo had arranged for them to share the tent alone, and she had to admit that she enjoyed sharing this time with him. There was intimacy and there was wonder and there was waiting, always waiting. She was now fully aware of the attraction between them, and it grew with every hour. During their long nights together, she was begrudgingly beginning to appreciate many things about the man who safeguarded her. His intelligence and education astounded her. In the darkness of the tent, as they lay near each other, Mateo would enlighten her about his life. It was amazing that anyone born in the nineteenth century could have such an encompassing knowledge of the world. He told her he had lived in Spain, where he had studied Castillian law. After several years in Europe, including briefly studying in France, the twenty-four-year-old man had missed the open spaces and the slow-paced life of his homeland. Upon returning, Mateo opened a law practice adjacent to his home and began receiving clients. Although most of his clients were the rich *gachupines*, or pure Spanish, such as Joaquin and his grandmother, and the *criollos*, or native-born pure Spanish, Mateo also found himself representing the *campesinos*, or poor workers of the region. It was while representing them before prejudicial courts that he had become interested in Joaquin's cause. After Mateo was burned out and tortured, it seemed only natural for him to join Joaquin. Corky was aware that it was Mateo's level head that kept the volatile outlaw's desire for revenge restrained, and she admired the lawyer's coolness under pressure.

He had a wicked sense of humor and a quick wit. More than once she had born the brunt of his jokes. Her mind went back to the time she had been trying to pick up some simple Spanish words to make her life easier in the camp, which was difficult at best even if one spoke Spanish. But except for Mateo and Joaquin, who had learned the King's English, no one spoke a word of English. Corky knew some Spanish from her required two semesters at college, but when confronted with actually having to speak and understand the language, she was at a loss. One day this became an acute embarrassment when Mateo came across her trying to communicate with the other camp women. She had been trying to explain that she wanted to clean the tent. With her limited Spanish she did not know the word for tent, only the word for house, "*casa.*" Apparently she said something wrong, because the other women started to giggle and give her sly looks. As she became more frustrated, the gales of laughter increased. She was almost at her wit's end when Mateo arrived. He smiled when one of the women said something and pointed at Corky. He answered in what she surmised was a witty reply because the women once again broke into laughter, but this time it was with genuine amusement. As he turned away, she quickly followed and grabbed his arm.

"What was that all about? What did I say to make them laugh at me? All I wanted was for them to know that I wanted some tools to clean the tent."

"Ah, *chica*," Mateo intoned with mock patience, "your Spanish needs a lot of work."

"And what did I say incorrectly?" Corky was now fuming and frustrated by his casual reference to her limited Spanish.

"You know the word *casa* means house, no?"

"*Sí*"

"The word *casa* also means married."

"Oh, it does . . ." Her words trailed off as the full meaning of what she had been trying to say flooded over her. She actually had been telling those women that she had been looking for "tools of marriage." And in a bawdy camp such as this one that could only mean one thing. . . .

"*Sí, chica*, would you care to look for these 'married tools' with me?" Mateo teased in a wicked undertone as he saw she understood what she had said, for her face was as red as the sunburn he had seen on her pale skin that day he had hauled her from the river.

"That won't be necessary," Corky returned quickly as she saw his eyes darken with passion. With a mumbled apology for her stupidity, she had hurried off.

That was just one example of his remarks laden with sexual overtones that made her feel young and foolish. This man could turn her inside out with the great knowledge he had of the world and of women. And because she liked intelligent, witty men with a sense of humor, she felt herself drawn irresistibly closer to his powerful masculinity. Whoever Mateo Armandez Rivas was, and whatever the future held for her, she knew she'd never forget the time they had shared. He was an outlaw, a hunted criminal, a man without a home; she was a woman who eventually must return to her own time. But she could imagine him dressed in blue jeans and a close-fitting T-shirt, helping her shop for old-world antiques, and suddenly, she realized that this man would be comfortable in any time, in any place, and in any century.

The silence of the night and her thoughts were suddenly shattered by the sound of riders approaching. The men sprang to their feet and, drawing their guns, plunged into the darkness.

When Three-Fingered Jack and Valenzuela rode into camp, the men reappeared, shouting their greetings.

Joaquin emerged from his tent, and Corky watched as he jubilantly greeted the men.

Jack and Valenzuela settled down on the other side of the fire, devouring the food and drink that had magically appeared. Corky listened as Three Fingers and Valenzuela, along with a battle-scarred Luis Vulvia, related their harrowing escapade.

On their way back to camp, they had lost five men in various skirmishes. Though the horses looked exhausted, they were in good health, they reported. Then, laughing, they each drew out a heavy bag of gold coins and handed them to Joaquin.

Shaking her head, Corky wondered how much longer their merriment would last as Joaquin broke open a cask of *pulque*, and they drank to their newest victory.

6

Two days later, most of the outlaws were preparing to leave. Corky had never been away from Mateo's protective presence, and she was apprehensive about his departure. If something happened to him, what would she do? For the first time, she realized how important he was to her safety. The old woman could do little if someone decided to do away with her. For the most part, the men and women in camp left her alone, but with Mateo gone, the dangers increased.

That night, as she lay beside Mateo in the consuming darkness, she suddenly rose on one elbow. "Take me with you tomorrow."

"It is out of the question."

"Mateo, please, I'm frightened without you here," she said quietly.

He was silent for a moment, then said, "No one has bothered you, have they?"

"No, you're always around so they wouldn't dare, but who knows? And maybe I could be of help." Bits and pieces of Joaquin's life came to her at times, and it was possible that she would remember something that would keep him and his men from harm's way. She sat up and looked at Mateo; the moonlight that scissored through the tent flap now bathed their faces in a soft glow.

Rolling to his side, he looked at her in the dim light. Once again she saw suspicion dominate his dark eyes. "And this is the only reason you ask to ride with us?"

"No, I'm coming along to spy on you," she taunted.

"As I thought."

"Oh, for heaven's sake, I'm not a spy. If I was going to do something, I would have done it by now."

Sitting up, he gently cupped her face in his strong hands. His eyes searched hers before he spoke. "How I hope you speak the truth, my most beautiful *querida*, for I have begun to desire you as I have no other."

Her heartbeat quickened, swelling to a rapid resonance that she feared he must be able to hear. She understood what his eyes were asking. More than that, she was certain her reply would bring an irrevocable change in their relationship.

As he drew her closer, his warm breath teased her ear. "And you, *mi bella amor*, do you also desire me?"

Suddenly, the unspoken question and tension which had been building ever since that night by the fire was irrevocably voiced out loud in the passion-filled darkness.

For an instant, she thought of evading his question. But she'd learned something in the weeks she'd spent with him, in his world, and in his era; she'd learned never to squander time. She'd learned to live every moment to the fullest. If she did not answer his question, if she did not tell him her true feelings, she knew without a doubt that she would regret the decision for the rest of her life.

She swallowed and forced herself to meet his gaze squarely. "I know it's illogical, Mateo, but if you are asking me if I want you to make love to me"—she took a steadying breath—"then I admit that I do."

"Ah, *mi querida*, may God forgive me, but I do with all my heart. It is something I have wanted since I pulled you from the river."

The corners of Corky's mouth lifted in a bittersweet smile. She had no idea when she'd be suddenly whisked back into the twentieth century without warning, or even if she'd come back alive; she only knew that she wanted to share this night with him.

She realized that she might never have this moment again. Whatever time she had with Mateo, she would make the most of it. They would make a memory that would sustain her for the rest of her life, whether she lived in the twentieth century or the nineteenth.

"Love me, Mateo." Her whisper caught in her throat as he crushed her lips to his.

He seemed to struggle for restraint when, after a moment, he moved away from her and took a deep breath.

"I disappoint you." It was her worst fear. She knew little about the ways to please a man and her confidence was shaken by his abrupt withdrawal. Perhaps, by kissing her, he had discovered how awkward and unskilled she actually was.

"Disappoint me? Is that what you think, *querida?*" He lifted her chin to smile tenderly into her eyes. "You could never disappoint me. It is I who must remember to go slowly, to treat you gently, to show you the ways of a man with a woman."

"I know you can tell I don't know much about . . . well, about how to . . . do things."

Her honesty was disarming. "We will go slowly, savoring, learning the ways to pleasure each other."

He gazed at her tenderly while his hands caressed her hair. It gradually became clear that he would not press her before she was ready to begin. He waited until he felt the barely perceptible surrender of her body beneath his questing hands.

Touching his lips to hers, he stroked and smoothed the tense knot at the base of her neck. Gradually, her lips softened and her neck became pliant. Her head tilted back, and her throat shone pale in the moonlight. Her apprehension was easing, while a new kind of tension was building deep inside her. Was he using this moment and her weakness as yet another means of gaining the truth? She couldn't bear it if that were true.

His lips trailed hot kisses down her throat, down into the deep V of her open blouse. She gasped at the unexpected sensation that bloomed inside her when his head lowered between her breasts.

He seemed to force himself to pause. She watched him lift his head as if with great difficulty. She saw the muscles of his neck tighten as he swallowed thickly. Taking her hand in his, he laid her palm on his chest.

She felt the pounding, hard and fast, and realized that he was as excited as she. Her fingers spread wide, and she let her hands roam over his bare chest, her slender fingers tangling in the thick, dark whorls of hair.

With deliberate care, his long fingers moved slowly to push the blouse off her shoulders. The brush of his knuckles as he continued to ease the garment over her bare skin caused ripples of excitement to undulate inside her.

She drew in a breath of air tinged with woodsmoke and wildflowers and the manly scent of Mateo Armandez.

He drew down her blouse, and the touch of

his fingers grazing over her breasts and down her arms sent a shiver over her skin like smooth water shuddering in the wake of a breeze.

Cupping his palms over her narrow shoulders, he warmed them. Then slowly, with his eyes on hers, his hands began to circle lower, exploring, testing, kindling the flames inside her until they leaped higher.

Her stomach contracted involuntarily at the sensations he incited within her. She wanted him to slow down and hurry at the same time. The agonizing anticipation as his thumbs brushed over her breasts in mesmerizing circles was almost too much to bear. She leaned forward and lifted her lips. He groaned as he took her sweet offering hungrily.

It was as if something inside him could no longer be contained. His lips opened, drawing hers apart as well. Their tongues joined, twisting, teasing, stroking in evocative play.

She clung to him, unable to tear her lips away, addicted to this sweet agony of stimulation.

His hands moved to the peasant skirt and slowly he began to ease the garment from her slim hips. She willingly assisted him as he sensually drew the woven material down her legs. As he rose before her, the blanket covering him fell away.

Painfully modest, she had slept every night fully dressed, while he had followed the tradition of sleeping with only a light blanket covering his nakedness.

In the moonlight, her eyes swept down the magnificent sight of him. Ridges of muscle tapered to slim hips. When her gaze started to drop shyly away from that most compelling view between his powerful thighs, he captured her hand in his.

"I will not hurt you. Here"—he guided her hand to him—"touch and do not be afraid, Cordilla."

The silky smoothness of his skin reassured her, and she let herself explore him, tentatively at first, then more boldly.

At the same time, he gently touched her, increasing his tempo, stoking the fires until they consumed her.

"Oh, Mateo . . ."

"There's more, *mi querida*. Permit me to teach you . . ."

"Oh, yes." She reached up, offering herself to him.

Levering himself above her, he entered her with controlled patience. She felt a sense of fullness, a completeness that she'd only imagined before. She realized that together they would make this night one she could cherish no matter what the future or past might bring her. She had made the correct decision. She released a long sigh that whispered of the feeling of rightness which now filled her body as well as her heart.

It seemed to be the signal he was waiting for. He began a rhythm that carried them into another dimension. His hands on her hips provided subtle encouragement until she, too, joined him in the magical cadence of lovers that defied time and reality.

The tempo built until behind closed eyelids, she saw the moonlight splinter into a hundred torchlights. And somewhere, far away, she heard him calling her name again and again and again.

7

MATEO was off again. As usual, Corky didn't know where he'd gone, but he'd promised to return by dark.

It was close to that now, and she eagerly awaited the sight of his white teeth flashing mischievously in his nut-brown face.

Strange, she thought, even with all their differences she was still passionately attracted to him. She hid a smile, remembering what she had to smile about. Here she was, caught in some kind of time warp that could reverse itself at any moment, suspected by every woman in camp, mistrusted by most of the men, and downright distrusted by Mateo, yet she was smiling.

She slid the pack of Tarot cards from her pocket and opened them, staring at the ancient symbols. They were smooth and worn from use, and the accompanying pages were brittle with age. She'd read the yellowed notes so many times that she'd memorized them. Her mind had gone over and over the moment that had somehow swept her through time.

Often, she'd thought about spreading the cards before her to see if they would sweep her back to the future, but she always hesitated. She wanted to return, she convinced herself, yet she was curious about what had brought her here. Was she on a clandestine mission, and if she was, when would its purpose be revealed to her? A day, a week, a year? Time no longer meant anything to her, and she had no idea how long she had been here.

She lifted the cards closer to the firelight, her thumb thoughtfully stroking the tattered edges. There were so many things she missed about her former life and the comforts she had always taken for granted: hot and cold running water, perfumed soaps, and deodorant.

She wanted to go back; her mother must be beside herself with grief. And she missed Dalia, and the long talks they had shared. And Cleo. She hoped someone was taking care of her cat.

But now, Mateo was interwoven into her life. Remembering the hours she'd spent with him, touching him, kissing him, her body flushed with love's passion, brought an ache to her heart. Being with him was more exciting, more sensual than she could ever have imagined. Whenever he was gone for even a few hours, she felt an emptiness she couldn't explain. And when he smiled at her, it was as if the world dropped away and there were only the two of them. She knew her thoughts were foolish. It was sheer lunacy to feel this way about a man who lived his life on the fringe of extinction—a man with whom she could never have a lasting relationship. Why then did she keep seeing him in jeans and a T-shirt cradling a child?

At the sound of approaching hoofbeats, she slid the cards back into her pocket and stood up.

Mateo was riding at the head of a small group of men. His gaze swung immediately to her as they entered camp, and she grinned.

As he slid from his horse, she found herself shamelessly running to him as she had done so often lately. Grabbing her, he swung her around in a dizzying circle, his lips nuzzling her ear. "Your hunger matches my own, no?"

"Desperately," she whispered in return. "Desperately."

He held her high so that their eyes met evenly before he gathered her close. "Then let us seek our solitude, *querida*," he whispered. He let her body slide down the full length of his until her feet lightly touched the ground, then his mouth took hers hungrily.

* * *

Corky was brushing her hair when she looked up, and her eyes met Mateo's as he entered the tent.

He paused in the doorway, gazing at her. "Your beauty fills me with longing. My mind is consumed with thoughts of you to the point that I cannot perform my duties properly."

"I worry about you when you're gone."

His smile was warmly teasing. "Worry? About Mateo Armandez, the scourge of the country? How the authorities would laugh."

He knelt on their pallet and drew her to him.

"But I do worry." Her fingers tenderly traced his features. "What would happen to me if something happened to you?"

"Ah, *mi amor*." His gaze caressed her sensuously. "You worry only for your safety?"

"No." She lowered her eyes, afraid he would see her true feelings. "I worry not so much for me, but for you. You could be wounded, or killed."

He caught her hand and pressed her fingers lightly to his lips. "This I will try to avoid."

She saw his smile fade as the flames of passion burned in his gaze. "And now I tell you my secret, *mi bella amor*. When Joaquin appointed me to watch over you, I was resentful."

"And now?"

"Now, I thank the fates that have brought you into my arms. The Old One says it is the cards, that it is because of Rosita's urgent prayers that you are here. But I think perhaps you are here for me alone."

"My being here has something to do with Rosita?"

"It is what the *Vieja* says. She says Rosita prayed for someone to intervene in Joaquin's life before he was seized by an untimely death. She says you hold a secret, a secret yet to be revealed."

"I know of no secret," she whispered, confused by the old woman's prophecy.

Mateo's features hardened in the lamplight. "Do not lie to me, *querida*. Now is the time, for the truth, as you know it."

"I speak the truth, Mateo," she answered wearily. "You'll just have to believe me, because I know of no way to prove my innocence. Don't you trust me?"

He looked at her for a long moment, his dark eyes filled with hesitation, then softening with affection. "Yes, *querida*, I do."

Then his mouth took hers roughly, urgently, and she lost herself in his passion.

Sometime during the night Corky awoke with a start. Sweat blanketed her forehead, though the air was mild.

As she sat up, trying to clear her mind, the pages from a book flashed through her brain. The boldly lettered text stood out as clearly as if a light had been switched on: Joaquin Murieta was about to be attacked again, only this time he would not survive.

The air suddenly constricted in the small tent. Mateo lay on his side, sleeping deeply, his even breathing blending with the night sounds.

How could she have forgotten what she had read and taught? Suddenly, it was all clear in her mind. However wild and farfetched it seemed, she knew now, with crystal certainty, why she had been transported back in time.

She couldn't change history, but she could make it work to Joaquin's advantage—and save Mateo's life.

"What is it, *querida*?" Mateo murmured, awakened by her restlessness.

"I have to talk to Joaquin."

"Joaquin—"

Scooting to the flap of the tent, she parted the canvas impatiently. "I have to talk to him right now."

Mateo sat up and reached for his pants. "I will take you to him."

Relieved, Corky realized that he had meant it when he said he trusted her now. Moments later they were striding across the clearing to Joaquin's tent.

"Joaquin, I would speak with you," Mateo called softly.

Joaquin's sleepy voice returned from the darkness. "Mateo . . . Do you take leave of your senses?"

"I am of sound mind. Please, allow me to enter."

Corky heard the sound of rustling, Rosita's disgruntled murmurings, then, "Come."

Mateo stepped inside, pulling Corky behind him.

Sitting up, Joaquin scratched his beard and glared at the midnight intruders. "Do you bring word of trouble?"

Nudging Corky forward, Mateo said softly, "Speak, *mi amor*."

"I know this sounds crazy," Corky began, certain that both men would think she'd gone completely mad, "but I know why I've been sent here."

A mysterious smile appeared on Rosita's face as she huddled closer to Joaquin.

Leaning forward, Joaquin fumbled for the lantern. "Continue."

"What is the date?"

"Today's date?"

"Yes, today's date. What is it?"

"The twenty-fifth, I believe." He blew out the match and adjusted the lantern wick.

"Of July?"

He nodded.

"Tomorrow you plan to ride to Panoche Pass, right?"

Joaquin exchanged looks with Mateo. "You told her this?"

"No, I spoke not a word of the plan."

"Mateo didn't tell me, I saw it—a few minutes ago."

"Saw it? How is this possible?" Joaquin scoffed. "The plans were made only a few hours ago."

"Listen to me, Joaquin." Kneeling, Corky made him look at her. "Your life is in grave danger. If you ride to Panoche Pass tomorrow, you won't return alive."

"What is this gibberish she speaks?" Joaquin derided.

"Hear her out," Mateo urged, suddenly aware that Corky was about to fulfill the old woman's prophecy.

"You are a man in love, your heart is persuaded to believe—"

"No, I know not how, but she speaks the truth."

"Joaquin, you must listen to her!" Rosita pleaded.

Joaquin's gaze slowly returned to Corky. "Tell me how you can know of my approaching death."

They sat on the blankets in the darkness, talking softly, and Corky could hear the nuances of disbelief, anger, and frustration in Joaquin's voice as she explained her vision, and what they must do to prevent it from coming true.

"This tale you tell," Joaquin said when she was finished, "how am I to believe such a story?"

"Summon the Old One. I think she knows more than she's been saying."

"The *Vieja* sleeps. She is old and very tired. I will not disturb her for such madness."

"Joaquin, she speaks the truth," Mateo insisted.

"And how do you know this for certain?" Joaquin waved his hand dismissively. "Go now, leave me to think on these strange ramblings."

With a sense of impending doom, Corky turned and made her way once again to the tent she shared with Mateo. He followed close behind. Both were lost in their own thoughts, she with the knowledge she now possessed, he with the realization that she was not of this time or of this place.

Mateo was sure she had not been sent as Joaquin's guardian angel, but there lay the mystery. Just who was this woman who had stolen his heart? Just what magical powers did she possess to be able to read the future? Although he was a learned man, he trembled with uncertainty, for here was a subject he knew nothing about. This woman, the one he had chosen above all others, must be a sorceress, and therefore evil. Did not his religious training in the Catholic faith demand that he shun such an individual? Lost in thought, he was unaware that Corky had stopped just outside the tent and was now looking at him searchingly.

"Mateo, please walk with me. I know I have said a lot of things tonight that have disturbed you. I think the time has come for you to know about these." She pulled the Tarot cards from her pocket.

Fear of what he would hear caused him to hesitate, but as she placed her slender hand in his larger one, he realized he would follow this woman anywhere. For this woman he would see hell's burning fires, for with this woman he had also seen heaven. Love was not enough;

complete trust was what made a man and a woman one.

He recognized the path to the bend in the river as the one where he had first realized his feelings for her, and suddenly he wasn't afraid anymore.

Corky sat on the grassy bank and gently pulled Mateo down beside her. Holding the Tarot cards in her right hand, she turned to face Mateo's quizzical frown.

"Do you know what these are?" she asked, handing the cards to him one by one.

"Yes. Are you a Gypsy?" he inquired as he took them from her.

"Oh, no." Corky laughed uneasily. "What I am about to tell you may seem farfetched and crazy, but I'm asking you to hear me out and keep an open mind before you dismiss what I am going to say."

Recognizing the earnestness in her voice, Mateo nodded.

In a hushed voice, beside the bend in the river, enclosed and protected by a night radiant with stars, Corky related the story of her fantastic journey through time.

"I don't know exactly how I got here, except I'm sure it was through these cards," she finished lamely, slowly taking the worn cards from his hands.

"It is enough to know that you are here," Mateo said when she had finished. "I have often wanted to know about the future. When I was visiting

Paris, I met a *loco* Frenchman named Jules Verne. He was filled with wonderful tales of ships that traveled under the sea, and of voyages to the past and the future. What an *imaginación!*"

"Oh, yes." She laughed. "Jules Verne was ahead of his time. He later wrote many books and some of his predictions came true. The ship he told you about is a 'submarine.' It can keep three hundred and fifty men under the sea for up to six months at a time."

"*Increíble*," Mateo breathed. "Tell me more of this future."

As the darkness turned to the dusky hues of dawn, Corky related to this nineteenth-century man, the modern technology of the twentieth century. When she finally finished, the sky was a brilliant blue and the camp was awake. Throughout the night Mateo had proved to be not only an avid listener, but an inquiring one as well. His quick and brilliant mind formulated questions in great detail, and Corky was once again struck by his ability to retain information.

"I wish I could see this future of yours," he said as he took her hand to lead her back to camp. "I would like to see the boats that sail under the sea and the metal birds that fly."

If only you could, my love, Corky thought as she walked beside him. If only you could.

8

EARLY the next morning, Corky heard riders leave camp before dawn. Bolting from her bedroll, she realized that Mateo was gone from her side.

When she stepped outside, the woman tending the fire was bent over laying slices of ham in a skillet.

"Who were the riders who just left?" Corky called.

Glancing up, the woman replied quietly, "Joaquin, Three-Fingered Jack—"

"Mateo?"

"Mateo tends the horses."

Whirling, Corky returned to the tent, relieved that Mateo was safe, but heartsick that Joaquin had ignored her warning.

While Mateo spent the afternoon making arrangements for the transfer of a herd of horses, Corky's apprehension mounted. Why had Joaquin refused to believe her? What if, because of his belief that he was immortal, he'd

83

ridden to Panoche Pass this morning? If only she could have convinced him not to go.

Before the sun set that evening, a rider rode into camp at a full gallop.

"Joaquin is dead! Joaquin is dead!"

A low wail went up from Joaquin's followers, and Corky felt her knees turn to dust as she reached for Mateo's arm. She had failed in her mission.

"Do you know this as truth?" Mateo demanded as the rider dismounted.

"I speak *la verdad*. I was just about to enter our camp when I saw it happen before my eyes. No one knew I was there, and that is why I escaped. Our *compañeros* were having dinner and resting their horses in the region of Panoche Pass, to the west of Tulare Lake. I could see that all seven of them had dismounted. Except for Joaquin, who was grooming his horse, the rest were around the campfire. Suddenly, Captain Love's Rangers rode in. The men bolted for the horses, all except Joaquin. The Rangers had their guns on the group when a lieutenant approached Joaquin.

"He rode up to where Joaquin held his horse, calm as a forest pool, and he asked him where they were traveling. Apparently at first the Rangers thought they had not been recognized, though I recognized the leader, Lieutenant Byrnes, whom I knew from before."

"Get to the tale, Juan," Mateo demanded.

The man studied the ground for a long moment before looking up again.

"The Rangers asked a few questions, and it seemed all was going well, when suddenly a fight broke out and both sides began shooting. When Joaquin yelled that every man should ride for himself, the men scattered for escape. Three-Fingered Jack rode into the forest, but he was shot by several of the Rangers. While they were shooting, Joaquin jumped up on his horse and rode off with a dozen or so men firing at him."

A woman in the crowd wailed with grief.

"Finish the tale," another urged.

"Where is Rosita?" Mateo suddenly asked, concerned that she might overhear the news of her lover's death before it could be broken to her gently.

"I will go for her." A woman started running toward Joaquin's tent.

"After a long chase," the rider continued, "the Rangers kept shooting at Joaquin, but they couldn't hit him. So they finally shot his horse, and it fell dead beneath him."

"What of Joaquin?"

"Joaquin leaped off and started running on foot, but the Rangers rode him down." He paused, lowering his eyes apologetically. "They fired many bullets into his body. *Caramba*, he was brave!" Juan summoned a proud grin. "Joaquin turned and shouted, 'Don't shoot anymore! The work is done,' and then he fell."

Silence followed Juan's words as the men and women stood with bowed heads, uncertain what to say or do.

"And Jack?" Mateo asked.

"He was pursued by the lieutenant and two other men. He ran five miles on foot before many shots brought him down. You should have seen him, *compañeros*. He leaped over the ground like a wild beast, outrunning the horses that sometimes stepped in the holes left by the prairie dogs.

"And when they cornered him, he wheeled around with his eyes blazing fire, and with a yell of defiance, he fired at them before Byrnes shot him through the head."

Turning, Mateo walked away, his shoulders bent with disbelief and the realization that the cause was finished.

It was late before Mateo came to bed that night. Drawing Corky into his arms, he held her tightly.

"If you could travel in time, anywhere you wanted to go, would you go back to your life before it was changed by the *Norteamericanos*, or would you move forward?" she asked.

He lay quietly for a few moments before answering. "If you had asked me that question a few weeks ago, I would have said I wanted to see again the faces of the men who had burned my home so I might exact my revenge. But now that I have held you in my arms, I desire only a future of peace, with you." He caressed her arm, before lifting her wrist and pressing a kiss in the palm of her hand. "Who knows what the future holds? For me, the future is now, and you are here."

Turning into his arms, she lost herself to his lovemaking.

* * *

The next morning she awakened with a purpose. Mateo had left the tent long before the sun had risen. When she went out to the fire, she found most of the camp already gathered. Many, she discovered, had been up all night, some packing, believing that with their leader gone, they were in danger of being discovered. Others appeared to be too distraught even to make the simplest plans.

As Mateo approached, Corky went to him. "Mateo, I want to see where Joaquin died."

"He is not there."

"Where was his body taken?"

"Cordilla—"

"Mateo, I don't believe that Joaquin is dead."

His brows knitted together angrily. "It is best not to dwell on this—"

"No, listen to me. According to history, Lieutenant Byrnes wanted to make certain everyone believed that it was indeed Joaquin Murieta who was killed. He was afraid that Captain Love would doubt his word, so he instructed that the head of Murieta be cut off and preserved in a jar of alcohol."

A stunned gasp went up from those who were listening to their conversation.

"How can you speak of this?" Mateo challenged. The long hours since word of Joaquin's death were manifested in his weary features.

"It's in my history books. The preserved head will be necessary in order for Captain Love to collect the reward, but it won't be Joaquin's."

Mateo's eyes narrowed with suspicion. "How can you know this?"

Her eyes met his, and challenged him to dispute her knowledge. "You said you trusted me."

"I do, but, *querida*, the words you speak—"

"Then take me to where Joaquin's alleged death took place."

Mateo weighed her words. "It is senseless—"

"Just agree to take me there . . . and get Rosita. She should come with us."

"Joaquin's woman is encumbered with grief! She can endure no more!"

"Please, Mateo." She reached out to take his hand. "Trust me. If I am wrong, then I err with the best intentions."

Remembering their conversation by the river and the fact that Corky had foreseen Joaquin's death forced Mateo to reconsider. Fifteen minutes later, they left camp with Juan leading the riders toward the region of Tulare Lake. Corky and Rosita rode hard to keep pace with the men's horses. They were inviting danger by riding *en masse* during the daylight, but there was no other way to confirm Corky's suspicion.

By the time they arrived at their destination, the sun was setting behind a bank of threatening storm clouds. Reining their horses to a halt on a small rise, the riders stared at the valley below.

"This is where our *compañeros* encountered the Rangers," Juan said.

"Are you certain?" Corky asked. Below them the tranquil setting bore no evidence of a recent battle.

"Of this I am certain. The Rangers took everything. I watched as they gathered up the horses, the saddles, the bridles, and the Colt revolvers. They even took the handmade boots off those who had fallen."

"And where was Joaquin?"

"He fell"—Juan pointed to a small hollow—"over there."

"You saw this?"

"I did not see him actually fall, but I heard what the men shouted as they . . ." He shifted in his saddle, glancing at Rosita. "As they removed his head."

"Why did you not tell us this before?" Mateo demanded.

Juan shrugged as he gazed at Rosita. "I wanted to spare her the pain. It was enough that he was dead."

"Mateo, please," Corky entreated. "We're here. It can't hurt to look."

Nodding, Mateo kneed his horse down into the valley. The others formed a solemn procession behind him.

Guiding her horse to the edge of the incline, Corky's eyes focused on the hollow for any sign of life. She couldn't believe that Joaquin had not taken her warning seriously. She simply *refused* to believe he would be so foolish.

9

A SHOUT rose from Joaquin's men, and Corky whirled to see Joaquin Murieta's horse burst into the small clearing. Astride the animal was a healthy and robust Joaquin with his head firmly attached to his shoulders.

He gave a jubilant shout and grinned, sweeping his hat off to his followers. "Grieve no more, my good and faithful men! Joaquin Murieta lives on!"

Mateo looked at Corky incredulously and her smile was one of jubilation.

The band assembled around Joaquin, calling out prayers of gratitude and thankfulness.

Drawing his horse closer to Corky, Mateo looked contrite. "I wish to apologize. Again, in my heart, I did not believe you."

"I know you didn't. But why should you?" Corky knew that the whole idea of her coming a hundred and thirty-eight years from the future could be pretty mind-blowing for anyone.

He gazed down at her, his eyes mirroring his

90

love. "Then it is true. You are able to foretell the future."

"Not really, but I know Joaquin perpetrated a hoax in order to convince the authorities that he was dead. It was the only way he could free himself from a life of crime so that he and Rosita could live in peace."

"This I do not understand—"

"Joaquin is as tired of anger and resentment as you are. History is vague about whether the head Captain Love had in a jar was really that of Joaquin Murieta, but it didn't seem to matter to the authorities whether the head was that of the real Joaquin or one of the other four who claimed his name. As long as the killings, robberies, and cattle-thieving ceased, and it appeared to the world that the sovereign state of California could protect its citizens, then the authorities were content to assume that Joaquin was dead. Indeed, the legislature was so relieved to be rid of Joaquin Murieta that they voted an additional five-thousand-dollar bonus for Captain Harry Love and his men."

"And what of Three-Fingered Jack?"

"Jack, I fear, is dead, just as Juan said."

"But Joaquin would have warned him about the attack."

"He most likely did, and Jack chose to ignore the warning."

Mateo's eyes returned to his leader, finding the events of the past few minutes incredible. "How could this be?"

"According to history, Captain Love had been

tracing Joaquin's movements for days. At Arroyo Cantoova, the Rangers encountered about twenty men with fifteen hundred horses, many which were recognized as stolen. When confronted, the leader gave such vague answers that Love was convinced he was onto Murieta's band. Not wanting to frighten them, Love decided to track them to make sure this was indeed Murieta's group of bandits. When the outlaws split, the group with the horses heading northward toward the San Joaquin River and a smaller group heading southward toward the Tejon Pass, Love decided to split his forces, also. He and a small group of men followed the horses northward while Lieutenant Byrnes, with the rest of the Rangers under his command, followed the bandits south."

Draping his arm around Mateo's shoulder, Joaquin finished the story as he and Rosita walked up to join Corky and Mateo. Corky and Mateo looked at each other, shaking their heads with disbelief. Joaquin seemed to be enjoying this!

Embracing Mateo warmly, Joaquin pounded his friend on the back. "This woman of yours . . . she is . . . *una bruja*, a witch! She knew exactly what would happen, and she saved my life!"

With one arm around his friend and one arm around his Rosita, Joaquin filled them in on how he had escaped.

Apparently, Joaquin had gone with the horses, sending his trusted look-alike lieutenant, Joaquin Valenzuela, with the southern party. Somewhere along the line, Joaquin had doubled back unbeknownst to Captain Love and had ridden up just as Lieutenant Byrnes ordered the head of Joaquin Murieta be removed for evidence.

"Joaquin, you are a fool," Mateo berated, "for not returning earlier and scaring us all into an early grave."

"Ah, *mi buen amigo*, after I saw the destruction by the lieutenant, I headed northward again to see to the horses. When I arrived, I saw that Love and his other group of Rangers had captured my men. I hid until I felt it was safe to escape."

"But Jack did not survive?" Mateo asked.

"It was an honorable death, *mi hermano*. Jack leaped like a deer over the ground, pursued by Lieutenant Byrnes and two others. He ran for miles before he fell, pierced by no less than nine bullets. I had warned him of the danger we faced and prayed that he would heed Cordilla's warning, but, alas, he did not."

Joaquin shook his head sadly. "When it was over, four were dead and two were taken prisoner. Lieutenant Byrnes rode among the dead, and as I watched, he identified one of the bodies as that of Joaquin Murieta. Captain Love was notified and they severed the head of a man believed to be me."

He continued, "I was reluctant to believe what Cordilla had told me last night, but I went to the *Vieja* and she told me of my Rosita's prayers for my safety, and that I could not ignore Cordilla's warning. While we were riding toward the valley, I became convinced that I should heed the warnings, and therefore, I promptly veered off. The others continued northward with the horses."

Corky knew he felt great sorrow at having seen his friends and comrades fall.

"The head of the one identified as Murieta was cut off to be carried back as proof of my death so that the reward could be collected."

"Then whose head was it?" Rosita asked.

Corky already surmised the answer from her knowledge of Joaquin's life. "More than likely Joaquin Valenzuela, who was often confused with Joaquin because of his responsibility in the governing of the band and important expeditions. Even though Valenzuela was much older than Joaquin, he was frequently taken for him."

"So," Mateo finished the tale, "the head of the leader, in this case that of Valenzuela, was removed."

"Yes," Corky replied.

"And what else do you know of Three-Fingered Jack?" Mateo asked her.

"According to one historical account, Jack's head was so badly damaged by a pistol ball that there was no use trying to keep it. Instead, his mutilated hand was amputated and preserved in spirits."

As Corky continued to listen to Joaquin recount how he had escaped the jaws of death once more, she could only feel a sense of relief.

The authorities were satisfied that Joaquin was dead, and now Mateo was free.

* * *

Later, Mateo stepped out of the tent and walked to the clearing where Corky sat on a blanket. "Come," he said, "we leave now, *querida*."

Corky looked up into his eyes. "Where are we going?"

"To the mountains. Our revenge is complete. Your history books tell you this, no?"

She smiled. "Some accounts say Joaquin died yesterday at twenty-two and that a grieving Rosita spent the remainder of her years with her parents in the mountains. Others say he lived on. I'm happy to know the latter is true."

"Ah, at this moment Rosita is far from grieving," Mateo conceded, his eyes filling with a sensual light.

Corky's smile faded as she scooted over to make a place on the blanket beside her. "Mateo, come, sit with me."

He obediently settled himself next to her. For a moment, they shared the beauty of the night. The stars overhead were bright in a clear sky, and it felt good to be alive.

"What do the stars tell you tonight?" he asked as he gazed at the august heavens.

"If they could tell me anything, it would be that I must return home."

He looked at her, his eyes clouding with pain.

"My mission here is complete, Mateo."

"Is this your wish, *querida*?" he inquired tenderly.

"Yes, I want to go home," she conceded.

Reaching for his hands, she held them, urgency filling her voice now. "Come with me." Then she added in a choked voice, "I can't bear the thought of losing you."

When he finally spoke, it was after much thought. "How can you be certain that you will not remain with me?"

"I'm not certain, but I want to try to go home. Oh, Mateo, I miss my mother and my friends." She gazed up at him, trying to convey every ounce of the love she felt for him. "Please understand, it doesn't mean I love you any less."

"I will try very hard," he returned quietly.

"Will you come with me?" Unexpectedly the vision of Mateo in a business suit flashed before her. Desperate, she continued, "It'll be scary at first. My world isn't anything like this one. It's big and confusing, but I'll be there to help you adjust."

"But how is it possible for me to go to your time?"

She was relieved that he hadn't completely rejected the idea. "I don't know if it is possible, but I have an idea. Right now, I just want the assurance that you love me enough to go with me if it's possible."

Reaching for her hand, he brought it to his lips in a courtly gesture, his eyes openly caressing her. "My love for you knows no earthly bounds. Tell me of this plan. I will follow if God wills."

Tears stung her eyes. She had been so afraid that he might refuse. There would be problems, of course. He would have difficulty adapting to a new life, but she would be there to teach him all he had to know.

As the moon rose higher, the old woman spread a blanket close to the firelight. Picking up Corky's deck of cards, she shuffled them, then handed them to Corky.

"Mix them carefully," she said in her ancient voice. "Then choose a wand card."

Closing her eyes, Corky recalled the instructions Dalia had read the night this had all begun. "Blonde hair and blue eyes, select a wand card."

Opening her eyes, she quickly chose a card and handed it to the Old One. Then a second card was added to the first, followed by four more, making a total of six.

"Is that right?"

"Your hand is true," the old woman assured her.

"This will work?" Corky looked anxious.

"*Vieja* makes no promises, but she will do the best she can."

Corky gave Mateo a smile of encouragement. "That's all we ask."

Carefully, the old woman laid the cards Corky had drawn out on the blanket in a pattern as old as time. One by one the cards revealed their magic.

"This one is mine," she stated as she laid the Queen of Swords at the top of the blanket, facing north. "This one is yours, Cordilla." She laid the Queen of Wands below and to the left of the Queen of Swords. She turned to Mateo.

"And this one is yours, *mi hijo*," she said as she placed the King of Pentacles directly across from Corky's, to the right and below her own. In the center, between Corky's and Mateo's cards, she placed the Lovers.

"Now we will see if returning to your time with him is possible," she breathed. There were two cards left, the Fool and Death. With utmost care she aligned the Fool to the southwest of the Lovers card. In the opposite right hand corner, she placed the Death card, facing southeast. With a pensive sigh, she sat back on her heels to view the completed geometric pattern laid out before her.

Corky felt her heart constrict in her throat when she saw that she had drawn the Fool card and the dreaded Death card. She turned an anxious gaze to the white-faced Mateo and squeezed his hand for reassurance. What did these last two cards mean? Were they fools for trying to travel together to the future, or was she a fool for trying to leave? The card of Death. She had read about it and remembered that whoever drew this card would die. Did this card mean Mateo would die if he was transported forward? That would make sense, she speculated. After all, they were leaping more than one hundred years into the future. Mateo would have long been resting in his grave, his bones turned to dust. Suddenly she was afraid; the logistics just weren't there. By asking him to come with her, she had made certain of his death.

The old woman turned and faced Corky and Mateo.

"I see from what the cards have said your desire will be fulfilled."

"But what about that card?" Corky whispered, pointing to the Death card almost directly below that of Mateo's.

"Ah, you of so little faith, so little understanding," she admonished. "Look, and remember. Notice this card. It is the card of Death, *la muerte*, but it is also one of life."

"How can that be?" Mateo interjected. "How can death also mean life?" Briefly, he thought of the Resurrection, but that had been God's miracle; here there were only cards and the words of a sorceress, *una bruja*.

"Ah, *mi hijo*, so little trust." She looked at him, but it was to Corky she directed her words. "One must trust in order to love. The cards have not lied. All that you wish will come true."

"But how?" Corky interjected. "That card is the Death card." She squeezed Mateo's hand, and a look of hopelessness passed between them.

"Look carefully," the Old One said as she pointed to the card. "Do you not see that the card is inverted? When it is inverted, it means that Death is destroyed."

"But what about the Fool?" Corky said. "Am I a fool to bring Mateo with me?"

"*Mi hija,*" the old woman patiently intoned, "the Fool represents the sun. As long as it lays in an upright position, as it does now, it is the source of life. However," she continued, "if the Fool had also been inverted, like that of the Death card, it would mean that one of you would die on the journey. As it is, if you both desire to go on this journey through time, all you have to do is wait." She mumbled what seemed to be an incantation and then all was silent.

Hope swelled anew as Corky drew a deep breath and waited. Overhead the clouds began to churn, obscuring the moon.

Moving closer to Mateo, Corky whispered, "Do you like ice cream?"

Mateo's features went blank as he looked at her.

"Or pineapple whips—or better yet, a Dairy Queen Blizzard made with Butterfingers or maybe some M&Ms?" It had seemed like *ages* since she'd had one of those.

His vacant stare deepened.

She laughed, tightening her grip on his hand. They'd have plenty of time for those things, and so many, many more exciting twentieth-century marvels to share.

And now, thanks to the Old One's wisdom, she would return with the man she loved. Once again she remembered the visions that always seemed to skirt her consciousness. A son, moonlight, and shadows filtering through her bedroom window as a sun-drenched arm enfolded her in love's embrace. She turned to Mateo and saw the trust in his eyes, and suddenly, she knew they had made the right decision.

A soft breeze rustled her unbound hair and she felt herself move, as if in slow motion, forward.

Epilogue

"MOM! I'm thirsty!" The sound of a three-year-old's plaintive wail echoed throughout the vine-covered cottage.

"In a minute, Matt!"

Corky pushed Mateo's feet to the side and set the bowl of popcorn on the bed between them. "How come he never yells for you?"

Mateo winked. "Because you're the pushover."

Leaning across the pillow, she kissed him. "Never a pushover, my dear. Easy, maybe, but never a pushover."

"Mom!"

Groaning, Corky rolled off the bed and went into the bathroom for the glass of water. When she returned from taking care of Matt, the evening news was coming on.

Shooing Cleo off the bed, Corky kicked off her scuffs and climbed under the covers beside her husband. Pinching the waistband of her lacy panties between her fingers, she lowered her

101

voice seductively, "Edible underwear. Interested?"

"Dad! There's something in my closet! I see eyes!"

Giving Corky a don't-go-away look, Mateo got out of bed to exorcise the nightly demon in his son's closet. The child's apprehension was a carryover from the time Matt had discovered the faded Mexican *sombrero* and *pistolas* casually tossed in the corner of the hall closet. When Mateo had laughingly put them on, his son, rather than squealing with delight, had shrieked in terror. Apparently, five years in the twentieth century had not diminished the ruthless outlaw appearance of the now conservative Hispanic named Mateo Armandez. The vestiges of the past had been hastily secreted away, but the vision of his father in all his former glory still frightened the little boy.

When Mateo returned, Corky had forgotten her edible underwear remark and was engrossed in a rerun episode of *Cheers*.

"Did you set the alarm?" she asked absently.

"Uh-huh."

"Remember, you have an early-morning meeting with a client. Did you take the Martin case?"

"Uh-huh."

She poked him in the ribs. "You have adjusted very well in becoming the typical American, uncommunicative male, are you aware of that? Is that all you can say? Uh-huh, uh-huh."

Grinning, Mateo hooked his arm around her neck and dragged her beneath the covers, upsetting the popcorn bowl atop the blanket.

"Now this is more like it," she said as his hands began to do delicious things to her. They kissed, savoring their first moment alone all day.

"Mateo?"

"Uh-huh," he mocked.

"Do you ever regret that you came with me? I know it hasn't been easy adjusting to all the changes."

"What do you think?" He kissed her again in a way that dispelled her worries.

"I think you're deliriously happy," she decided. "As you well should be, having an adorable, caring, totally devoted wife, a thriving law practice, a wonderful child—" She broke off, laughing, as he tackled her again.

Later, much later, when they lay in the dark holding each other, she thought about her life, and how happy Mateo Armandez had made her. It was still hard to believe that her mother had bought her blow-to-the-head amnesia story so easily, but Edith had been so relieved to have her daughter back safely that she didn't question the flimsy explanation of Corky's disappearance.

Dalia hadn't been such a pushover. To this day, she didn't believe the amnesia story and still pestered Corky from time to time to tell her what had really happened during the time Corky had disappeared from the face of the earth and met such a fantastic man.

But Corky had never told anyone the truth. For one thing, she knew that Dalia would accuse her of making the whole thing up.

"No." She smiled languidly as Mateo rolled to his side and she rolled to hers, their hands still closely entwined. "No one will ever know the real story of how we met."

"Did you say something, *querida*?" he murmured sleepily.

Wincing, she pulled a popcorn kernel from beneath her elbow and tossed it on the floor. Cleo bounded off the foot of the bed and gobbled it down noisily.

"Nothing, dear." She sighed. "Only that I love you."

Lori Copeland

When LORI COPELAND started writing romance novels ten years ago, she never thought about writing historical or time-travel books. Now they are two of her favorite genres.

For All Time is the first time-travel story she has attempted in a shorter format, and she found it wondrously fun to write. She hopes you will enjoy your brief time with Mateo, Corky, and the men and women who fought so valiantly for justice, and that perhaps when you've finished the story, you will look more kindly upon Joaquin Murieta than the history books have.

Timeswept Love

Catherine Creel

1

"THE poor man died of a broken heart, so they say. Big and strong and the most handsome young chief ever to be seen in the Highlands. He was the best, and the last great leader of the Clan MacDonell. Mark my words, Rory MacDonell met his end because of a *woman*!"

Elizabeth MacKenzie had heard enough. She tossed an obligatory glance up toward the portrait of the Scottish chieftain, which was also being scrutinized by the other, far more fascinated members of her tour group assembled in the dimly lit great hall. She exchanged a frustrated look with her friend Tracy, then seized the opportunity to escape. The guide's dramatically high-pitched voice droned on behind her as Elizabeth stole away to wander Castle MacDonell alone.

Broken heart, her mind echoed, and she smiled ruefully at the woman's histrionic words. No one had ever truly died of a broken heart, she mused with a sigh. If such a thing were possible, then she wouldn't be here now in this dark, drafty old castle deep in the Scottish Highlands. And Garrett Cantrell, damn him, wouldn't be back home in the Dallas summer heat with a leggy, wasp-waisted blonde and a broken engagement to explain.

It was Elizabeth's own fault, of course. She was the one who had called it off two months ago. But she'd had good reason—more than enough fuel for the fire, as her grandmother would have said. Her hopes and dreams had been shattered beyond repair. Garrett had certainly seen to that.

As she drifted across the hall, her slow and directionless steps mirrored her wandering, troubled thoughts of the man she had nearly married. She had actually come to believe that Garrett preferred her to the flashy, fun-loving women Tracy had told her he'd dated all through high school and college. Looking back now, she realized that what had happened between them in the end was inevitable, as she was far too serious and introspective for him. Their relationship should never even have started. And it wouldn't have if she hadn't allowed Tracy to drag her along to a friend's party at the Deep Ellum Cafe seven months ago.

Fate had dealt her a surprise that night—in the form of the attractive, sandy-haired former quarterback for Southern Methodist University who had returned to Dallas to join his brother's advertising firm. She had fallen hard the first time she had seen Garrett Cantrell, Jr., and according to him, his own reaction had been equally powerful. She hadn't even known about his rich and well-connected family then, but even if she had, it wouldn't have mattered. Nor had his openly disapproving parents' opinions counted, once she'd been confronted with them. Nothing had mattered but the love they had shared. Or rather, the love she *thought* they had shared.

Her deep blue eyes clouded with renewed pain at the memory of his unfaithfulness. God help her, what a fool she had been. What a naive, trusting little fool.

Tracy was right, Elizabeth told herself as she drifted farther and farther from the group. She *was* a hopeless romantic. She wanted it all—a true and everlasting love, a man both strong and compassionate, a partner in life who wasn't afraid to let her match his strengths with her own. Her late grandparents had known that kind of love, and she could still fondly recall heartwarming details of their relationship. Growing up in their care, she had often studied photographs of her parents—who had died shortly before her fifth birthday—and wondered if they had also shared a special love. Why couldn't *she* find what her grandparents had found together? And how could she ever settle for less?

Ironically, this vacation was supposed to help her forget her heartache, and if she hadn't felt so miserable, she wouldn't have agreed to leave her catering business in the care of Tracy's sister at the peak of the summer season to come to Scotland to "recuperate." These past three weeks had been an absolute whirlwind of shopping, exploring, and learning a great deal more than she had expected about her ancestors' homeland.

And she was grateful that Tracy had come with her. She had been a delightful companion, which was no surprise, since the petite brunette had been Elizabeth's closest friend since the seventh grade. They were business partners as well. While Elizabeth did the actual supervising and bookwork, Tracy dealt with the clients. It had always struck her as odd that they should get along so well, considering that they were complete opposites.

Her lips curved into a faint, indulgent smile. Tracy Tyler had always been outspoken and gregarious, a real "live wire" who seldom bothered to hide her feelings. If not for Tracy, Elizabeth might have gone to pieces after learning of Garrett's betrayal. It was Tracy who had insisted that they forget about their business for a while and take a vacation together. But Elizabeth knew their hastily arranged getaway was really for her benefit, and her friend's generosity of spirit had prompted her to make every effort to pull herself out of her melancholy.

It was still difficult to ignore the dull ache in her heart, though, especially today when every portrait, every blessed stick of furniture provoked another tale of marital anguish or unrequited love from the tour guide. The woman was certainly into the spirit of her job. . . .

"Lizzie!"

Tracy's loud whisper startled her from her unpleasant reverie. She whirled, coloring guiltily as her friend advanced on her with a reproachful frown.

"Where are you going?" Tracy demanded, shooting a quick glance toward the wide, circular stone staircase in the far corner of the hall. "Mrs. Stewart is taking us upstairs to see the bedrooms."

"I think I'll stay down here."

"Why?"

"I'm feeling a bit tired, that's all." Elizabeth smiled. "But you go ahead with the group. You can fill me in on the gory details later."

"All right," Tracy said with visible reluctance. Folding her arms across her chest, she frowned again. "But it was *your* idea to come here, remember? I've had just about all I can stand of ghosts and clans and 'great bonny lairds'!"

"I know," Elizabeth murmured, her gaze conveying a touch of wry amusement. "And I promise—no more castles."

"I'll hold you to that. Besides, we're going to spend the next two days prowling all the stores in Inverness."

"No more shopping! I'm already going to have to buy another suitcase to get everything home." She looked down at the clingy, red woolen sweater and above-the-knee-length skirt she had found in one of the dozens of Edinburgh's kilters' shops. The clothes fit her to perfection, and she felt a certain pride in knowing that the tartan of the skirt—a blend of blue, green, red, and white—

was the traditional plaid of the MacKenzies. "We won't be able to wear these outfits until the dead of winter back home."

"Who cares?" Tracy glanced over her shoulder and saw the gray-haired, ebullient Mrs. Stewart leading the tour group up the stairs. "I'd better be going. Heaven knows, if I got lost in this place, I'd probably never be able to find my way back down here. You can send out a search party if I haven't returned in an hour."

"I give you my word I won't leave without you," Elizabeth vowed with mock gravity. She watched as Tracy, rolling her eyes heavenward, pivoted and hurried to join the others upstairs.

The deserted great hall was quiet now except for the wind whistling through the cracks in the thick stone walls and rattling the window latches, as if the castle's long-ago inhabitants resented the intrusion of strangers in their domain. It was eerie, Elizabeth thought, and the gray, overcast afternoon added to the mysterious, rather unearthly atmosphere. She almost wished she were back at the hotel in Inverness, curled up with her newly acquired first edition—or so the bookseller in Aberdeen had claimed—of poetry by Robert Burns.

A sudden, involuntary shiver ran the length of her spine and, wide-eyed, she scanned the room that had once served as the center of domestic life for dozens of generations of MacDonells. She could easily imagine the former occupants sitting at the long table on the dais enjoying their dinner, or dancing to the music of bagpipes and harps. The round, multi-towered keep itself was more than five hundred years old. And looks it, she reflected with another faint smile of irony.

Still feeling strangely restless, she wandered off to the right of the hall. She crossed through an arched doorway into one of the smaller rooms separated from the main living area by a dividing wall nearly as thick as the ones of the keep. Her gaze lit with mingled surprise and pleasure at the roaring fire blazing beneath a mantelpiece of solid oak. Its warmth chased away the damp chill and set the room aglow with soft golden light. The furnishings had obviously seen better days but were of undeniable quality. A large, upholstered gold-velvet sofa held reign in the center of the room, flanked by tables of carved mahogany. A sadly threadbare carpet covered the floor, and a number of ancient photographs and oil-painted landscapes hung on the papered walls. Overhead a tarnished brass-and-crystal chandelier merged its token illumination with that of the fire.

An infinite variety of other items lay scattered about, some of which indicated the several hundred years of MacDonell rule in this region— Highland clan crests, ancient weapons, tartans, tapestries, and a few smaller paintings of deceased MacDonells. But the frayed draperies and the water-stained plaster ceiling attested to the regrettable fact that the castle had fallen into a state of disrepair even though the National Trust for Scotland had rescued it and opened it to the public. The air in the room held a slight mustiness, joining with the more pleasant aromas of woodsmoke and potpourri.

An old wooden rocking chair before the fire seemed to beckon to Elizabeth. She hastened forward, but stopped as her eyes were drawn to a painting above the mantel. Her breath caught in her throat.

This portrait of Rory MacDonell was far more vivid, far more lifelike than the other one she had seen in the great hall. The powerful young Highland chieftain who stared back at her was tall and devilishly handsome, with dark red hair and deep, emerald-green eyes flecked with gold. His tanned, chiseled features were rugged yet aristocratic, and he wore his clan's tartan with a pride that came through even on canvas. He was without a doubt the most striking man she had ever seen—and he had been dead for four hundred years.

"He died of a broken heart," she murmured, repeating what Mrs. Stewart had said. She found it difficult to believe that such a *masculine* man had been led to his deathbed by emotions. It was far easier to envision his being killed in battle, or even being run through by a jealous husband. The thought made her smile, but her amusement was fleeting, for in the next moment she felt a sharp, inexplicable stirring of her heart.

Unable to tear her gaze away from the portrait, she sank into the rocking chair. One hand raked her thick, long black hair away from her face while the other inched up toward the necklace she had worn every day since her deceased grandmother had given it to her some four years ago. From a delicate gold chain hung a pendant depicting a mountain aflame, the clan crest of the MacKenzies. The pendant had been in the family for a long time; exactly how long was anyone's guess. She had never really felt compelled to research her ancestral roots as so many others did. Until now.

"Rory MacDonell," she whispered, and a strange, startlingly forceful yearning rose deep within her. Fingering the necklace, she stared in fascination at the painting. If only she could have known him. What would it have been like to be loved by this wild Scottish chieftain? Judging from the fire in his eyes, she mused with an uneven sigh, it would have been heaven on earth. His wife would have enjoyed the kind of loyalty and passion about which most women fantasized but seldom experienced.

Then again, what did she know of passion? She had never even been intimate with a man. Her admittedly old-fashioned standards had earned her a great deal of teasing from Tracy, and a great deal of pressure from Garrett. She was the last of a dying breed and knew it. And yet, there had been times with Garrett when she had almost surrendered to her sexual needs. She was, after all, a normal, healthy, twenty-four-year-old female. But her determination, not to mention her moral convictions, had always stopped her. She wanted the whole dream and Garrett hadn't been willing to wait.

Mr. MacDonell, why couldn't you have been born four hundred years later? she lamented silently, then shook her head at her own foolishness at being attracted to a man who was nothing but a memory. Other women tourists had no doubt stood in this same room and found themselves bewitched by the likeness of the young chieftain. Laughing, Elizabeth imagined that the gorgeous Scotsman turned over in his grave every time some impressionable female tramped through his beloved home and gawked at his portrait. She wondered what he thought of her.

Another sigh escaped her lips as she leaned back in the rocking chair and closed her eyes. Suddenly feeling tired, she loosened her grasp on the pendant but did not let go completely, her mind full of visions of the man in the portrait as she drifted toward sleep. Her last thought was of the woman, whoever she might have been, whom Rory MacDonell had loved and lost.

2

ELIZABETH awoke with a start, surprised that she had fallen asleep. Alarmed by the unfamiliar surroundings, she took a quick survey of the room. The castle, she recalled, and relaxed her tensed muscles. She was at Castle MacDonell, waiting for Tracy.

The fire still blazed comfortingly beneath the mantel; the likeness of Rory MacDonell still commanded her attention. But . . . but something was wrong. Very, very wrong . . .

"What on earth—" she murmured, breaking off her words when her mind, numbed from sleep, finally acknowledged a startling reality.

Though the room was the same one in which she had fallen asleep, the furnishings had changed. The velvet sofa was gone, in its place a small, rough-hewn table and benches. Her eyes flew up toward the ceiling. The chandelier had mysteriously disappeared, as had the photographs and the lamps and even the carpet on the floor. Surely her eyes were deceiving

119

her. She couldn't have been asleep for long, and anyway, why would anyone transform the room while she slept?

She hastily looked down and was shocked to discover that she was no longer sitting in the rocking chair, but rather in a heavy, uncushioned wooden chair with a low, curved back. Strangely enough, she was still wearing the same sweater and skirt, the same woolen knee socks and thick-soled leather shoes. *She* hadn't changed—but everything else had.

"I must be dreaming," she whispered. That was it, of course. She was lost in one of those awful nightmares, trapped in that hazy, ill-defined world between sleep and consciousness. And yet she felt very much awake.

Her heart leapt in growing panic, and she stood abruptly and gazed up at the portrait again. Rory MacDonell's eyes seemed to burn down into hers. In fact, she could have sworn the look on his handsome face was one of mocking amusement.

Desperate to escape the cruel joke her mind was playing on her, she offered up a silent prayer for enlightenment and turned away.

"Tracy?" she called out, her voice tremulous and edged with a note of fear as it echoed in the firelit room. "Can anyone hear me?"

She told herself to remain calm, but it was impossible. Her legs feeling perilously weak, she hastened back through the arched doorway and out into the cool, sinister shadows of the great hall.

A sharp cry broke from her lips when she collided forcefully with someone just beyond the doorway. A pair of strong hands, a man's hands, closed around her arms to steady her. Grateful for their support, she quickly regained her balance and opened her mouth to offer an apology for her own carelessness.

She looked up at her rescuer, but the words caught in her throat. Her eyes widened while the color drained from her face. She gasped in stunned disbelief. *Rory MacDonell himself stood before her.*

"Dear God, it can't be!" she breathed. It was nothing more than an apparition, she pronounced inwardly, a ghost haunting her for daring to invade his private, well-guarded home. But the hands on her arms were real. *He* was real! Rory MacDonell, in the flesh, was holding her captive while his fiery emerald gaze raked over her.

He was even more magnificent in person. The portrait, she dazedly concluded, didn't do him justice. His thick auburn hair was lit with gold from the torches flickering all about the hall, and she could literally feel the heat emanating from his virile, hard-muscled body. He was dressed exactly as he had been in the painting, in a short, saffron-colored linen tunic with long sleeves and a flowing length of wool plaid, identified by Mrs. Stewart as the *feileadh mor*. The MacDonell tartan of red, white, and black was draped over one shoulder and belted at the waist, and he wore a matching pair of breeks, and leather brogues on his feet. A flat blue cap sat atop his head. To say that he made an impressive figure would have been a considerable understatement. He looked every inch the fierce Highland chieftain he was.

Elizabeth swallowed hard as his fingers branded her skin even through the heavy wool of her sweater. Her luminous gaze locked with the gleaming intensity of his, and she felt as though he could see into her very soul.

The dream had taken a dangerous turn. She shook her head, certain that she was either sleeping or crazy or maybe even both. Plunged into shock, she could only stand and hold her breath, waiting for him to break the spell.

"So, you have come skulking about like a thief in the night, have you? 'Tis nothing more than I would expect from a MacKenzie!" he ground out.

Speechless, she blinked at him. His voice was wonderfully resonant and deep-timbred, and he spoke with a heavy Scottish brogue that was somewhat difficult to understand. But there was nothing in the least bit confusing about his anger as his hands tightened with punishing force on her arms.

"And by the heavens above, your father has sent you to me looking worse than a Lowland strumpet! Have you no decency, woman, to come dressed thus? Your appearance is an insult to us both!" His searing gaze flickered contemptuously up and down the length of her. "I am well surprised he did not send you forth with naught but a *leine* on your back, for you are near enough to that now! But if he thinks to shame me into calling off the bargain, he is even more of an old rascal than I've thought him to be these twenty years past!"

"I—I don't know what's happening, but I am not who you think I am!" Elizabeth stammered breathlessly. Her head was spinning, and she was afraid she would faint. How could she faint if she were dreaming? It had to be a dream . . . it *had* to be!

"You are Elizabeth MacKenzie, are you not?" Rory MacDonell demanded, his green eyes narrowing suspiciously down at her. His spies had told him that Angus MacKenzie's daughter was beautiful, but their descriptions had fallen short in praise of her beauty. Perhaps what lay ahead would not prove so distasteful after all. "Well? Speak, woman! Are you not Elizabeth MacKenzie?"

"Yes, but I don't understand! I don't know what's going on, or how you got here, or why—"

"I warn you, MacKenzie," he cut her off brusquely, "do not seek to play me for a fool. I want this marriage no more than you, but we are both bound by duty and honor to keep the bargain."

"*Marriage?*"

"Aye. Though it be the devil's own union, we must act in complete obedience. The contract has been signed, as well you know. The MacDonells and the MacKenzies will be joined together in peace this day, just as you and I will be joined together in wedlock." His gaze filled with a near savage light when he decreed in a low, simmering tone, "Too many men have died already. And by all that is holy, if I should find myself saddled with a wife who is both shrewish and daft, then so be it!"

Elizabeth gasped again as he suddenly began propelling her none too gently toward the staircase. She struggled within his iron grasp, trying desperately to hang back and prevent herself from being dragged up the wide stone steps, but it was no use. Rory MacDonell was much too strong—and determined.

She began to panic in earnest now. "No! Please, stop! Listen to me—my name *is* Elizabeth MacKenzie, but I am not the woman you're supposed to marry! I was simply here visiting the castle with my tour group, and then the others went upstairs, and I fell asleep, and—"

"Stop your blathering, woman!" His temper blazed to a dangerous level, and ignoring her protests, he continued to pull her up the stairs.

"I'm not blathering!" Though she still wavered between incredulity and dismay, her own temper was a match for his now. Her deep blue eyes kindled with fire while she clawed at the large, powerful hand on her arm. "I don't know who the hell you think you are, but this little charade has gone far enough! Let go of me this minute, damn you, or I swear I'll scream! I'm trying to tell you that—"

"Speak to me like that again, mistress, and you will feel the flat of my hand on your backside!" he threatened tersely. " 'Tis clear to me now that your father has sadly neglected your education. If you have no mind to be rewarded with the skelping you so richly deserve, then you had best watch your tongue!"

"You're insane!" she gasped out, a shiver of very real fear dancing down her spine.

"That I may well be." The merest smile touched his lips when, pausing briefly in their wild flight up the torchlit darkness of the staircase, he turned to her and said in a tone laced with meaning, "But 'tis not my mind you should worry about, lass. I would not be worthy of the name MacDonell if, come morning, you have any cause to complain of what takes place between us this night."

Elizabeth felt sudden warmth flooding her body. She'd had no previous encounters with spirits of long-departed Highlanders, but she was nevertheless quite sure they didn't go around boasting of their sexual prowess. Nor was it possible that they could make her feel what *this* one was making her feel. The situation, whether dream or some distorted reality, was growing more and more incredible. She had to find a way out.

"Help!" she shouted on impulse, her voice rising shrilly in the massive, stone-walled castle. "Please, somebody help me!"

"Scream all you like, my bonny *Ealasaid*. There are few about at present, and not a one of them would dare to interfere with their *Ard-Righ* and his bride."

"I am not your bride!"

"Are you not?"

They came to a halt and Elizabeth found herself thrust unceremoniously inside a small, candlelit room with three rows of benches on either side of a narrow aisle and a single window of stained glass depicting the tabernacle of Solomon. There were three other strangers, all men, waiting in the chapel.

"On to the wedding," Rory decreed masterfully, leading his reluctant bride forward.

"No!" she protested. "This is ridiculous!" She tried to pull free, but he was relentless. Almost before she knew it, she was standing with him before a simple wooden altar.

"I pray you, my child, offer no resistance, but instead submit yourself freely to this marriage," exhorted a kindly looking man whose portly frame was encased in a full-length, belted robe of brown wool. His brow creased into a frown of shocked disapproval as his gaze flickered over her scandalously brief attire, but his brown eyes were full of compassion when he said, "This union will bring peace to your families. It is your duty to—"

"I am not marrying this man or anyone else!" she told him, shaking her head with such vehemence that her long hair, naturally curly and as black as midnight, bounced about her face and shoulders. "I don't know who any of you people are, or who put you up to this, but I'm not about to stay here and be a part of your cruel, asinine joke! I am an American, and if you don't let me out of this place at once, I'm going to pay a visit to my country's consulate and press charges with the local authorities!"

"*Cum do theanga!*" Rory commanded in a voice that was whipcord sharp.

"What?" she gasped in angry bewilderment. She had no knowledge of Gaelic, but the way he spoke left little doubt that the words weren't at all complimentary.

"Keep your tongue!" He clamped an arm around her waist, holding her captive against his side while he gave a curt nod. "Have done with it, Parson!"

"Dearly beloved brethren, we are gathered together here in the sight of God and in the face of His congregation, to knit and join these parties together in the honorable estate of matrimony . . ."

Dear God, this can't be happening, thought Elizabeth. She didn't know what was real anymore. Dimly aware of the minister's words, she felt her knees threatening to buckle beneath her again. She stood in the strange, ancient-looking chapel as if transfixed, her body refusing to acknowledge her mind's warning to turn and run before it was too late. What was the matter with her?

The ceremony flew onward to its inevitable conclusion. The bride was instructed to please and to obey her husband, they were both reminded that God had brought them together for procreation and the upbringing of children, and a short homily was given on the evils of fornication. When the minister came to the part where he asked about any impediment to the union, Elizabeth finally came to life again.

"*I* am the impediment!" she declared, her whole body quaking with the force of her outrage. "I never saw this man before in my life, and—"

" 'Tis understandable that you would be unwilling, my child," the man of God offered in a consoling manner. But he went on as if she had never spoken at all. His expression was solemn as he instructed the groom in the care and keeping of his wife, and he smiled in satisfaction when Rory gave the proper response.

"Even so, I take her before God and in the presence of His congregation."

Turning to Elizabeth, the minister asked if she would accept the young chief of the Clan MacDonell as her true and lawful husband.

"I most certainly will *not!*" She emphasized her defiance with a sharp jab of her elbow to her handsome captor's ribs. He muttered an oath and shot her a look which promised retaliation, but she would not be silenced. "You can't do this! For heaven's sake, we aren't back in the Middle Ages! This is 1993, and I'll be—"

"1993?" the minister echoed with a frown of pure bafflement. "I know not of what you speak. 'Tis the year of our Lord 1593."

"*What?*"

"Enough!" snapped Rory. He scowled darkly and charged the parson to continue.

"You must consent to the marriage," the man advised Elizabeth.

Although still reeling with shock at his announcement of the date, she began to understand at last. She wasn't lost in a dream at all. Somehow, she had been transported back in time, back across four hundred years of life and death and the endless seasons of the earth. . . .

It all made sense now. Or rather, it *would* have, if only she believed in such things. But time travel? No, it couldn't be! The concept was nothing more than make-believe, something that existed only in books and movies.

And yet, a voice deep inside her brain pointed out, how else could she explain the changes in the room downstairs where she had fallen asleep? How could she explain the odd-sounding language and the sudden, puzzling disappearance of the tour group? And most important of all, what about the man beside her? He looked exactly like the Rory MacDonell in the painting. *Exactly*.

"We are waiting, my child," the minister prompted with only a hint of impatience.

"I . . ." she tried to answer, but could not. She looked up at Rory. His splendid green eyes were brimming with a fierce combination of anger and desire and something else she could not put a name to. Her heart pounded wildly in her breast.

"She is mine," he declared with quiet authority.

"So be it." The minister sighed, anxious to do his duty and avoid further bloodshed among his long-divided flock. Heaven be praised, the accursed feud would end that night. "You are husband and wife now. May God bless your union. Live in harmony and never forget, my children, to honor our Lord with every undertaking of your marriage."

The ceremony over, the two men stepped forward to make their mark in the parson's book as witnesses to the marriage, Elizabeth realized.

Wasting little time in claiming his rights, and without a word, Rory MacDonell took a visibly stunned Elizabeth MacKenzie into his arms and brought his lips crashing down on the parted, unsuspecting softness of hers.

3

HER blood turned to liquid fire in her veins while Rory's warm, strong lips moved sensuously over hers. His kiss demanded a response, and his arms held her captive with such fierce possessiveness that she felt almost lightheaded. Acutely conscious of his tall, powerfully muscled body pressing against her, she stifled the moan that rose low in her throat and swayed against him in unspoken surrender. Her arms crept up to his neck.

What was happening to her? She had never felt like this when Garrett had kissed her. As a matter of fact, she had never felt like this with anyone. Her whole body seemed to be going up in flames; her senses were reeling out of control. She wanted this madness to go on forever.

"But a taste of things to come, sweet *Ealasaid*," Rory promised huskily, using the Gaelic form of her name again as he released her at last. No longer a reluctant participant in a marriage he had only hours before denounced as a necessary evil, he kept a firm hand on his wife's arm and told the minister, "You have my gratitude, Parson. And now, 'tis time my bride and I were off to bed."

"To bed?" Elizabeth echoed with a sudden, sharp intake of breath. Her eyes widened, while her heart twisted with renewed alarm.

She hadn't thought about *that*. Everything was happening so fast. How was she supposed to be able to think clearly? She was trapped in the sixteenth century, trapped in a till-death-do-you-part relationship with a man whose damnably compelling portrait had turned her whole world upside down. Since it was anybody's guess how long this bizarre situation would last, she'd have to try and get her feet squarely on the ground.

Her amorous new husband, however, was obviously intent upon sweeping her off her feet. Enough was enough, she groaned inwardly. She wasn't about to let herself become his wife in fact as well as in name, no matter how much she liked being kissed by him.

Surely, she thought as her mind raced to think of a way out of the predicament, they wouldn't actually consummate the marriage. After all, he was nothing more than a stranger—a stranger whose very touch set her on fire, but a stranger all the same. She hadn't made love with Garrett, a man she had intended to spend the rest of her life with; why in heaven's name would she do so with *this* man?

"No! I'm not going to bed or anywhere else with you!" she declared, furiously jerking her arm free. Her next words came out in a tremulous rush. "I don't know how any of this happened, but I don't belong here! Surely you've noticed that I don't talk like you, and that my clothes are definitely out of place. I was touring the castle with a group of people from Inverness, and I fell asleep in one of the rooms downstairs, and then I woke up and everything was different! Don't you understand? I've come from the future, from four hundred years into the future! I was transported back through time, and I've got to find a way to—"

Her explanation ended on a loud, startled gasp when Rory suddenly seized her about the waist and tossed her face-down over his broad shoulder. He was beginning to wonder if her rantings were those of a lunatic, or if she merely wanted him to believe her cursed with insanity in order to worm her way out of the bargain. Whatever the truth of the matter, it was too late. The vows had been spoken. Their marriage, whether made in heaven or hell, was a reality neither of them could escape.

"Be gentle with her, my son!" the minister cautioned with a worried frown. "The poor lass is no doubt feeling the strain of these two weeks past since her father put his name to the marriage contract." Either that, he added silently, or she was as daft as her grandmother had been—God rest the poor woman's soul. Indeed, the women of Clan MacKenzie had long held the reputation of being high-spirited. His mouth twitched in wry amusement at the thought. It was clear that

Rory MacDonell would have his hands full with his own bonny MacKenzie.

"Put me down!" Elizabeth shrieked. She squirmed and kicked, pushing angrily against his back, but his arms were wrapped about her legs so securely that there was no possibility of escape.

Impervious to her defiance, Rory gave the parson a curt nod. "Aye," he said, his eyes darkening with intent. "She can flyte at me until the cock crows, but it will not keep me from the bedding." He turned away from the altar now, his long, purposeful strides directed toward the doorway.

"Let me go!" Elizabeth demanded breathlessly, her struggles intensifying. "You can't do this to me! I'm not really your wife! I *can't* be!"

His only response was to carry her out of the chapel and back down the stairs. She fought him the whole time, but to no avail. He flung open a door, stepped inside with his far-from-subdued burden, and kicked the door shut with his heel.

From her uncomfortable vantage point, Elizabeth saw that they were in a smaller and more luxurious room now. A blaze emitted warmth from a hooded fireplace, a large window reflected the darkness that had crept over the glen, and a dozen candles burned in a tall brass stand. Beautiful, richly colored tapestries covered the walls, while several woven mats offered a respite from the bone-chilling cold of the stone floor. Matching chests flanked the bed that stood against the middle of the wall across the room.

The bed. Elizabeth's wide, apprehensive gaze shot to the impressive piece of furniture, a massive four-poster, draped with embroidered hangings. On the wooden canopy above was a carved representation of the Clan MacDonell's crest, a raven perched on a rock, which she had noticed during the tour.

"To prove that I am a generous man," Rory told her, "I will grant you a moment of privacy. But only a moment." He finally set her on her feet, though his hands held her arms. A faint smile played about his lips, and his eyes glowed warmly down at her. "The garderobe is there." With a nod, he indicated the location of a short, right-angled passage in the thickness of the wall. It had been a source of considerable pride to his father that the castle boasted of a permanent latrine that was flushed by water from tanks above. The memory provoked a spark of indulgent humor in his gaze. "We MacDonells are not so savage as your clansmen would have you believe."

"I don't have any clansmen!" she insisted angrily. The blood still pounded in her ears as she struggled to regain control of her highly erratic breathing. She swept the disheveled mass of black curls from her face and tugged at her sweater.

"You wear the crest of a MacKenzie," he pointed out. His hand gestured to the pendant about her neck. " 'Tis a fine piece of workmanship. A gift, no doubt, from your father."

"My grandmother gave me this necklace when I was still in college!" She took a deep, steadying breath and battled a fresh wave of panic. "Look, I—I don't know if I can explain this! I know it sounds crazy, but you've got to believe me! I'm not the woman you were supposed to marry! I was born in Dallas, Texas, in the year 1969, and—"

"You are beginning to wear thin my patience," he warned softly. Once again, he wondered if her strange behavior and equally strange manner of speaking were designed to convince him of her unsuitability as his mate. He strode past her, moving to the window. "Be quick with your preparations, Elizabeth."

"Preparations?" she repeated numbly. "What are you talking about? Haven't you heard a word I've said? I'm not who you think I am! I'm telling you, you've married the wrong woman! And you're out of your mind if you think I'm going to go through with this little 'celebration' you've got planned!"

"It strikes me, sweet bride, that we are well-matched for lunacy," he quipped in a low, mocking tone. He turned slowly to face her again, his hands moving to the belt at his waist. "But take care, for there may yet be a method to my madness."

"Wha-what are you doing?" she faltered, her eyes growing enormous as her delicate oval face blushed.

"Have you not been told of the wedding night?"

"There isn't going to be any wedding night!"

"Och, you are a carnaptious woman," he muttered, frowning in exasperation. He drew off the belt, unfastened his plaid, and stripped it from his body. "Do you know nothing then of what takes place between a man and his wife?"

"Of course I do!" she retorted, her color deepening. "And that's exactly what I'm talking about! I didn't want to be your wife at all, and we certainly aren't going to—"

"You have nothing to fear, lass," he assured her. He removed his flat-soled shoes and the full, knee-length shirt, and now stood before her clad in nothing but his tartan breeks. His powerful arms and broad chest gleamed like bronze in the softly lit room.

Elizabeth swallowed a sudden lump in her throat and tried, unsuccessfully, to prevent her gaze from traveling over every plane of his magnificent body. The tight woolen garment molded his lean hips and long, athletic legs to perfection, and there was certainly no ignoring the bulge between his muscular, trim thighs. The warning bell deep in her brain sounded louder than ever.

"Do you remove your clothes yourself," Rory now asked, "or mayhap you would prefer that your new lord and master perform the honor? There is no lady's maid to assist you this night." He had given orders that the household servants were to be dismissed after the wedding.

He wanted no witnesses to the bedding of his reluctant bride. "The choice is yours. But rest assured, the outcome will be the same however you choose."

That was the final straw. Murmuring something unintelligible, Elizabeth spun about with the intention of getting out of the room as fast as her legs could carry her. But Rory was upon her in an instant. He swept her up in his arms and carried her to the bed.

"*No!*" she choked out, hot tears springing to her eyes as her throat constricted with dismay. "Please, you've got to listen to me! This is all some terrible mistake!"

" 'Tis no mistake," he disputed firmly. "You know as well as I that we had no choice. Our marriage will finally bring peace to the clans. I will not deny that the bargain was, until this night, a bitter and loathsome prospect to me. But I am of a different mind now."

He lowered her to the plump feather mattress and she squirmed beneath him. She cried out in helpless, frustrated anger when he imprisoned both of her wrists in one large hand, pulled her arms above her head, and began tugging at the hook-and-eye closing on the waistband of her plaid skirt.

"Stop it! Damn you, Rory MacDonell, you have no right to do this to me!"

"I am your husband," he reminded her quietly.

"And you think that gives you the right to . . . to *rape* me?"

"Rape?" He scowled, then allowed a brief, crooked smile to touch his lips. His eyes burned down into the glistening, fiery blue depths of hers. "No man worthy of the name MacDonell has ever found it necessary to force a woman. No, my sharp-tongued lass, it will not be rape. I mean to love you well this night."

"Let me go!" she countered vehemently, but gasped when he suddenly yanked the skirt downward to her knees.

Although she had dispensed with a bra and slip that day, she was wearing a pair of long silk underwear and a matching camisole for warmth. Rory frowned at the unfamiliar garments in bemusement, but he wasted little time in removing the skirt *and* the lingerie.

Still suffering the after-effects of a mysterious, unintentional journey back across four centuries, she discovered that her strength was no match for his. It didn't matter how much she struggled or how many curses and protests she flung at his handsome head. In the end, she was powerless to prevent him from stripping her completely naked.

Somewhere in the deepest recesses of her mind, she realized that he was quite proficient at getting a woman out of her clothes. An inexplicable twinge of pain pricked her at the thought and she tried to shield her body from his gaze, but he forced her arms above her head again.

His green eyes smoldered with desire and admiration as they surveyed her. Too impatient to delay the bedding while attempting to win her over with words, he told himself that she would not be tamed by endearments alone. But tamed she would be. With that thought in mind, he drew off his breeks. He stretched out beside his beautiful, defiant bride and held her against him once more.

Elizabeth inhaled sharply at the contact of bare flesh upon bare flesh, a sensation that was at once startling and wickedly pleasurable. Their bodies fit together as though they had been made for one another, his tall, lithely muscled frame welcoming every curve of her slender yet well-rounded softness.

"Aye, we are a fine match indeed, sweet *Ealasaid*," he murmured in a soft, vibrant tone that sent a delicious shiver coursing down her spine.

Her struggles abruptly ceased now. She could only stare at him in breathless anticipation, and he did not disappoint her.

Lowering his head, he captured her lips and she moaned low in her throat. After an embarrassingly brief hesitation, she entwined her arms around his neck and, obeying her instincts, arched beneath him while his mouth ravished the sweetness of hers.

The kiss was even more earth-shattering than the first one and she thrilled to the invasion of his hot, velvety tongue. All thought of resistance melted away as she answered with her own desire. What she felt was more than physical; it transcended understanding and even time itself.

Strangely enough, it was as if she had been waiting for Rory MacDonell her whole life.

Passion flared between them, all flash and fire and the heat of the moment . . . and yet more enduring than either of them dared to hope.

Rory's hand glided over the alluring curve of her hip, roamed boldly, possessively across her firmly rounded buttocks, then moved up to the rose-tipped fullness of her breasts. Moments later, his lips had joined his fingers in a rapturous assault upon her flesh. His mouth closed about one of her breasts, his tongue swirling about the delicate nipple while his lips suckled as greedily as a baby's.

"Oh, Rory!" gasped Elizabeth, desire blazing through her like wildfire. Her fingers threaded almost convulsively through the gold-flecked thickness of his auburn hair, and she trembled beneath him as a deep, unfamiliar yearning built to a fever pitch within her. She didn't know how or why this was happening, but it no longer mattered. For the first time in her life, she was being swept away on the wings of passion. And it felt right. *So very, very right . . .*

The sweet-savage madness rapidly intensified. Rory's mouth returned to claim hers in a kiss that soon had them both silently begging for mercy, while his hand crept down between her thighs. His warm fingers delved within the beckoning triangle of soft raven curls, and gently, albeit masterfully, began to stroke her.

She shivered at the first touch of his hand, but in a matter of seconds her hips were moving restlessly against his skillful caress, her legs parting wider of their own accord as he took her to dizzying new heights of passion. She clasped him tighter and kissed him with such innocent, heartfelt fervency that his own passion was sent spiraling toward the uppermost limits of human endurance. As he had said, they were well-matched. In every way.

And then, when neither of them could bear any more of the exquisite agony, Rory's hands slipped beneath Elizabeth's hips while he positioned himself between her thighs. She opened her eyes for a moment, looking up at him with a mixture of desire and uncertainty. He smiled softly down at her. His own gaze held an unspoken promise.

He eased himself into her at last, expertly sheathing his manhood within her honeyed warmth. She cried out at the pain, but the discomfort was short-lived, quickly replaced by a pleasure more intense than she would have believed possible. His hips tutored hers into the age-old rhythm of love. Her fingers curled feverishly on the bronzed hardness of his shoulders as she met his thrusts with a newfound boldness. They soared higher and higher, lost in a world of their own making.

Heaven and earth came together in that huge canopied bed, offering them a fulfillment that was truly explosive. Elizabeth gave a soft, breathless cry and collapsed back against the pillow. The sensations were so powerful, so unlike anything she had ever experienced, that she felt as though she had been on the very brink of death. In the next instant, Rory tensed above her, his seed flooding her with its warmth. She gasped anew and clutched at his arms for support.

In the soft afterglow of their first tempestuous union, the young chief of the MacDonells rolled to his back in the bed and tugged his well-loved bride close. There was no need for words. They both knew that what had happened was a rare gift.

Elizabeth released a sigh of mingled weariness and contentment. Her eyes swept closed, and she smoothed an appreciative hand across Rory's hair-covered chest. His arm circled her slender waist possessively.

He had "loved her well," all right. Now she understood why he had been so impatient to get her into bed. Her body tingled anew at the sweet memory of their lovemaking. It had felt natural, lying in his arms like that . . . as natural as listening to the soft crackle and hiss of the fire, smelling the pleasant aromas of woodsmoke and spices, and most of all, feeling her husband's heart beating against her cheek.

Her husband. Filled with wonderment at the thought, she sighed again and snuggled closer to his hard warmth. She was too tired to argue or to question or to analyze any more that night. The "whys" and "wherefores" no longer seemed to matter. Rory MacDonell, her wild, devilishly appealing Highlander, was a dream come true.

As night deepened and the candles burned low, the newlyweds drifted off to sleep, their breaths mingling in the firelit darkness. Elizabeth's last waking thought, oddly enough, was of Garrett. For the first time since she had broken off their engagement, she offered up a silent prayer of thanksgiving for his betrayal.

4

ELIZABETH stretched languidly in the warm bed, then gasped. Her eyes opened in surprise when her fingers brushed against the bed's heavy brocade hangings. The memories of the night came flooding back to her.

Dear God, had it really happened? Her own wonderfully traitorous flesh was proof that it had. She was naked beneath the covers, and she ached in places she hadn't even known existed until now. Rory had made love to her twice more before dawn, and would have done so a third and maybe even a fourth time if she hadn't pleaded exhaustion. Each *houghmagandy*, as he had called it, had been more exciting, more wickedly enchanting than the last.

Her face colored when she recalled, with vivid clarity, the things her hot-blooded new husband had taught her. She would never have believed it possible to learn so much about passion and pleasure in only one night. Their desire for one another had been insatiable, positively insatiable.

She turned her head on the pillow and frowned when she saw that she was alone. Rory's side of the mattress still bore the faint indentation of his body, and she heaved an audible sigh. She slowly pulled herself into a sitting position, her long black hair cascading riotously about her face and shoulders. Soft morning light streamed in through the window, and the room was filled with the unmistakable aroma of food.

"Tha ar bracaist deiseil."

She started at the sound of that familiar, splendidly deep-timbred voice and her gaze shot to where Rory stood before the fire. Lowering his hand from the mantelpiece, he slowly pivoted to face her. He had drawn on his breeks, but nothing else.

"What did you say?" she asked, her own voice a bit breathless. She instinctively snatched the covers over her naked breasts. It was one thing to forget all about modesty in the magical, nighttime darkness; it was quite another to face him like that in the light of day.

"Our breakfast awaits," he translated, a smile tugging at his lips. "Bridget was as prompt as ever." He nodded toward the tray of food on a small table in front of the fire.

The sun's rays lit gold in his dark red hair, and his skin glowed from a recent scrubbing. If anything, thought Elizabeth, he looked even more captivating than she had remembered.

"Up with you, woman," he commanded with mock sternness. " 'Tis the forenoon already. Would you have my gillie think me bewitched?"

His gaze danced with a touch of ironic humor when he envisioned his faithful steward's reaction to his tardiness. He had never risen so late in the morning before. But then, he had never taken a wife before. The prospect of spending a lifetime of nights with his beautiful, raven-haired *Ealasaid* filled both his heart and his body with warm pleasure.

"I—I didn't hear anyone come in," Elizabeth stammered weakly.

"Mayhap because you were bone-weary." He smiled again and reiterated. "Come. Though it would please me more to tumble you back into bed, I have duties which require my attention. And you, my bonny bride, require a bath."

"A bath?" She swallowed hard and tried to ignore the way her pulse raced. Inching carefully from beneath the covers, she took the sheet and wrapped it around her. She joined Rory before the fire.

"You are a braw sight in the morning, lass, with your hair all tousie and your sweet lips begging for a kiss."

There was no mistaking the passion in his low,

resonant tone as he pressed her down onto one of the benches which had been drawn up to the table. He then took a seat on the opposite bench.

"You must be hungry."

"I suppose I am," she confirmed, nodding slightly. Her eyes suddenly took on a faraway look. "I haven't eaten anything since yesterday morning." Yesterday morning, her mind repeated. It seemed years ago—four hundred, to be exact.

"Aye, the wedding was no doubt much on your mind." His heart twisted with compassion at the thought of her fear. "I am sorry, Elizabeth, that the marriage was not of your choosing. But I cannot be sorry we are wed. In truth, I have no regrets for what took place between us last night," he declared solemnly.

She offered no response as her gaze fell beneath the searching intensity of his.

" 'Tis not my habit to take meals in my solar, but I thought you would be wanting an extra measure of privacy this once. If the porridge and oatcakes are not to your liking, I will—" He broke off when she suddenly gave a soft laugh, and a puzzled frown creased his handsome brow. "Have my words given you amusement?"

"No!" she said, shaking her head while her eyes continued to sparkle mirthfully across at him. The absurdity of the situation wasn't lost on her. "It's just that I find this . . . well, unusual to say the least. I mean, here we are, sitting down to breakfast together like any other newlyweds, talking about what we're going to eat and how glad we are that we got married in the first place."

"Why should we not speak of such things?"

"Because we *aren't* like other newlyweds! Damn it, this is all so terribly confusing, and—"

"Elizabeth," he interrupted, his tone warning her to watch her tongue.

"Oh, Rory!" she murmured. She stood up, then watched while he rose to his feet as well. Tilting her head back, she gazed up into his fathomless green eyes. "What I told you last night was the truth! It's obvious that you made a bargain to marry a woman named Elizabeth MacKenzie in order to settle some feud between your clans. Well, I'm not the Elizabeth MacKenzie you were expecting! I don't know what happened to her, but—"

"By the heavens, I will hear no more of this!" he ground out angrily.

"Yes, you will!" She startled him with her flash of spirit. "And this time, Rory MacDonell, you're going to listen! You've got to believe me when I say that I was somehow transported back in time! For heaven's sake, I wasn't even born until nearly four hundred years into the future! We can't have a life together, not when I don't belong here!"

A life together. Those particular words burned in her mind, their significance hitting her like a bolt out of the blue. Her heart leapt in renewed fear. What about her own life, the one she had unwillingly left behind? What about her catering business and her friends and—dear God, what about Tracy? Poor Tracy must be worried sick at her disappearance and had probably called the police by now. There would, of course, be little evidence to aid them in their investigation. It would look as if she had simply vanished.

Her thoughts raced back to the man she had married. No matter that he had taken the most precious gift she had to offer, no matter how important this marriage was to his clan, she couldn't stay with him. She had to find a way to return to her own time!

"Why do you still seek to shame me, and yourself?" demanded Rory. His eyes darkened with pain as well as anger. "Have I not treated you gently?"

"Yes! Oh, Rory, yes, and I—"

"Then why must you continue with this talk of another Elizabeth MacKenzie? Why the devil must you make such *gorach* claims?" Though he would not yet acknowledge it, a small part of him already suspected that she was not what she seemed. His thoughts returned to her clothing and her speech, so unlike his own. But that she should have come from another time and place? No, he could not lend credence to such an explanation. He could not!

"I only want you to believe me!" she insisted, her eyes filling with sudden tears. She had been through so much these past twelve hours; at this rate, she'd be lucky to have any strength left by nightfall. Or when she was finally able to return home. "Please, you've got to try and understand! I can't stay here! I've got to get back to the twentieth century where I belong! And you've got to help me!"

"You will not leave me!" he proclaimed, his voice raw with emotion. In one swift motion, he rounded the table and grabbed her. His eyes gleamed fiercely down into the wide, luminous blue of hers. "Aye, mistress, 'tis true! You belong to me! I know nothing of this 'time travel' of which you speak, and if you persist in this foolish babbling of yours, I will keep you locked in this room!"

"No!"

"I warn you, never again speak to me of leaving! Are you truly so addled that you cannot understand what is at stake? Our marriage is all that stands between another declaration of war between our clans! The lives of many a MacDonell and MacKenzie depend on our union! Would you destroy the peace, Elizabeth? Would you accept the blood of others on your hands?"

"I—I don't want to see anyone killed!" she faltered, her throat constricting painfully.

"Then do not seek to break the truce with your own selfish whims! By damn, woman, do you understand nothing? The die has been cast! You *will* perform your duties as my wife! You will see to my household and entertain my guests— and you will warm my bed!"

"I'm not your slave, Rory MacDonell! You have no right to give me orders! I don't know how long this ... this mix-up is going to last, but if you think I'm going to bow and scrape in the daytime and play the whore at night, you're out of your mind!"

"You had best guard your tongue," he warned in a tone of deadly calm. "Else you may well find yourself treated with far less respect than is due the wife of a MacDonell!"

He thrust her roughly away from him and stalked from the room. Elizabeth winced as the door slammed shut behind him. Hot tears stung her eyes once more as she ran to the bed and flung herself onto its rumpled softness.

It was nearly noon when she climbed from the four-poster again, ate her cold breakfast, and made use of the garderobe. Before long, a knock sounded at the door. A fair-haired young woman entered. Shyly giving her name as Jean, she told Elizabeth that she was to be her lady's maid, then added that a bath had been ordered. A big, wooden tub was soon produced and filled by two other maids, who dropped a quick curtsy to their new mistress before they scurried from the room, giggling like schoolgirls.

Relieved that she was left alone to bathe, Elizabeth tossed aside the sheet and lowered herself into the water's soothing warmth. Troubled thoughts flooded her mind as the water engulfed her. She wasn't sure what sort of behavior should be used in dealing with the servants; it was impossible for her to consider them anything less than her equals.

Still, she knew enough about history to be aware that a certain protocol was followed by the lady of a castle. And she was, after all, the lady of the castle now. She had so much to learn, she realized with a sigh. The only things she had learned thus far were that she was a pawn in a battle of wills between two belligerent clans, and that the success of her marriage was, quite literally, a matter of life or death.

How could she possibly hope to fit in, to function in an age she knew so little about? Her surroundings had changed, and yet she hadn't been transformed to match them. Even though she had been hurtled back to the sixteenth century, she was still a twentieth-century woman. True, she had always been old-fashioned, but *this* was ridiculous. She was the wife of a man who had been dead for four hundred years . . . only, he wasn't dead now. He was very much alive and very much a force with which to be reckoned.

Her conscience was stung by the way she had responded to her "husband's" lovemaking. More than a little amazed at her newfound sexual freedom, a freedom that owed itself entirely to Rory MacDonell, she took up the cake of heather-scented soap and scrubbed at her skin until it was pink and glowing. She washed her hair as well, then dried off with the thick, soft, woolen towel waiting beside the tub.

Jean had brought her a long gown of light-colored tartan, with scarlet sleeves trimmed with gold lace. Wondering how Rory had come by the garment so easily, she couldn't help feeling a sharp pang of displeasure as she drew it over her head and belted it at the waist. She was puzzled to find no stockings or undergarments, and she made a mental note to ask Jean about them the next time she saw her. She'd also have to ask about what they used instead of toothbrushes, about cosmetics and medicines and a thousand other things she had always taken for granted. Until she could get back to her own life, she'd have to know the basics of existing in an era which offered few conveniences. Life in the past was certainly going to be a challenge.

She retrieved her clothing from the floor beside the bed and withdrew her wallet from the pocket of her skirt. Emptying its contents on the table, she stared down at the coins, paper money, and driver's license she had brought with her but never used. She reached into the other skirt pocket and found her passport, and the charm bracelet her grandmother had given her for her ninth birthday. The clasp had broken just after she had boarded the tour bus with Tracy yesterday morning. Every one of the objects provided a link to the future, and they looked considerably out of place in the room.

Turning away with a frown, she wandered over to the window. In spite of her uneasiness, she gazed down into the courtyard and her eyes lit with interest at what she saw. Grooms were sweeping out the stables, a woman was washing sheets and tablecloths in a wooden trough, and the smith was already stoking the fires of his forge. As she watched, it seemed as if people had materialized out of nowhere to add their efforts to the bustle of activity.

A true Scottish kingdom, mused Elizabeth. And Rory presided over it all.

"I trust you are feeling better?"

She turned at the sound of his voice. Her heart leapt wildly at the sight of her husband, in spite of the fact that he had left her only an hour ago.

"Yes, thank you," she answered solemnly. "I was watching everyone in the courtyard."

"There will be ample opportunity for you to begin wreaking your woman's havoc on the morrow," he teased. Quite breathtaking in his Highland costume, he closed the door behind him and started toward her. "I fear I must be away now. But I will return before the gloamin'."

"The gloamin'?" she echoed in puzzlement.

"Och, woman, you know it is the twilight!" His eyes glinted harshly. "This playacting of yours would try the patience of a saint!"

"Where are you going?" she asked, ignoring his reprimand.

"Word has reached me of a kinsman's ill fate. I must speak with his sons." He opened his mouth to say more, but his gaze suddenly fell to her belongings on the table. "What is this?" he muttered, his brows furrowing in puzzlement. Reaching out, he picked up the charm bracelet.

Elizabeth remained silent and still, her eyes full of hopeful anticipation as she watched him examine the engraved gold disks, then the other telltale items. She held her breath and prayed once more that he would finally accept the truth.

His gaze darkened with a near savage gleam, then shot to where she stood outlined by the bright golden sunlight warming the glass panes.

"How is it you came by these?"

"They're mine! They were in the pockets of my skirt when I came back through time!"

"By all that is holy, are you a witch then?" he demanded hoarsely, looking at the strange objects. They could well be charms used to cast spells. Countless women had been put to the torch in Scotland for practicing black magic these thirty years past. Could it be that his own wife possessed unholy powers? He could not deny to himself that she was unlike anyone he had ever known. As she herself had said, her manner of speaking was strange.

"*Are you a witch?*" He smoldered again as a sharp pain sliced through his heart at the thought.

"Of course not! Oh, Rory, why won't you listen to me? Look at the money, look at the date on everything! And my charm bracelet—read the inscriptions! Surely now you can see that I've been telling you the truth?"

"You ask me to believe what is impossible!"

"I used to think it was impossible, too, until it happened to me!" She hastily closed the distance between them. Her eyes were full of a heartfelt appeal as they met the steady, magnificent green fire of his. "I could tell you so many things that haven't even happened yet . . . about airplanes and automobiles and space travel . . . about wars and famine . . . about great inventions which will change life for everyone! And about your own country! I don't know as much as I should about Scotland's history, but I do know that it will be united with England someday in the near future and she will rule the better part of the world!"

Rory ground out an oath and seized her arms in a hard, punishing grip, only to release her again as though the contact had burned him.

"We will speak more of this when I return!" he promised, his tone dangerously low and level. He spun about and strode toward the doorway.

"Please, don't go yet!" she called after him. "Rory, wait!"

But it was too late. He had gone. She was left alone with an aching heart—and the certainty that, without his help, she would never return to her own time. Rory MacDonell held her fate in his hands.

5

AFTER four weeks had passed, Elizabeth wondered if she would spend the rest of her life in the sixteenth century. On several occasions she had visited the same room where she had been transported, sat in the same chair, and stared up at Rory's painting while fingering her pendant. She had tried to go home, but nothing had happened. Absolutely nothing.

Her mind and emotions were in utter turmoil. She certainly had no wish to be the cause of further bloodshed between the MacDonells and the MacKenzies, but if she did somehow manage to get back to her own life, she ran the risk of starting yet another feud. It was an awful responsibility, and one she would have given anything to transfer onto someone else's shoulders. There were times when she truly despaired of ever finding a solution to the dilemma facing her.

There was a great deal more to her problem than the question of sacrifice, however. Her feelings for Rory were equally chaotic. She had begun to discover the many fascinating traits of the man she had married. He was a good clan chief, often riding out across the rugged, windswept countryside to inspect his lands and to dispense encouragement as well as justice. It was obvious that he was well-loved and respected by his kinsmen. Compassionate and tender, firm and evenhanded, he was a man unlike any she had ever known. She had gained a considerable measure of admiration for him.

And affection. She couldn't deny that she had come to care for him. In spite of her expressed determination to leave him, he had crept into her heart. She presided over his household during the day—no easy task, given the fact that even the simplest chores were done in a completely different way in the sixteenth century. And she shared his bed at night, though not like some quiet, submissive female. He seemed both surprised and delighted by her assertiveness, and yet he still refused to believe her.

She had persistently confronted him with the articles she had brought with her, only to be met with continuing disbelief and suspicion. He would not accept her story, and to make matters worse, he continued to accuse her of being either a witch or a clever, calculating actress. Tempers flared whenever she tried to talk to him about returning to her own time.

Wondering if tonight would be different since it was their one-month anniversary, Elizabeth drifted off to sleep in front of the fire. She awoke when Rory scooped her up gently in his arms and carried her to bed. Once there, he spoke to her of the day's travels and then pressed a long, lingering kiss on her lips, signaling that he was no longer in the mood for conversation.

Elizabeth, however, was of a completely different mind. She had spent the afternoon contemplating her situation, and now felt terribly confused and despondent. Pulling free, she told Rory in a voice choked with emotion that she had not yet given up hope of going home. Passion turned to anger at that point and, once again, a heated argument erupted between them. He would not heed her pleas for help, and she would not allow herself to surrender to his embrace. She watched in helpless frustration as he rolled away from her, indicating that the "discussion" had ended.

Her troubled gaze crept heavenward while she listened to her husband's steady breathing. Sleep eluded her for quite some time, and it was nearly midnight before she slipped into welcome unconsciousness.

The first gentle rays of the dawn had set the horizon aglow the next morning when a loud knock sounded at the door to the bedchamber. Rory was on his feet in an instant, uncaring of the fact that he was naked as he hurried to fling open the door.

"The MacKenzies!" the well-armed man who stood there burst out. "May God strike them down for their treachery, they have come to lay siege to the castle!"

Elizabeth gasped and sat up in the bed. She watched in growing alarm as Rory, grinding out a curse, jerked on his breeks.

"Rory? Dear God, what are you—"

"Stay here!" he commanded tersely. He donned his shoes and his *leine*, then grabbed up the great, two-handed claymore on his way out of the room.

Elizabeth hesitated only a moment before scrambling from the bed. She dressed in the long tartan gown and, barefooted, gave chase. She wasn't about to sit and wait while Rory MacDonell went off and got himself killed. By the heavens above, she swore, what would happen to her if he ended up dead? She couldn't allow that to happen! And furthermore, she was supposed to be an instrument of peace between the clans. Maybe her intervention would put a stop to the hostilities.

Rory gazed out over the mist-cloaked glen, assessing his enemies and steeling himself for the battle ahead. The MacKenzies were an impressive sight to behold as they approached the castle's outer walls. Their force was some two hundred strong, each man among them wearing the same tartan and armed with shield and sword. Leading the unexpected assault was the burly, black-haired giant Angus MacKenzie, the clan's chief and father of the woman Rory had married.

Angus spurred his horse ahead of his men and jerked the animal to a halt before the iron gate. He scowled murderously up at the battlements, where dozens of Rory's men had taken positions with bows and arrows. More men awaited below the keep, ready to defend both the castle and the honor of their name. They were outnumbered, but they had the definite advantage of being within the protection of the thick, towering stone walls.

"Come forward, MacDonell!" bellowed Angus, his voice ringing out in the cold morning light. "I would have a word with you—aye, you scheming, black-hearted young rogue—before I split your skull in two!"

"What talk is this, MacKenzie?" Rory demanded, frowning darkly as he stepped up to the edge of the battlement. Looking down in furious bewilderment at his enemy, who was now his father-in-law, he shook his head and pronounced, " 'Tis a strange way to be greeting your new *cliamhainn*! Why do you seek to break the peace between us? Is not your own daughter within these castle walls?"

"My daughter has fled to Edinburgh, as well you must know by now! The poor lass preferred banishment from all she held dear to sharing the bed of a MacDonell!"

"The devil you say! She has shared my bed these four weeks past! And lest you doubt it, you may put forth the question to any man herein! We were wed at the appointed hour, with the parson's blessing and in the sight of God!"

"What nonsense is this?" shouted Angus, his dark eyes narrowing in mingled rage and suspicion. "Are you such a coward then, Rory MacDonell, that you must lie your way from a fight? I have waited these many days for you to strike and avenge yourself for her betrayal, but I will wait no more! Let the first blow be mine! The bargain between us—"

"*The bargain has been fulfilled!*"

Rory jerked his head around to see that Elizabeth had climbed up behind him. His handsome face grew thunderous, and his low, simmering tone was for her ears alone.

"Get below, woman!"

"No!" she retorted defiantly. Ignoring his wrathful glare, she took her place beside him and declared to all assembled, "My name is Elizabeth MacKenzie, and I have been the wife of Rory MacDonell for a month now!"

"Spare yourself the same judgment as the others, lass!" Angus warned, his bearded features displaying both disbelief and disgust. "You are no MacKenzie!"

At Angus's emphatic denouncement, Rory knew that he had, indeed, married the wrong Elizabeth MacKenzie. She had spoken the truth about that, he told himself in amazement. Had she spoken the truth about traveling back through time as well?

"By the heavens—" he breathed. His incredulous gaze fastened on his wife's beautiful face. He forgot about the danger of attack for a moment, forgot all else save the woman beside him. If she truly was what she claimed to be, then would she leave him? And dear God above, what would happen to them all if she did?

He realized in that moment that she had captured his heart. The days he had spent with her had been the happiest of his life and he couldn't bear the thought of losing her. Indeed, a miracle *had* been granted them. He would give thanks for it every day of his life.

"I swear to you that I am a MacKenzie!" Elizabeth insisted to the leader of the opposing clan. Acting on sudden impulse, she reached up and unfastened her necklace. She held the pendant aloft. "See for yourself—I am wearing the clan crest! And may I be struck dead where I stand if my name isn't truly Elizabeth MacKenzie!" she added, tossing the pendant down to Angus, who caught it and glowered up at her. Surprised at her own courage, she prayed that her melodramatic challenge would help.

" 'Tis not impossible, I suppose," Angus conceded reluctantly, examining the piece of jewelry in his hand. He could not deny that the crest, a mountain inflamed, was that of the Clan MacKenzie. The lass also had the look of one of his own. Whatever her identity, his young adversary seemed to be well-pleased with the outcome. Mayhap there could be peace between them after all, Angus thought as hope sprang to life within him.

"My wife speaks the truth!" Rory now affirmed. Although she was not the Elizabeth MacKenzie he had agreed to marry, she was his wife. A surge of protectiveness welled deep within him. She was his, and he would keep her! "She is a stranger to you, aye, but the blood of a MacKenzie runs hot and strong in her veins! Before God, I proclaim my acceptance of her! The truce must not be broken! And so, Angus MacKenzie, get you home again!" he exhorted with a faint smile down at the man who had earned his begrudging respect along with his enmity these twenty years past. "There can be no battle this day—no, nor any other day so long as we desire an end to the feud!"

As the other Highlander visibly wavered at this point, Elizabeth held her breath and watched him. She moved closer to Rory, her hand closing on his arm while a terrible tension rose in the air.

Finally, Angus spoke. "Aye!" he shouted, his face splitting into a broad grin. "We shall have peace between us, MacDonell!" The MacKenzie chieftain tossed the pendant to one of the MacDonells. The man climbed up to the castle wall to return it to Elizabeth, who hung it around her neck.

A great cheer went up from the men on both sides of the castle. Rory slipped his arm around Elizabeth's waist. They watched together as Angus MacKenzie reined about and led his kinsmen homeward again.

"I should skelp you well and proper for your disobedience!" Rory threatened his bride gruffly, knowing that he could never lift a hand to her in anger.

"I had no intention of being widowed yet!" she parried, unrepentant. Her eyes were alight with affectionate humor as she tilted her head back to look up at him. But she sobered in the next instant, asking softly, "Now do you believe me, Rory?"

"I fear I am beginning to," he admitted reluctantly. He kept his arm around her shoulders while he led her toward the stairway. "I have never held with mystery and magic, Elizabeth. But you are here with me, and I cannot find the explanation within my own mind."

"I know it's incredible . . . I know it doesn't make any sense." She released a long, pent-up sigh and told him, "I have tried to get back, but I can't. Maybe it happened because we were meant to be together. You were born too soon— or I was born too late. Either way, it just happened! Don't you see? It could be that we were meant to love each other, Rory. I don't know. Time doesn't seem to matter anymore."

"And so it never will again. You are mine forever!" he vowed masterfully, drawing to an abrupt halt in the shadows of the corridor and sweeping her up against his virile, hard-muscled warmth. His gaze seared down into hers. "You are mine, bonny *Ealasaid*, and with God as my witness, a MacDonell holds what is his!" He paused for a moment before asking, "Why do you want to leave me? Do you not love me?"

"I . . . I'm not sure what I feel," she answered. "If only I belonged here." She raised a hand to the rugged perfection of his face, her fingers tracing lightly, affectionately upward to where a strand of his dark red hair had fallen across his forehead. "But, oh, I *could* love you, Rory MacDonell."

She searched his face and glimpsed an incredible sadness in his eyes—and an understanding she had not yet acknowledged.

"But you do, Elizabeth," he whispered.

The next few weeks were spent in a captivating whirl of passion and discovery. During the day, there was an endless amount of work for Elizabeth and Rory to supervise—fetching fuel and water, gathering supplies, cooking and cleaning and mending, writing letters, checking accounts, making weapons, guarding the outer walls, keeping the roof and battlements in good repair, settling personal disputes, and arguing political matters. Guests had to be welcomed and entertained, and there was always the possibility that some other clan would decide to test the strength of the MacDonells.

In spite of the ever-present threat of danger, Elizabeth was happy. She had fallen in love with Rory MacDonell and at last understood why she had been unable to resist him on their wedding night. Her fate had been sealed the first moment she had studied his portrait. Loving him was no longer just a possibility; it had become the most important reality of her life.

Everything had changed since that day on the battlements, when she had stood beside her husband and faced the MacKenzies. Rory had finally accepted the truth about her, and with his acceptance had come the freedom to love. When she had realized that, she had experienced a tremendous inner struggle, as though her old life was battling with the new one she'd found with Rory. After all, she had reminded herself, she still didn't really belong in his time—her world was so different from his—and yet he needed her, just as the clans still needed her to ensure peace. Her life had never held as much purpose as it held now, and she could not abandon her responsibilities.

But it was her love for Rory that forced her to make the final decision. She wanted to spend the rest of her life with him, to share his bed and have his children and grow old with him. How could she ever think of leaving him? Nothing else seemed to matter anymore. She knew she would give up everything to be with him. *Everything*.

God help her, she had fallen in love with a man from another century. She loved him with all her heart . . . with her very soul. And she knew that, whatever the past, present, or future held, her feelings for him would never change.

Rory had made no secret of his own feelings, either. He made sweet, captivating love to her each night, then lingered with her in the mornings, demanding to know everything about her childhood as well as her more recent life before she had appeared in this century. There were times when it was obvious that he found her words difficult to comprehend, but he listened with rapt interest and saw fit to interrupt her with a question only on a couple of occasions.

Now, though, as she lay beside him in bed and spoke of Garrett, he was none too pleased.

"Did you truly love this man?" he asked, his green eyes darkening with jealousy at the thought.

"No," she was able to reply honestly. "I thought I did, but I realize now that what I felt was nothing more than infatuation. I suppose I just wanted someone of my own. I was a fool to think I could ever settle for anything less than the real thing."

"More fool I for believing a woman such as you to exist in the world I know." He drew her closer to him. "You are like no other, sweet Elizabeth."

"I'm glad you finally noticed." She smiled, her eyes twinkling merrily at him. "You wouldn't fit into my world, either, you know. In the twentieth century, men don't go around forcing women to marry for the purpose of ending feuds."

"Do they not?"

"No. And I can't think of anyone who can lay claim to the title 'lord and master.' Women have the same rights as men."

"The devil you say!" he exclaimed in disbelief, pulling away in order to search her face closely.

"I'm perfectly serious! Throughout the next four hundred years, Rory MacDonell, women are going to demand, and receive, the right to own property and to earn a living, to vote, and even to hold political office. They no longer have to answer to their husbands—unless they want to, of course."

"You may well speak the truth, but *this* husband has methods to ensure the compliance of his woman," he boasted, his mouth curving into a slow, tenderly wolfish smile.

"Is that so?" she challenged in a seductive tone. "Well then, perhaps you'd care to offer a demonstration."

"Aye, that I would."

And he did.

After they had gloried in the passionate enchantment of their love once again, Rory divulged more of the mysteries of his own life. Elizabeth was fascinated by his stories of a boyhood spent hunting and riding, learning to fight like a true Highlander, and helping his father with the endless responsibilities of a clan chieftain. Her heart twisted at the discernible pain in his voice when he spoke of the bloodshed he had witnessed. He had spent the better part of his adult years in warfare of one kind or another.

"No wonder you were so anxious to put an end to the fighting between the MacDonells and the MacKenzies," she murmured. "I think now I can understand why you were willing to marry someone you had never met before."

"I thank God above that Angus MacKenzie could not control the will of his daughter."

"So do I. And I feel sorry for that 'other' Elizabeth."

"Why should she have your pity?" he asked in puzzlement.

"Because she missed out on *you*."

She was rewarded for her deeply felt sentiments with another kiss. And then Rory climbed from the bed at last, chastising her in mock, husbandly irritation for having tempted him to madness again. She gave a soft laugh and joined him in his search for his clothes.

Finally, on this particularly bright summer day, they emerged from the solar just in time for the noon meal. It was served in the great hall by Jean and the plump, dark-haired, young Bridget. Elizabeth took her usual place beside Rory at the long table perched atop a dais. They feasted on smoked herring, peas, fruit from the castle orchard, freshly baked bread, and homemade ale. Although not exactly formal, the atmosphere was quietly elegant—a far cry from the mannerless feeding frenzy Elizabeth had once imagined.

When they had finished, she told Rory that she was anxious to explore more of the castle. There were many rooms she still hadn't gotten around to inspecting, even after all this time. She was surprised when her husband confided a reluctance to let her out of his sight.

"But why?" she asked, troubled by the sudden shadow crossing his face.

He clasped her hand within the strong, possessive warmth of his own as they moved away from the table. "My mind is uneasy this day." He had never before been a man ruled by his fears, but the gift of her love was too new to trust to chance.

"Nothing is going to happen, Rory."

"Still, Elizabeth, I—"

"You mustn't worry," she insisted reassuringly. She lifted her hands to rest on his chest when he stopped and drew her to him. "I promise not to leave the castle. And I know you've got work to do. Remind me later to tell you about a quaint old custom called a 'honeymoon.' Or have you already heard of it?"

"Aye," he confirmed with a perfectly devastating smile. "Mayhap we will travel to Edinburgh in a few days' time."

"I don't care where we go, just as long as we're together."

"My thoughts are the same as your own."

"Then you'd better take your hands off me now, Rory MacDonell, or neither one of us will get anything done!"

He gave a low, mellow chuckle and obediently released her. She watched as he disappeared through one of the passages near the foot of the staircase. Her eyes softly aglow, she turned her own steps toward the kitchen.

The delicious smells wafting through the castle beckoned her. As she had already discovered, there were actually two kitchens—one for baking, the other for roasting meat, preparing fruits and vegetables, and boiling giant cauldrons of stew. Each day, a small army of kitchen servants drew water, fetched spices and other ingredients, plucked geese and cleaned fish, and kneaded a mountain of dough.

Elizabeth smiled to herself at the intriguing sights, sounds, and smells. She was always amazed at the smooth efficiency with which the tasks were performed. Making a mental note to return later, she set off on her exploration.

She followed no definite course, but instead strolled from room to room, scrutinizing the interiors and speaking to everyone she met. She was greeted in return with genuine pleasure as Rory's kinsmen expressed their gratitude for her presence there, especially since the MacKenzies had gone away without a fight. They also confided to her that their *Ard-Righ*, their beloved young chief, was obviously happier than he had ever been before. For that reason alone, they pledged her their undying loyalty and devotion.

Filled with deep satisfaction, Elizabeth took her time, allowing herself the luxury of a respite from her usual routine. By late afternoon, she finally decided to call a halt to her wanderings. She stepped out of the chapel, where she had spent the past several minutes gazing up at the stained-glass window and remembering her highly unusual wedding. It was difficult to believe she was the same woman who had stood before the minister in a state of shock. So very much had changed.

Lost in her thoughts, she was surprised to feel a sudden tug, and her eyes widened with dismay when she detected the sound of fabric ripping. She glanced down, frowning at the sizeable tear in the soft plaid wool that had caught on a splintered piece of wood in the chapel's narrow, arched doorway.

With a huff of exasperation at her own carelessness, she gathered up her long skirts and headed back to the solar. The room was empty, but the bed had been made, and a newly stoked fire blazed in the stone hearth.

Elizabeth's gaze was drawn to the clothing that had been laundered, folded neatly, and placed on the covers of the four-poster. They would look every bit as out of place as they had nine weeks ago, but she had little choice at the moment. Musing with an inward smile of irony that she'd have to behave like any other wife down through the centuries and pester her husband for some new dresses, she hastened to exchange her torn gown for her sweater and skirt. She pulled on the silk underwear and knee socks as well, then sailed forth from the room again with the intention of finding a needle and thread. Her skills as a seamstress were almost laughable, but she could at least manage to repair the gown until someone else took pity on her and did a more capable job.

She was already on her way across the great hall when a sudden noise caught her attention. It was a muffled sound, one she couldn't describe. She decided to investigate, her instincts leading her toward the same room where she had been transported back through time—and where she had tried to reverse the process. She would always be thankful that it hadn't worked.

She halted at the entrance, and her gaze made a quick, encompassing sweep of the room, but she saw nothing. Her eyes moved up to Rory's portrait the moment she stepped through the doorway. She smiled at the sight of it and crossed to the chair in front of the fire. Sinking down on its uncushioned hardness, she breathed deeply and continued to stare at the painting. The likeness truly didn't do him justice, she reflected again. But then, how could any artist hope to capture Rory MacDonell's vibrancy, his incomparable fire and spirit and utter manliness?

It didn't seem possible that she had once sat in this exact spot and had been swept back to the late sixteenth century. So much had happened since that day. Her marriage to Rory MacDonell had brought her love, just as it had brought peace to the glen. In that one split second in time, two worlds had been changed forever.

She still wondered what Tracy had thought when she had returned downstairs and discovered her gone. If only there were some way she could explain.

She wished she could ease the pain and worry and confusion she knew her friend must have been feeling since her disappearance.

Her hand crept up to her pendant and she shifted her deep blue gaze to the fire. All about her, life in the castle went on, but her thoughts were elsewhere.

She closed her eyes, breathing deeply again as a sudden, inexplicable weariness descended on her. She didn't want to sleep, and yet she could not prevent herself from slipping away.

6

"LIZZIE? Lizzie, wake up!"

With great difficulty, she opened her eyes to find Tracy bending over her.

"Come on!" her friend urged impatiently. "We're going to miss the bus!"

"Tracy? What—" She broke off abruptly, her gaze filling with shocked dismay as it darted up toward the portrait. *Rory!*

"You look as if you've seen a ghost!" her friend remarked with a soft laugh. "Wait until you hear some of the stories Mrs. Stewart told us. Some of *them* are certainly spooky enough to curl your hair." She took Elizabeth's arm and gave a gentle, insistent tug. "I can't for the life of me understand how you could fall asleep with the wind howling like that, but you've got to wake up so we can get back to Inverness. I'll be damned if I'm going to spend the night in this haunted old rattletrap!"

"How . . . how long have I been asleep?" Elizabeth stammered dazedly. Dear God, was it all only a dream?

175

"About an hour, I'd say."

"An hour?" she echoed, her head spinning.

She was pale and shaken as she finally pulled herself to her feet. Feeling an acute sense of loss, she looked at the painting again. Rory MacDonell's eyes seemed to be boring down into hers. It had been so real. So very, very real. . . .

"If you're so enchanted with this place, you can come back tomorrow. But I've had enough. Now let's go!"

Lost in a trance, Elizabeth was scarcely aware of her own movements as she allowed Tracy to lead her across the room. But she held back when they reached the doorway.

"No, I—I can't leave!" she cried brokenly.

"What do you mean you can't leave? I'm telling you, Elizabeth MacKenzie, you're out of your mind if you think I'm going to let us miss that blessed tour bus!"

"It couldn't have been a dream," Elizabeth murmured aloud, hot tears filling her eyes when she turned back toward the fireplace. "It couldn't have been!" The room was the same as she had remembered it—in the twentieth century. The velvet sofa, the old photographs, the chandelier . . . everything was the same. And Rory MacDonell's compelling portrait still hung above the mantelpiece.

"A dream?" Tracy's mouth curved into an affectionately teasing smile. "Don't tell me you've gone and fallen in love with one of the ghosts of 'bonny auld Castle MacDonell'?"

"Oh Tracy, it was so real," she whispered. Her heart ached terribly, and she could hear the blood pounding in her ears. "I—I was married to Rory MacDonell!"

"Well then, I'd say that was *some* dream. You must really be tired!" Her friend slipped an arm around her shoulders and guided her firmly out of the room at last. "We'd better get you back to the hotel right away. Honestly, you don't look so well. Thank God we won't be touring any more castles."

Elizabeth could not summon the strength to resist. She moved through the great hall, then outside where she and Tracy boarded the waiting bus. Throughout the short drive to Inverness, she sat silent and still, greatly troubled by memories that weren't memories at all. *A dream . . . nothing but a dream.*

It was already starting to get dark by the time they reached the hotel. Tracy announced her intention to get something to eat in the hotel's restaurant, while Elizabeth managed a wan smile and said she'd rather wait and order from room service later.

Once inside her room, Elizabeth finally surrendered to the powerful, overwhelming urge to cry. She collapsed facedown on the bed. Her arms clenched the pillow while sob after sob rose in her throat and tears flowed unchecked down the flushed smoothness of her cheeks.

How could it have been nothing more than a dream when she could recall every detail, every word and smell and taste with such vivid clarity, she wondered in agonizing bewilderment. And how was it possible that she could still remember Rory MacDonell's touch so well? His kisses still burned on her lips . . . her body yearned for his.

"Oh, Rory!" she choked out. Now she understood what it meant when people claimed that their hearts had been broken. Her own heart was filled with unbearable pain, her very soul crying out in anguish. Not only had she and Rory lost one another, but there was every likehood that, without her presence within the castle walls, the feud would commence once more.

Rory MacDonell met his end because of a woman. Had Mrs. Stewart's words set her off on a wild flight of fantasy? Or was it something else? She had been thinking about Garrett—maybe that's why her mind had concocted the journey back through time. After all, she had wished for a man like the one in the portrait, hadn't she? He had apparently fit her idea of the perfect cure for Garrett's betrayal. God help her, he had fit it all too well.

She wept bitterly, until no more tears would come. Lying there in the silent, deepening blackness of the room, she felt empty inside. How could she ever forget what had happened—or rather, what she had imagined?

If only she could go back. But then, there was nothing to go back *to*. These past weeks existed only in her mind. Rory MacDonell had been dead for four hundred years. She had fallen in love with a ghost, just as Tracy had playfully suggested. Only, there was nothing at all humorous about the reality of her feelings. She loved him. She would always love him.

"Dear God, what am I going to do?" she implored in a hoarse whisper. "Please, help me!"

She closed her eyes again and buried her face in her hands. Not since her grandmother's death had she felt so miserable and full of despair. If she had to lose Rory, too, how could she ever hope to know happiness again?

"Elizabeth."

A startled gasp broke from her lips. She could have sworn she'd heard someone calling her name. Lowering her hands, she opened her eyes and sat up. She held her breath and listened.

"Elizabeth!"

There it was again, only stronger this time. It was Rory's voice, she realized, her whole body flooding with joy. Rory MacDonell was calling her back!

She knew then that the miracle was a true one. It had happened. Thank God, it was real!

She had to return to the castle right away, and she had to let Tracy know what she was planning to do. Her eyes lit with sudden comprehension. That was why she had been transported back to the future—*to let Tracy know.*

Scrambling off the bed, she turned on the lamp and hurriedly withdrew a pen and a piece of paper from the nightstand drawer. Her hand skittered across the page as she did her best to explain the whole incredible story. She knew Tracy would have difficulty accepting the truth, but she hoped that in time she would understand. At the very least, Tracy would have the letter to show to the authorities, and she would have the catering business, as well as all of Elizabeth's belongings in Dallas.

Elizabeth finally set the pen aside, folded the paper, and stuffed it into an envelope. There was no reason to delay any longer. She raced out of the room and down the corridor to the elevator. Once on the ground floor, she handed the envelope to the desk clerk with instructions that it was to be given to Miss Tracy Tyler in Room 304 first thing in the morning.

Her heart was beating wildly as she raced outside to hail a taxi. It was quite late, and she grew frantic after her first three attempts failed to yield any results. Finally, a cab pulled up in front of the hotel.

"Where would you like to be going, miss?" the gray-haired driver asked. He was polite, but his words were so heavily accented that she had to venture a guess at half of them.

"To Castle MacDonell, please!" she replied, sliding onto the back seat and closing the door.

"Castle MacDonell?" he repeated, frowning. "I'm sorry, miss, but it isn't open to the public after—"

"I know! Please, just hurry!"

With an eloquent shrug, he complied, pulling away from the hotel and heading out against the steady stream of traffic that flowed into the capital of the Highlands on this blustery, overcast night.

To Elizabeth the ride seemed endless, and her heartbeat quickened when she finally sighted the castle in the nearing distance. Towering above the beauty of the surrounding glen, it looked gloomy and ominous in the cold night air. There were no lights burning inside, and if not for a single mercury lamp fastened high on a pole in front of the building, she would have had to face the prospect of making her way across the grounds in total darkness. But she would have done it, and gladly. She'd have walked through fire if it meant she could be with Rory again.

"It won't be opening until the morning," the driver informed her, his voice edged with worry. "You can't stay out here by yourself, miss. Let me take you back to the city."

"Thank you, but I'll be fine!" she assured him. She got out of the taxi and reached into the pocket of her skirt to pay him. Until now, she had forgotten about leaving her money and identification on the table in the solar. And sure enough, both pockets were empty—except for a single, twenty-pound note which she had somehow overlooked. She handed it to the driver and said, "You don't need to wait—I'll be staying!"

"Staying? Are you sure?" He didn't make a habit of questioning his customers about their destinations, no matter how bloody odd they might be, but there was something about this pretty, bright-eyed young American that made him think of his own daughter.

"Absolutely!"

She cast him a brief, preoccupied smile, then turned away and hastened toward the castle. The puzzled Scot watched until she had disappeared around the back. He hated to leave her, yet there really wasn't much he could do if she had set her mind on whatever nonsense had brought her there. Promising himself to notify the police all the same, he shook his head in reluctant acceptance of the situation and drove away.

Elizabeth's steps seemed to be guided by an invisible force. Although it was very nearly pitch-black at the rear of the building, she moved confidently toward one of the windows. Finding it unlocked, she opened it and climbed inside. She was pleased to see a soft, flickering glow coming from the room where she had faced her destiny that afternoon.

She followed the beacon of light, her heart hammering with apprehension and excitement as she stepped through the doorway. Rory's portrait was spotlighted by a small, low-wattage lamp attached to the upper edge of the frame, and she saw that the embers were still glowing in the stone fireplace.

Praying as she had never prayed before, she hurried across to take her place in the rocking chair. She raised her eyes to the painting, and her fingers shook as they grasped the pendant. "Please, God, please let me be with Rory!" she whispered fervently.

She could live without modern conveniences. She would suffer no second thoughts about giving up her comfortable lifestyle for one that might well be full of pain and hardship. All that truly mattered was Rory. She'd rather die than live without him. He needed her, and his people needed her.

Please! her soul cried out once more.

She knew that miracles rarely happen twice throughout the course of a lifetime, never mind a single day, but just as rare was the kind of love she had found with her wild Highland chieftain. A love like that could move mountains and alter the course of history. A love like that, she believed with all her heart, could transcend time itself—as long as Rory's love was as strong as her own. Together, they could cross the boundaries of time.

His name was on her lips when her eyes swept closed, and before she even knew what was happening, she had fallen into a deep, dreamless sleep.

"Elizabeth!"

The sound of Rory's voice penetrated the darkness and she struggled toward it.

"By the heavens, Elizabeth, can you not hear me?" he demanded in growing concern.

She opened her eyes and saw him kneeling before her, felt his strong arms around her, and looked at his handsome face bent close to hers.

"Yes, Rory," she answered softly. "I hear you."

"God be praised," he exclaimed in a voice raw with emotion, "you have come back to me! I have searched for you these many days past! I believed you to be lost to me forever . . . I love you more than life itself! Never leave me again, Elizabeth! *Never!*"

"I won't," she promised tremulously, her heart stirring with the certainty of her words. "For I love you with all my heart."

Without hesitation, she yanked the gold chain from about her neck, opened the small silver casket on the table beside the rocking chair, and tossed the pendant inside. She closed the lid and locked the box.

She was home.

At half past ten the next morning, Tracy Tyler hurried anxiously inside Castle MacDonell. Having received Elizabeth's letter only an hour earlier from the desk clerk, she had read and re-read it. She was convinced that her friend had suffered some kind of intense emotional breakdown while visiting the castle the day before.

It was to be expected, of course, Tracy told herself. After all, Garrett Cantrell, self-serving, egotistical bastard that he was, had hurt Elizabeth deeply. No wonder she had fantasized about some dashing, long-dead Highlander. *But she was carrying things too far.*

She'd have to find the poor girl before she did something stupid, Tracy thought in growing alarm. And she'd probably better notify the local authorities as well. It was clear that Elizabeth needed help desperately.

"Mrs. Stewart?" she called out, hoping that the tour guide had either seen her friend or could offer some information about her whereabouts.

Voices drifted out to Tracy from the same room where she had found Elizabeth sleeping yesterday afternoon. She frowned and headed across the great hall.

The venerable Mrs. Stewart stood before the fireplace, surrounded by the eight female members of the morning tour group from Inverness. All eyes were fastened on the magnificent portrait that hung above the mantelpiece.

"And here, of course, you see another likeness of Rory MacDonell, one of the castle's former owners. This one, I think you will agree, is much more finely detailed than the one we examined in the great hall."

"Didn't you say he died of a broken heart?" one of the women asked, visibly perturbed at the thought.

"Yes, but I should, perhaps, offer a slight clarification," Mrs. Stewart responded with a knowing smile. "Though it sounds quite romantic to make such a claim, there are a few things worth knowing about the handsome Mr. MacDonell. You see, he *did* pine away for his dear wife, but only after they had been married for some fifty-odd years, a considerable accomplishment in those days. He couldn't bear to live without her, I suppose, and followed her in death within a week's time."

"And what was his wife's name?" Tracy demanded, coming forward now. She felt a sudden, unaccountable need to know the name of the woman who had married Rory MacDonell—*Elizabeth's* Rory MacDonell.

The answer, when it came, was both startling and strangely comforting.

"Why, it was Elizabeth. Elizabeth MacKenzie."

Catherine Creel

CATHERINE CREEL's first historical romance novel was published in 1979. Since then she has written fifteen others and admits that she has often felt as if she belonged in an earlier time.

A native Texan, she is proud to be able to count both Davy Crockett and Colonel William Travis among her ancestors, and credits her cowboy grandfather with giving her the love of storytelling. In addition to writing, she enjoys traveling, collecting movies, and reading about history.

Catherine still lives near her grandparents' Fort Worth ranch, where she spent most of her childhood. Happily married for eighteen years, she and her husband have three children under the age of ten and a very tolerant cat.

Destiny's Spell

Kay McMahon

A SOFT smile crinkled Nicolas Charboneau's ruggedly handsome face as he stood by the open patio doors, staring out across the rose garden at the beautiful sunset. Although this wasn't his first time in France, it was his first visit to Lisette and Jacques Forgét's country estate, and they were already promising to make it a vacation he would never forget.

"A costume ball," he stated, his dark eyes sparkling as he turned to look at his host. "Your wife is off finding a costume for me to wear and the two of you think I'll actually dress up in tight breeches, hose, and a lacy shirt?"

Forgét shrugged. "Well, it is what was customarily worn at the time of the French Revolution."

"Mmm," Cole murmured as he came back across the room to sit down near his friend.

As a professor of French history at Illinois State University in Normal, Illinois, Cole knew all about the tradition, the language, and the

191

battles that were a part of the country's past. It didn't mean that he wanted to reenact any of it. He was more into skiing the French Alps, skydiving, and hiking rough terrain. About the calmest thing he had ever done in his spare time was motor across the United States on his 1000cc Hurricane touring bike and camp out under the stars. If his friend had suggested anything similar to that kind of excitement, he would have eagerly agreed. But a costume ball?

"I know what you're thinking, Nicolas," Forgét predicted, "but I assure you the party will have its rewards."

"Oh?" Cole questioned skeptically, grinning.

Rising, Forgét grabbed the decanter off the buffet and refilled his companion's glass with wine. "How long has it been since you've seriously dated anyone?"

The question caught Cole off guard, and he frowned. "Not since Nancy, three years ago."

"And you like it that way?"

Nancy Sedbrook had been the first woman in Cole's life to break his heart. They were already making plans for their wedding, when one day, out of the clear blue, she had handed him back his ring with the announcement that she would be marrying someone else the following week. He had been devastated and had walked around in a daze for months, until a friend of his had asked him why he was wasting his time and energy on someone like Nancy. There were plenty of other women in the world who would love to date him, no strings attached. It hadn't taken him very long at all to find that out.

"Yes," he answered. "I like it that way."

Forgét smiled broadly as he sat back down. "And what better country than France for you to fully enjoy the art of love? With your good looks and charm, you'll have to fight the women off."

"Thank you, but I'd rather do it wearing jeans, my friend," Cole replied, laughing.

A commotion in the hall interrupted their conversation, and the two men quickly came to their feet as Lisette Forgét walked into the room.

"Nicolas!" she called excitedly as she hurried over to him and accepted his warm embrace. "It's so good to see you again. I'm sorry I wasn't at home when you arrived, but I had some important errands to run."

"There's no need to apologize," he assured her. "You were expecting me this morning, and I would have been here on time if my flight out of New York hadn't been delayed." He held her at arm's length and looked her up and down. "You're still just as beautiful as I remember."

Cole had met the Forgéts during the fall semester, when they came to Illinois State as a part of Jacques' lecture tour on French art. They had become fast friends within minutes of meeting each other, and it had been Lisette's idea that Cole pay them a visit the following spring. It hadn't taken much insistence on her part to get him to agree, and Cole didn't regret his decision.

"And you're still quite the flatterer," she

charged, giggling. She slipped her hand into his and looked at her husband. "Has Jacques told you about the party we're having this Saturday in celebration of Bastille Day?"

Cole frowned playfully. "Uh-huh. But I'm hoping you're going to tell me that you couldn't find a costume in my size."

Lisette's eyes sparkled. "Jacques told me you probably wouldn't like the idea, but I promise the party will be fun. And yes, I found a costume. I had Antoine take it to your room." She glanced at her husband again. "And that's not all I found."

Jacques rolled his eyes. "Don't tell me. Something for the château." He frowned at Cole. "I swear she'll spend every sou I earn before she's done."

Cole smiled. "It looks to me as though it's money well spent. Lisette has done a marvelous job refurbishing the place. Everything in it looks to be original."

"Then wait until you see this," she declared as she rushed from the room.

A moment later she returned, followed by one of the servants carrying what appeared to be a huge painting wrapped in a thick cloth. While Lisette pulled the strings free, the servant set up an easel, and together they placed Lisette's latest purchase on its stand near the patio doors where it would catch the full light of the late-afternoon sun.

"Are you ready?" she asked, smiling.

Both men nodded and she lifted the covering

off the gold-framed portrait.

For an instant Cole thought he was seeing double, until he realized that the painting was of two exquisitely beautiful young women, twins. One was seated, the other standing behind and off to one side of her sister. They both wore dark green gowns with low necklines and white lace trim across their full bosoms. Their hair, a rich chestnut brown, was piled high on their heads with ringlets cascading down the back and interlaced with strands of pearls. Their skin was a flawless ivory, and around their necks they each wore matching black velvet chokers with white cameos in the center. The young women were identical in every way, yet there was a subtle difference between the two that Cole couldn't quite pinpoint.

"Who are they?" he asked, moving closer. "Do you know?"

"Oh, yes," Lisette assured him. "Their names are Danielle and Dominique Dubois, and this château was built by their father for his bride in 1770. The previous owners told us about it and how they had had to sell off some of the furnishings when they fell on hard times. It took until today for me to track down this painting. Isn't it superb?"

Cole nodded but didn't speak as he studied the two faces staring back at him. They had the same shaped nose and chin and high cheekbones, the same arch to their brows, the same long neck and square shoulders. They were alike in every way . . . except one. Suddenly, he saw it. Thick, black lashes trimmed beautiful, dark brown eyes, yet one twin—the one who stood with her hand resting on the back of the chair— had no sparkle in the depths of her gaze. He wondered what had made her so sad.

"There's a story that goes along with the painting, Nicholas, if you'd like to hear it," Lisette offered.

"Very much," he replied without looking away.

"The one seated is Danielle. The other is Dominique, and the portrait was painted shortly after their father, Guilbert Dubois, announced his daughters' engagements. Danielle was happy with her father's choice for her, but Dominique hated her young man. Perhaps that's why she appears to be so sad."

For some odd reason Cole felt himself becoming angry. "You're not going to tell me that after their marriage he beat her, are you?"

"Oh, no. They never got married," Lisette quickly assured him.

A smile started to lift the corners of his mouth, but he pushed it back. "Why not?" he asked, turning to take his seat in the chair beside the sofa where Lisette had joined her husband.

"You must remember, now, that this tale has been passed down from generation to generation. How much of it is true, we can only guess."

Cole nodded his understanding, took a sip of wine, and waited patiently for the telling of a story he was sure would stir his sense of adventure.

"Not long after the engagements were announced, the French Revolution started. Dominique and Danielle were off visiting relatives in Corsica at the time, and upon their return home, they learned that their neighbors, nasty people who hated the Duboises, had accused their parents of being traitors. *Lettres-de-cachet*—secret warrants for their arrest—were served and they were taken to the Bastille in Paris.

"Because the two girls were so different in nature, Danielle wanted to flee the country, while Dominique plotted a way to rescue their parents. *Her* fiancé, Siffre Chevalier, being the coward that he was, had already escaped to England, but Danielle's betrothed, Jean-Luc D'Rillon, refused to run, even though his life was in as much danger as the twins'."

Cole looked at the portrait again. Only this time he decided that it wasn't sadness he saw in Dominique's eyes, but a rebellious strength. He also marveled at the sensation he felt . . . as if he were actually falling in love with her. "I suppose this story isn't going to have a happy ending," he commented.

"Well, it was a time of unrest and violence," Jacques remarked. "If one believes in ghosts, then I'm sure Dominique's spirit wanders through the château late at night."

Cole smiled lopsidedly. "A pleasant thought," he replied, as he absently toyed with the college class ring on his left hand. "I haven't been given her bedroom, have I?"

Lisette shrugged. "We're not really sure whose

room it was. But don't worry. No one's ever been murdered in their sleep."

"But there's always a first time?" Cole added, chuckling. "So what happened next?"

"The details are a little sketchy, but the gist of it and the *most* exciting part is that Danielle—afraid she, her fiancé, and Dominique would all be killed—sought out the help of a witch."

Cole's eyebrows dipped downward. "You're not going to ruin a perfectly good story by trying to convince me that witchcraft really works, are you?"

Lisette laughed. "I can't say one way or the other. Danielle never used it."

"What do you mean?"

"Apparently—or so it's been told—she asked the witch for a chant that would send Danielle, and whoever else she wanted to take with her, back in time where they would be in no danger. But because the witch was evil, she cast a spell on Danielle, and Danielle died a horrible death."

Cole grimaced. He wasn't curious enough to question what kind of horrible death. Instead, he asked, "And what happened to Dominique?"

Lisette bobbed one shoulder. "We don't know for certain. Her name was never mentioned again—as if, well . . ."

A cold feeling came over Cole. "You mean there's a chance this beautiful creature was beheaded like so many of her fellow countrymen?"

"It's possible, I suppose," Lisette replied. "The

records are not clear on that, only that somehow her parents were set free and taken from the country. It could have been Dominique who freed them, or someone else. She could have gone with them or she could have been . . . executed. We just don't know."

Cole shook his head as he refocused his attention on the beautiful face in the portrait. "What a tragic story," he murmured.

"Yes, it is," Lisette agreed as she cuddled up against Jacques. "And I agree with my husband. It wouldn't surprise me to see Dominique's ghost at the top of the stairs some night."

A sadness for a young woman who had lived and died over two hundred years ago closed around Cole, and while he sipped his drink he wondered what it must have been like to have lived during a time of such turmoil.

The butler interrupted their mood with the announcement that dinner was being served. Everyone agreed that they were hungry and set aside their wineglasses to follow the servant from the room. But as Cole neared the door, he paused and looked back at the portrait one more time, vainly wishing he could have lived in Dominique Dubois' century. He never would have abandoned her the way her fiancé had done.

At the top of the long marble staircase a short while later, Cole and the Forgéts bade each other good night and entered their respective bedrooms. But before Cole shut his door, he paused to glance back down the hallway at the stairs, half expecting to see a beautiful brunette with dark eyes standing there. Once he realized what he was doing, he chuckled to himself and gave the door a healthy nudge.

The covers on his bed had been turned down and though it looked inviting, Cole found that he wasn't ready to go to sleep. Kicking off his shoes and tossing his jacket on the chair, he rearranged the pillows against the headboard and stretched out on the mattress to study the furnishings in his room. He was hoping something would give him a clue as to whose bedroom it had been when the Duboises owned the property. A cheval mirror stood in one corner beside the stone fireplace. The armoire, a dresser, a wash-stand, the canopy bed, and a dressing screen were somewhat standard in any room of the eighteenth century, and he let out a disappointed sigh once he realized that the gold-colored cover-let, the gold, brown, and beige tapestry hanging on the wall behind him, and the autumn-colored rug on the floor were new. The chandelier over-head wasn't filled with a multitude of candles, but with tiny electric lights that he had turned on with the switch by the door. He was certain that everything resembled the way the room had once been, but that perhaps the only authentic pieces were the furniture. Whoever had lived here wouldn't recognize much about the bed-chamber if he or she were to see it now.

Noticing that the door to the armoire stood slightly ajar, Cole remembered Lisette saying that she had had his costume brought to his room. Curious to see just what he was expected to wear, he swung his feet to the floor and crossed to the wardrobe to push the door open all the way.

He immediately spotted a dark green garment bag hanging beside his own clothes, which he had unpacked earlier. Grasping the hanger, he twisted the swivel hook and dropped the bag over the top edge of the closet door to unzip it. Inside he found a pale peach jacket with long tails and expensive silver-and-beaded embroidery along the lapels and hem, a matching pair of breeches, a white ruffled shirt with lace cuffs, white hose, and a silver brocade waistcoat. On the floor of the closet he noticed a walking cane propped up in the corner and three differently shaped boxes, which he guessed contained shoes, a hat, and more than likely a wig, the last of which he was sure he wouldn't wear no matter how much Lisette insisted. He hated the idea, and since his own hair was long enough to tie back at the nape with a ribbon the way many men of that time period wore their hair for casual dress, it would have to do. Everything else . . . well, that might be fun.

Curious to see what he would look like dressed as a French aristocrat, he pulled the garments from their hangers and laid them across the bed to don in their proper order. To his surprise, the clothes fit him almost perfectly, and he hurriedly collected the shoes from their box and stepped into them. They were a little snug, and he didn't particularly care for the high heels and big silver buckles, but to wear anything else would be out of style.

"Well, you've gone this far," he murmured to himself as he eyed the two remaining items in the armoire. "You might as well try the wig."

He groaned after he lifted the lid and peeked inside. Although it was a fairly plain wig—white, powdered, and with double curls over each ear and a ponytail tied with a black ribbon—it was still too feminine for his liking. And hot! How uncomfortable his ancestors must have been wearing such a thing on a warm summer day.

Standing before the cheval mirror, he awkwardly settled the periwig on his head, then stood back to study his appearance. It was still Cole Charboneau under all the lace and ruffles and beaded trim, and what he saw—he humbly admitted—wasn't really that bad. He took a deep bow as if he'd just been introduced to a lovely young lady, remembered his hat and cane, and quickly retrieved them from the armoire. With the tricorn in one hand and the gold-tipped walking stick in the other, he returned to the full-length mirror and bowed again. This time his playfulness went awry, for as he bent low and held out his left hand, the end of his cane struck a stone under the mantel. He felt it move, heard the mortar rain down on the wood floor, and saw the damage he'd done once he straightened to look.

"Damn," he mumbled as he tossed aside the

hat and cane and moved closer to examine the spot.

He couldn't understand how a simple tap with a wooden stick could have caused that much destruction, and once he'd made a thorough inspection, he realized that the masonry around the stone had been cracked *before* he hit it. Nevertheless, he felt responsible, and after he had cleaned up the dust from the floor, he wiggled the stone in an attempt to shove it back into place. It wouldn't budge, and he frowned.

Thinking that perhaps someone else had had the same problem and had put the stone in backward, Cole began to work it from side to side as he pulled on it. After a bit of effort, he freed the square piece of rock and automatically reached out to run his fingers around the opening to sweep it clean of any loose particles. Once he'd done that, he blew out any remaining dust and froze when he spotted something hidden within the dark cavity. An eerie feeling came over him and he just stood, staring and hesitant, until his curiosity chased away the chill across his shoulders. With only a hint of reluctance, he set the stone on the mantel and carefully withdrew what was inside the compartment.

The first article was a small leather-bound book, which he tucked under his arm once he realized there was something else hidden there. The second item was a yellowed piece of paper rolled in a tight tube and tied with a piece of faded red ribbon. Hurriedly sliding the strip of satin from the scroll, he crossed to the bed and sat down.

The message, written in French, was a poem of sorts, and since it made no sense to him, he laid it aside without finishing it to read the book instead. He had only glanced at the first few lines of the first page when a burst of excitement ran through him. He continued to read, first skipping a paragraph or two, then a number of pages, and finally all the way to the end.

"My God," he breathed. "It's Danielle Dubois' diary!"

The sudden discovery made him bolt from the bed to study his surroundings with a more critical eye. *This* had been the room where a young girl from the eighteenth century had slept and cried and dressed for a ball. She had been sick here, laughed here, and more chilling than that, this had been the place where she had scripted her innermost secrets! And now, two hundred years later, an American of French descent, a lowly professor from Normal, Illinois, was privy to it all.

Remembering Lisette's tale, Cole hurried back to the bed and the small book he had tossed down. His hostess hadn't been able to fill in all the details and had even admitted that those she recited might not be wholly accurate. Perhaps Miss Dubois had omitted a few of the important facts as well, but the difference was that whatever was written on those pages was fact—recorded by a young woman who had lived them, and Cole was about to learn the truth.

At first the flavor of her text was light and cheery. She spoke of her comfortable life and her hopes for a bright future. Several times she mentioned her twin sister and how opposite she and Dominique were, that she was the weaker of the two and that her sister was always arguing with their father. The notes became happy when Danielle talked about her fiancé, Jean-Luc D'Rillon, and their impending marriage, but just as quickly the tone clearly showed Danielle's fear when she wrote about the outbreak of riots and their parents having been arrested and imprisoned in the Bastille. Then several days passed without an entry. When she took pen in hand again, it was to record her secret visit with a woman who practiced sorcery.

"I have spoken with Zora," Danielle wrote, "a known witch, who lives near the Pont Notre-Dame bridge in Paris. I have asked for her help, since I fear for Dominique's life and for the life of my beloved Jean-Luc. They are plotting a mission that will end in ruin, and I cannot let that happen. She has given me a chant that will send us back in time, but I am afraid it will work to our disadvantage, as Zora cannot promise me an exact date."

Cole paused to look absently across the room. Even though he didn't believe in witchcraft, he wondered if what Lisette had told him about the spell that killed Danielle might not have been true after all. Dismissing the thought with a shake of his head, he began reading where he had left off.

"I can save my family. It is in my hands now, but I do not know if I will have the strength to see it through, as I have taken ill."

The rest of the pages were empty. Cole closed the book and set it down, noticing again the piece of yellowed parchment lying on the bed next to him. He carefully unrolled it and began to recite the words aloud.

"All things wicked, all things pure,
Send them hither, two by two.
Elements of wonder, it will unfold.
Send thy mortal beings to a place untold."

Suddenly a gust of wind rattled the windowpanes and seemed to shake the entire house. Curious, since he hadn't remembered hearing anything about a storm being predicted for the area, Cole absently picked up the diary and the scroll, and returned the articles to their hiding place for safekeeping before he crossed to the window to look outside. In the distance he could see the velvety black sky with its sprinkling of stars, but no clouds of any kind, and he reached up to unlatch the window. In that same instant and before he had lifted the sash, he was hit with a blast of cold air that took his breath away and spun him around. Everything in the room began to whirl, and he shivered as an electrifying sensation shot down his spine and made his flesh tingle. The wind intensified, and he raised one hand to shield his face as his world collapsed around him and the sights and sounds vanished into nothingness.

IT started with a pounding in Cole's temples, a trip-hammer beat that grew in volume and spread downward along each vertebra in his spine. The black void that had paralyzed him paled to a chalky gray, and once he found the energy to open his eyes, he saw a stream of silvery moonlight falling across the floor in front of him. He groaned and shut his eyes again.

He wasn't sure what time it had been when he and the Forgéts had parted company, but it had been dark enough for him to turn on the lights. So why were they out now? Had there been a power failure?

Uncomfortable lying face down with one arm underneath him, Cole mustered the strength to roll over. The movement aggravated the pounding in his head, and he gritted his teeth until the nausea passed. While he lay there, he wondered if the strong wind he had felt just before he passed out had anything to do with the power being off, especially since the sensation had been similar to what he thought being electrocuted must feel like.

Perspiration dotted his forehead, and he raised the heel of his left hand to wipe it off, startled for a second when something soft swept his face. Opening his eyes, he relaxed when he saw the lace cuff of his shirt, and a rush of memories filled his brain as he clumsily pushed himself up to sit there for a moment with his arms braced behind him.

Several minutes passed before the ache in his head subsided enough so that he could contemplate getting up. He had packed a bottle of aspirin in his shaving kit, and if he could get to it without falling down, he'd take some. Leaning forward, he rubbed his eyes with the tips of his fingers, including the soft spots along the bridge of his nose, his cheekbones, and finally his temples. He remembered the wig he was wearing when his fingers brushed against its curls. Growling, he seized it by the crown and flung it away. He hadn't liked it from the start, and he liked it even less now.

Twisting around, Cole came to his feet, staggering a little when his head began to spin. Blindly reaching out, he grabbed the bedpost to steady his balance. A moment passed before he was sure of his footing and could straighten and take a deep breath.

"Damn," he muttered. "I don't remember ever having a hangover this bad."

The soft moonlight spilling into the room cast enough light for him to see the washstand, and that the black bag holding his shaving cream, razor, after-shave lotion, and most importantly the aspirin, wasn't there. Thinking that perhaps he had knocked it to the floor when he fell, he glanced down and noticed for the first time that there was something different about the rug. He couldn't quite decide what it was, and he reached for the light switch by the door.

It was darker in that section of the room, and after several failed attempts to find the little plastic knob midway up the wall, Cole crossed to the windows and flung open the draperies. His temper was wearing thin, but it disappeared completely once his eyes focused on the yard below his room. He clearly remembered the circular concrete drive the cab had taken to deliver him to the front steps, and the fountain situated in the middle. Now, it seemed, both were gone. Stunned, Cole blinked, rubbed his eyes, and looked again.

"What the hell . . . ?" he muttered as he studied the brick road leading straight to the front door and the grove of trees that nearly concealed it. A second later the hair on the back of his neck stood out when he heard, then saw, a landau, its driver, and a team of horses cross his line of vision and halt at the main steps of the château. Jerking away from the window, Cole hid behind the thick draperies to watch as a servant—dressed in breeches, hose, white shirt, black-tailed coat, and one of those damnable powdered wigs—hurried from the mansion to open the carriage door. The passenger, a tall man garbed in a full-length black cape and tricorn, stepped down and quickly went inside. Cole collapsed against the wall.

"*What* is happening?" he whispered, raising his chin in the air as he took a long breath to calm his jittery nerves.

Only then did he discover the reason he'd been unable to find the light switch. The chandelier, with its dozens of tiny light bulbs, was gone. Jerking upright, he hurriedly looked about the room.

"Oh, my God," he murmured.

There wasn't a lamp on the nightstand. The armoire and dressing screen had traded places. An oil painting hung where the tapestry had been, and instead of an old, musty odor, everything smelled fresh and clean. Guessing the truth, he raced to the armoire and swung the doors open, his shoulders sagging when he found it full of gowns, hats, and ladies' shoes.

"This is all a dream," he assured himself. "That's what it is. You're just asleep, Cole. You'll be all right just as soon as you wake up." He glanced around the room again, noting the differences, and resignedly shook his head. It was no dream. It was real.

The cold grayness of the room seemed to mock him, and he stumbled to the bed to sit down, his head still pounding. He didn't believe in witch-craft—nobody did. Yet what other explanation could there be?

Remembering the diary and the scroll that

had caused the catastrophic change in his surroundings, he left the bed and hurried to the
fireplace. Working the stone loose, he stuck his
hand inside and smiled to himself as his fingers
touched the leather book and lifted it and the
scroll from their dark haven. It hadn't occurred
to him until that very moment that he had no
idea how far back he'd been thrown in time, no
idea whether Danielle was still alive, or if her
twin was already on her way to the Bastille.
Carrying the items to the window where the
light was brighter, he frowned once he noticed
that both pieces lacked the yellowing signs of
age. What more proof did he need that he'd
become a time traveler?

Idly thumbing the pages of the book, he considered his choices, none of which he liked. His
adventurous side dared him to step back and
enjoy the situation in which he'd found himself, while his common sense told him he didn't
belong here. Sure, he spoke flawless French and
his dark looks wouldn't give him away, but
he was bound to say or to do something that
would. Then where would he be? Standing in
line waiting to be burned at the stake as a war-
lock or at the steps of the guillotine with all the
rest of the French aristocrats? No, the only way
for him to get out of the mess he was in was to
find the witch. If Zora had the power to send
someone back in time, she certainly would have
the ability to send him into the future.

A noise coming from somewhere in the
château reminded him that he wasn't alone,

and that to be discovered now, before he had the opportunity to talk with the sorcerer, would cause him too many problems . . . especially if he was found in Danielle's bedroom! Rushing to the fireplace, he quickly jammed the diary back into the small hole. But he hesitated in placing the scroll alongside it. Once he left this room, he would probably never be able to retrieve the items again, and Zora might require proof of his claim. Guessing that perhaps the piece of paper on which the woman had written the chant would be enough, Cole slipped it in his pocket, slid the stone back into place, and moved to the door. His next hurdle would be getting out of the château before someone spotted him.

Yellow candlelight from the sconces in the hallway flickered across the floor and down the marble steps. Leaving the safety of Danielle's bedroom, he paused long enough to insure that he wouldn't get caught descending the staircase. From below he could hear voices drifting out from one of the rooms on the main level, and although he couldn't exactly hear what the man and woman were saying, there was an urgency in their hushed tones.

Deciding to chance it, he started down the steps on tiptoe, his right hand running along the banister's railing to guide him while his gaze traveled the assortment of paintings hanging on the wall—ones that hadn't been there the first time he'd used the stairs. At the bottom, he glanced around the great hall, noting the same fireplace as before, but that the credenza, the huge gold-framed mirror, and the Oriental rug on the floor were new . . . to him, anyway.

Because Jacques had shown him around the château while they had waited for Lisette to return, Cole knew where all the exits were, and since the heated conversation he'd overheard seemed to be coming from a direction close to the front door, he elected to cut down the hall, through the dining room, and out through a back way. As he started to move, the sound of footsteps forced him to duck inside the recessed entry into an adjoining room where the shadows would hide him. A second later a man and a woman stepped into the giant foyer, and Cole's desire to make a hasty departure vanished the instant he saw the woman's face.

"Dominique," he breathed, certain it was she and not her twin just from the way Danielle had described her in the diary. There was a subtle strength in the way she carried herself, a firm determination in the lift of her chin, and of course, those incredible eyes, the black silky hair, the ivory skin. Why, she was even more stunning than the painting had represented, and the attraction he had felt for her then multiplied twofold now. He was no longer looking at a reproduction in oils, but at a living, breathing goddess in lace and satin.

Suddenly, his fascination with her changed to irritation, and he turned his face away from her. He had enough troubles of his own without adding more. Yet he knew he wasn't going to be able to walk away. The story Lisette had told him about Dominique meant that very soon she would be placing herself in danger and that he had it in his power to stop her.

"Damn," he hissed softly. This wasn't going to be easy. Leaning forward slightly, he glanced her way again. He couldn't very well walk up to her and tell her he was from the future and that by accident he had wound up here . . . in her house. She'd never believe him. She'd just think he was crazy.

Cole watched as the man with Dominique took her hand and pressed a light kiss to the backs of her fingers before he reached for the doorknob and let himself out. Could he possibly be Siffre Chevalier, Dominique's fiancé? Cole wondered. Had he arrived before the coward's exodus to England? Cole hoped not. Chevalier would just get in the way otherwise.

Ducking back when Dominique turned in his direction, Cole waited for the sounds of her footsteps on the marble stairs. A moment later he heard a door from up above click shut, and he let out a long sigh. He couldn't be sure, but he hoped it meant she was retiring for the night, and that he would have time to do a little investigating. If he was going to help, he would have to have some questions answered first. So where should he begin?

He thought of asking a servant, since they always seemed to know more about what was going on in the house than their employers ever did. But he also knew they would be reluctant to tell a stranger anything that might harm one of the Duboises. Dismissing that idea, he decided he'd solve two problems at the same time. He'd borrow a horse from the stable and ride to Paris, where he'd pay Zora a visit, and while he was there, he would question her about Danielle, the diary, and the fate of the elder Duboises.

Once Cole left the château and stepped out of the shadow of the huge walnut tree in the side yard, he glanced back over his shoulder at the second-story windows. What he didn't need now was to be seen by Dominique or one of her servants. Discovering that the manor was completely dark, he relaxed a little and hurried his steps. When he reached the stable doors, he rushed inside and waited for his eyes to adjust to the change in light.

At the far end he could see two or three horses tethered in their stalls. Deciding not to waste time trying to figure out which in the group was the fastest runner, he approached the first and grabbed a blanket from its hook.

He was nearly finished saddling the mare when a sound coming from the direction of the stable doors warned him that he wasn't alone. Leery about moving in the slightest, he just stood there, waiting. A second later, the soft light of a lantern flooded the confines of the stable, and he frowned, wondering if he would have a chance to explain before he was shot.

"Raise your hands where I can see them," the dulcet, French-speaking voice commanded.

Cole didn't have to look to know who had made the demand. He had heard her voice before. Smiling, he obliged her.

"Now, turn around . . . slowly."

Again Cole did as he was asked. But the moment his eyes had focused on the shapely figure standing in the doorway, the smile faded and all he could do was stare. She was the most incredible-looking woman he had ever seen, and he silently marveled at how just looking at her warmed his blood. He knew he should be concerned about the loaded flintlock she held pointed at his midsection or perhaps even about what story he would tell her, but the nearness of her muddled his brain. The pale amber light from the lantern she held in her other hand caressed her silkened skin, her perfectly sculptured face, her dark brown eyes, and the knot of dark hair on the top of her head.

"What's your name and what are you doing here?" she asked.

The question penetrated his trance. He blinked, took a breath, and said in his best French, "Nicolas Charboneau, and I was about to borrow one of your horses."

The sound of the stranger's deep voice tickled the flesh down the back of Dominique's neck and across her shoulders. Until then she had thought that no other man in the world was as handsome as her father. But before her now stood one who contradicted that claim. His dark hair, a little shorter than most fashionable men wore it, glistened in the lamplight. The look he gave her with those deep brown eyes seemed to melt her bones. His lean jaw, high, wide-set cheekbones, and squarish chin stirred her very soul and brought a warm blush to her cheeks. He was tall—taller than most—with wide shoulders, narrow hips, and long, muscular legs. His clothes fit him perfectly even though they were a bit disheveled, and while most of her acquaintances, dressed in similar garb, had a regal air about them, *this* man presented a rakish nature merely by the way he openly stared at her and appeared indifferent to the pistol aimed at him. Suddenly the name he had given struck a familiar cord.

"Charboneau?" she repeated. "From Marseilles?"

Her lilting voice dulled his immediate reaction to the question, but once Cole realized the error in her thinking, he seized the opportunity to explain his presence. Marseilles was a coastal town in the south of France. He remembered Lisette telling him the twins had been in Corsica visiting relatives when their parents were arrested, and since Marseilles was the seaport to the island, it meant Dominique was probably familiar with the town and its people. Therefore, there was a chance she knew the Charboneaus from that area and if he wasn't careful, he might give himself away.

"A long-lost cousin, perhaps," he replied, deciding to rely on his own family's ancestry for help in convincing her he really belonged there. "I'm from a small town southwest of Paris."

She appeared to accept his answer, but she didn't lower her weapon.

"And why are you here . . . in my stable . . . stealing one of my horses?" she asked.

He contemplated moving closer and trying to make a grab for the gun. But he knew he'd have to be careful. She didn't strike him as the type to be easily manipulated. "I realize you don't have to believe a word I say," he began, "but my story isn't much different from everyone else's these days. I was away on business when the revolt started, and upon my return, I learned that my family had been arrested and most of our things confiscated. I have no money and my horse came up lame two days ago." He paused a moment to study her expression. It remained unchanged and he feared she hadn't bought a word of his story. "I needed to borrow a horse to get to Paris, as I was told my family was being held in the Bastille. It is my intention to free them." For dramatic flair and to play on her sympathy, he looked away and sighed. "If they haven't already been executed."

A sadness flickered in her eyes, but still she didn't lower the pistol. "You're correct, Monsieur Charboneau," she admitted. "A great many share your tragedy." She watched him for a moment, a look of doubt wrinkling her smooth brow. "In fact, it is so common these days, who's to say you're not telling the truth?" She paused a moment, then added, "And who's to say I should believe you?"

The smile returned to Cole's lips. Dominique was not only beautiful, but quick-witted, and that was a pleasant change from the type of women he'd been dating the past couple of years. But was she a cold-blooded killer? Could she simply pull the trigger, watch him die, and then walk away? He doubted it. He lowered his hands and started walking toward her.

"So, what do you suggest we do with me?" he challenged, noticing how the look of confidence in her eyes changed to panic as he drew near.

"That's close enough," she ordered, but he kept coming. "Did you hear? I said not another step!"

He was on her in a flash, easily twisting the gun from her delicate fingers as he crushed her slender frame against his massive chest.

Dominique gasped and thought about screaming, then changed her mind. Who would come to her rescue? There was no one left except the cook, an old woman of sixty, and Monsieur Beauprés, the aging butler.

"I'm not going to hurt you," she heard the handsome stranger promise.

Common sense warned her not to take him at his word, that there was something odd about him. Yet her womanly instincts begged her to give him the opportunity to prove himself. Suddenly angry, she shoved at his chest. But instead of gaining her freedom, she succeeded in pulling his shirt apart. She felt a matting of soft curls beneath her fingers and the rippled strength of muscles under her palm. Her face flamed. "Unhand me, sir," she demanded.

Cole had never come across a woman as feisty as Dominique or as reluctant to be held in a man's arms. But then, they did things differently in the eighteenth century. "Only if you'll swear to me that you'll give me a chance to explain."

His nearness was suffocating her. She could feel every inch of his hardened frame pressing against her, and while it was rather pleasant, at the same time it horrified her. "All right," she conceded, closing her eyes and turning her face away. "Just let go of me."

Cole wished she hadn't agreed so quickly, since he was enjoying the feel of her lush curves against him. Unwilling, but knowing he must, he dropped his arm. "It's a long story," he said, taking the lantern from her, "and it's chilly out here. Why don't we talk inside?" He sensed her hesitancy and added, "I'm not going to steal the silverware, if that's what you're thinking. Here . . ." He handed back the pistol. "You can shoot me if I try anything suspicious."

Dominique stared at the flintlock for a second, then at her unexpected company. If he were a scoundrel, he wouldn't have trusted her with the pistol, and he wouldn't be dressed like an aristocrat. Perhaps she shouldn't trust him, but she decided to take the chance. There was something curious about him, and she wanted to find out what that was. "I never had time to load it," she admitted in hardly more than a whisper, before she turned away from him and started out of the stable.

Laughter tightened the muscles in Cole's

throat, but he remained silent as he fell into step behind her.

The short walk back to the château and the yellow glow of the lantern awarded Cole the chance to indulge himself. Since Dominique had elected to stay several steps ahead of him, she was unaware that he was watching her every move. Her full skirts swayed provocatively and teased him with a brief glimpse of trim ankles beneath their hem. Her narrow waist accented her slender back, and her upswept hair exposed the long, slim length of her neck, a spot he found himself longing to kiss. The gentle night air carried the fragrance of her perfume his way, and the scent of it intoxicated him.

They entered through a side door, and she led him into the parlor, where she laid aside the pistol and took the lantern from him. Using its flame, she lit the long, white tapers in two separate candelabra, set one on the table next to the settee, and carried the other to the buffet.

"Would you care for a glass of wine, Monsieur Charboneau?" she asked, her hand resting on the decanter. When he nodded, she poured two glasses full and returned to where he stood. "Please. Sit down," she offered, lowering herself into one of the wing chairs near the hearth.

The soft candlelight caressed her silkened skin, and for a moment Cole entertained the thought of never going back to the twentieth century. Even though he was out of his element, Dominique was here, and wherever she was, he wanted to be right beside her. *That* revelation amazed him. After what Nancy had done to him, he had doubted he would ever feel this way about a woman again.

"How did you know I was in the stable?" he asked.

Dominique smiled softly. "I saw you in the yard from my bedroom window."

"And you came to confront a stranger, a man, all alone?" He waved a hand. "Where are your servants?"

Dominique casually sipped her drink. "Most of them have fled. There *is* much social unrest, you know."

He decided to hold onto the truth awhile longer and to make the kind of inquiries that would help him to realize just how far back in time he had gone. "What about your husband?"

"I'm not married."

"You mean you live here alone?" He could tell the question had hit a nerve when she looked away and appeared to be fighting back tears.

"My parents were arrested several days ago, Monsieur Charboneau. They, along with hundreds of others, are being held in the Bastille." She looked at him again. "As are yours, I believe you said."

He nodded, but wouldn't repeat the lie. He took a sip of wine, and suddenly remembered the man he had seen with her in the foyer. "There was a gentleman here earlier. I saw him leaving as I was heading toward the stable. A friend?"

She shook her head. "My fiancé, Siffre Chevalier."

He saw her frown, as if the mere mention of the man's name offended her, and Cole decided to find out for sure. "I'm disappointed," he said.

"Disappointed?" she repeated. "About what?"

"To hear you're engaged," he answered with a smile.

She stared at him, her dark brows drawn low over her beautiful eyes. "What is it you really want from me, Monsieur Charboneau? If you're so concerned about your parents, why are you wasting time here? Why didn't you just knock me aside, take the horse, and ride out? Is it because you're not who you say you are?"

Cole knew that sooner or later he would have to be honest with her. He didn't think now was the time, but she had backed him into a corner. "I guess you could say I'm here to help."

"Help?" she questioned. "To do what?"

He stared at her for a long moment. "Dominique, where is your sister?"

The color left her face. "How do you know my name? And who told you I had a sister?"

"Is she dead?"

Tears flooded her eyes and she jumped to her feet. "Get out!" she demanded, swinging a hand toward the door.

Now he knew exactly where he was in time. Lisette's version had said that the elder Duboises had been imprisoned *before* Danielle sought out Zora's help, and the diary confirmed it. Dominique's reaction, her tears, practically told him that the meeting had already taken place, and that her sister had succumbed to her foolishness.

"She went to see the witch, didn't she?" he pressed, rising. He hated being cruel, but he guessed it was the only way he could convince Dominique of the truth about himself. "And Zora killed her. Danielle is dead and only by a few days. I'm right, am I not, Dominique?"

Tears glistened in her eyes and spilled down her cheeks. "Who are you? Why are you here?"

His heart ached at the sight of her. He hadn't meant to hurt her, to make her cry, and he was suddenly wishing the chant had been off by a couple of weeks. If he'd arrived earlier, he could have prevented her pain.

"A friend, Dominique," he said softly. "I'm a friend, and I'm here through a twist of fate. Let me help you."

"To do what? My parents have been arrested and my sister is dead. There's nothing you can do to change any of it." She crossed to the buffet and refilled her glass. She took a sip, frowned, and turned back around. "How did you know about the witch? That my sister went to see her, I mean."

Motioning toward her chair, Cole waited until she had sat down again, then took his own seat. He remained quiet for several more minutes while he stared at the glass in his hands, and then he sighed, glancing up. "Do you believe in witchcraft, Dominique?"

There was something about the man's eyes, the shape of his face, his thick black hair, that made Dominique's heart beat faster every time she looked at him. He was soft-spoken, gentle, and seemingly sincere. Yet, he was still a stranger, someone who had appeared from out of nowhere, and she knew she should make him leave. "I believe a witch is responsible for Danielle's death," she answered.

"Then you believe a person has the power to change things," he supplied.

Dominique nodded.

He was gaining ground with her, but he doubted she would receive his next question with the same easy acceptance. "The sort of power that could transport a person from one time period to another? Say, a century or two?"

Dominique wasn't sure what he meant, but it made her very uncomfortable. "What are you trying to say, Monsieur Charboneau?"

Remembering the scroll in his pocket, he withdrew it and handed it over. "Have you ever seen this before?"

She unrolled the piece of paper, glanced at it, frowned, and gave it back to him. "No. What is it?"

"It's the chant Zora gave your sister, the one Danielle had hoped would save her family. It would have worked, Dominique," he pledged, "if Danielle had had the chance to use it."

Her lovely face remained expressionless. "What would it have done?" she asked calmly. "Change the century we live in?"

He could see she didn't believe a word of it, and rather than argue fruitlessly, he set aside his glass, reached for hers, and set it down, too, as he stood and took her hand.

"I want to show you something," he explained when she resisted. "It won't take a moment and I'm sure it will help convince you that I'm speaking the truth."

She cocked one dark eyebrow at him, then nodded.

Picking up one of the candelabra, he led her out into the foyer. But when he started up the steps, she came to an abrupt halt.

"I swear to you," he quickly spoke up, "that I'm not going to harm you. If molesting you was all that was on my mind, I would have taken advantage of you in the stable." She seemed to relax and he quickly added, "There's something in Danielle's bedroom that you must see. I could tell you where to look, but I'm not sure you would find it. It's better that I point it out. All right?"

She didn't respond. Instead, she held out a hand, indicating that he should go first and she would follow. He bowed his shoulders slightly and started up the staircase, Dominique a few steps behind him.

Dominique watched him closely as they went: his broad shoulders, narrow hips, and firmly muscled legs; how his clothes complemented his build; and that his shiny dark hair, even though it needed to be brushed and pulled back in a ribbon, gave him a distinct air of masculinity.

There was a magnetism, a sensuality about him, that stirred a strange desire in her and made her act against all logic. She shouldn't be following him upstairs, but she couldn't help herself.

At the landing she noticed that he didn't hesitate as he walked directly to Danielle's room and went inside. How would a stranger know which of the many rooms on the second floor belonged to her sister? As far as she knew, he'd never been on their property before tonight, much less inside the château. Frowning, she stepped into the doorway and halted.

He had lit a candle and was standing in the middle of the room.

"Are you aware that your sister kept a diary?" he asked.

She nodded.

"Do you know where she kept it?"

Dominique thought writing down one's thoughts on paper was a foolish and somewhat childish thing to do. She'd told her sister as much, but her criticism had never seemed to bother Danielle. As a result, Dominique not only didn't know where Danielle had stored the book, but Danielle had never shared with her any of what was written in it, either.

"No," Dominique replied.

He raised a hand and pointed at the fireplace. "Under the mantel. You'll find a loose stone there. Pull it out and inside you'll find her diary," he instructed.

Dominique eyed him for a moment, then crossed to the hearth. She located the stone after a second or two and wiggled it loose. Glancing at Cole one more time, she bent slightly and reached in. To her surprise, her fingers touched the small volume and she pulled it out, tears instantly choking her when she recognized it as having belonged to Danielle.

"How did you know . . ."

"I've been here before," he announced.

Dominique frowned. "When? Danielle would never have let you into her room."

He shook his head and motioned for the door. "Let's talk downstairs."

Dominique led the way, the diary clutched tightly against her bosom. She had never taken an interest in what her sister would record. Now the words were very precious to her, and she wasn't about to let the book out of her sight.

They entered the parlor and sat down near the fireplace again. He offered her a fresh glass of wine, which she accepted, and she took two sips as she braced herself for what Nicolas Charboneau was about to tell her.

While he spoke, she tried very hard to concentrate on what he was saying and not on how a faint dimple in the corner of his mouth appeared whenever he said certain words. Or how dark his eyes got when he was excited or troubled. The deep timbre of his voice tickled each vertebra in her neck, and the manly scent of him flooded her mind. Of a sudden, she realized he had stopped talking, and that he was staring at her. Embarrassed, she took another drink of wine and frantically tried to recall everything he had said, none of which made any sense. It did, however, explain how he knew which room had belonged to Danielle and where Dominique would find her sister's diary.

"Two hundred years?" she questioned. "You're from the twentieth century?" She tried not to smile. "And I suppose you're going to tell me you *flew* here from wherever it is you're from." She looked at his attire. "It's nice to know my wardrobe will still be in style."

"I know it sounds crazy, Dominique," he admitted. "And dressed as I am, there's no way to prove it." He sighed heavily and collapsed in the chair. "I'm still waiting to wake up. I'm sure this is only a dream."

She could see the frustration in his dark eyes, and despite the absurdity of it all, she felt compelled to believe him. Opening her sister's diary, she skipped to the last page, and in Danielle's own handwriting, she was told practically the same story this man had recited. But there was one thing wrong with it.

"Danielle writes that the chant would send her back in time, but that the witch couldn't give her an exact date," she observed. "If that's true, then why are you here . . . now, at this time and place? Wouldn't you have gone wherever Danielle was intended to go?"

"I went where the chant sent me," he replied, excited now that she seemed on the verge of accepting his tale. "You see, Dominique, it doesn't matter who uses the chant or where he or she is at the time. Whoever reads it will be hurled backward in time. If I were to say the words again right now, I'd be gone . . . perhaps to the sixteenth century."

She frowned, quiet for several moments as she closed the diary and ran her hand across its surface. "So in order for you to go home, you'd have to have a new chant, one that would send you forward in time."

He smiled broadly and nodded.

"And you were stealing a horse to get to Paris, to Zora?"

He nodded again.

"How do you know she'll help you? She put a curse on my sister."

Cole shrugged. "It's a chance I'll have to take."

"Because you have a wife and children waiting for you?"

He had a mother and father who would miss him, and all of his students at the university, and Jacques and Lisette, and his buddies from high school who met each year in late August to hunt in Canada, but no wife, no children. Here he was, nearly thirty years old, and he wasn't even considering settling down. No one woman since Nancy had interested him that much. He looked at Dominique. Until now.

"I'm not married," he replied, finishing his wine.

A long silence passed between them, broken by the chiming of a clock in the foyer.

"It's late," she observed. "Too late to go looking for Zora and much too dangerous for someone dressed as you are to be traveling the roads to Paris in the dark." She set aside her wineglass and rose. "You're welcome to spend the night, if you wish. In the morning you may take the horse."

"Dominique," he called as he stood and set down his glass. "You believe me, don't you?"

She stared at him. "I'm not sure," she said after a while. She smiled softly and tapped the book she clutched against herself. "But thank you for this."

"You're welcome," he replied.

Their eyes locked and held for a long moment, and Cole had to fight a strong urge to go to her and take her in his arms. He wanted so much right then to kiss her, to ease the pain she was feeling, to let her know that half of him wanted to go back where he belonged and the other half wanted to stay there with her, a dilemma he was sure no other man had ever had to confront.

"Come," she said. "I'll show you to your room."

They walked across the foyer and up the stairs in silence. Pausing outside the door next to Danielle's room, Dominique bid him good night and waited until he had closed the door before turning for her own bedroom. With her hand on the knob, she paused again, glanced back over her shoulder, sighed, and went inside.

STANDING in the doorway to the dining room the next morning, Cole drank in the sight of the lovely woman sitting at the table. Her chestnut hair was nearly all concealed beneath the small, white lace cap she wore, but the soft amber color of her gown, with its tight bodice, low-cut square neckline, and puffy sleeves left little to the imagination. She was all woman, and one who easily stirred a passionate longing in him.

He wasn't sure if he'd slept at all the night past, but a hot bath and shaving the stubble from his face had helped refresh him. Monsieur Beauprés, the butler, had been instructed to bring Cole a change of clothes—garments Cole had to assume belonged to Dominique's father—and to his surprise, they fit him well. He had brushed back his hair and tied it with a dark blue ribbon that matched his jacket and breeches, and even though it wasn't what he customarily wore, he felt at home. He would thank Dominique for her

232

kindness; then they would sit down and have a serious talk.

He watched her sip her tea, not quite ready to spoil the moment by announcing his presence. Then she returned the cup to its saucer, touched the corner of her mouth with a linen napkin, and casually looked his way.

"Come in, Monsieur Charboneau," she invited with a soft smile.

As he approached the table and the chair she had motioned for him to take, Cole noticed how her gaze traveled the length of him and back to the top of his head. Her perusal was one of approval, and it pleased him.

A servant entered the room, distracting them both, while a plate of steaming food and a cup of tea were placed in front of Cole. The aroma made his mouth water, but although he would have enjoyed eating breakfast, their talk was more important. He watched the servant leave the room, and when he was sure they wouldn't be overheard, he settled his gaze on the beautiful face staring back at him.

"At least drink your tea first," she interrupted. "My father always says a man thinks better when his stomach isn't empty."

"He does, does he?" Cole teased.

Dominique nodded, smiling.

"And what would your father say if he knew what his daughter was planning?"

The smile left her face. "Planning?" she repeated.

"Yes," Cole continued. "You and Jean-Luc, to be precise."

"Danielle's fiancé?" She laughed nervously. "Whatever are you talking about, Monsieur Charboneau?"

He glanced toward the door to make certain the servant hadn't returned for some reason. "I'm talking about how you and Jean-Luc are planning to free your parents from the Bastille. It isn't wise, Dominique."

Her temper flared. "And what would you have me do? Nothing? They've been accused of treason."

"By hateful neighbors," he finished. "I know. But getting yourself caught trying to free them won't do anyone any good."

She frowned. "Who said we would get caught?"

He remembered the story Lisette had told him and sighed. "I don't honestly know that you will, but I can't just stand aside and allow you to try."

"You don't have a choice," she stubbornly replied. "And how did you know that's what we were planning? Danielle's diary spoke of a mission, nothing more. And *she* was only guessing. We never told her our plans."

He reached out and touched her hand to comfort her. "The tragedy that struck this family will be passed down from generation to generation, Dominique. I heard the story *before* I found your sister's diary."

Her face glowed. "Then you know what will happen to my parents. Tell me, Nicolas, please!"

"I know that they will escape, but I can't say

the same for you or Jean-Luc," he answered, letting go of her small hand. "The tale is unclear about that, and it's very possible you will be captured and put to death." The idea pained him and he scowled. "I won't let you go."

His declaration brought a soft blush to her cheeks and she averted her eyes. When she had mentioned the plan to Siffre, he had simply stood there stuttering and stammering. He never once forbade her to get involved. Now this stranger, this man who claimed to come from a different world, showed more concern for her well-being than her own fiancé. It flattered her. And it made her feel warm inside.

They were interrupted at that moment when the servant entered the room.

"Excuse me, Mademoiselle Dubois," he apologized.

"What is it?" she asked.

"Monsieur D'Rillon is here to see you."

She waved a hand. "Send him in, and tell Nanette we'll need another place setting."

"Yes, miss," he replied with a slight bow before departing.

Cole wasn't sure he was ready to meet Jean-Luc D'Rillon just now. He hadn't quite convinced Dominique of the truth about himself, and working against the two of them would make it that much harder. But since he didn't have a choice, he would make the best of it. When the tall, thin Frenchman entered the room, Cole rose and stood quietly aside while D'Rillon greeted Dominique.

Introductions were made and although the man's handshake was firm, Cole noticed the cautious expression on his face, as if he already sensed something unusual had happened. They all took their seats, Jean-Luc next to Dominique and across the table from Cole. Once they were settled, Dominique smiled and turned to the man next to her.

"I found Monsieur Charboneau in the stable last night about to steal one of our horses," she said, her tone light and playful.

"Oh?" Jean-Luc questioned as he allowed the servant to pour him a cup of tea but waved off the plate of food.

"Yes," she continued. "He wanted me to believe he needed to get to Paris to free his parents from the Bastille."

Jean-Luc frowned. "I don't recall any Charboneaus on the list."

"That's because he wasn't telling the truth," she explained.

Jean-Luc had known the Dubois family from the time the twins were little girls. He'd grown up on the estate next to theirs. He'd shared secrets with the sisters, laughter when they were happy, tears when they were sad. As far as Jean-Luc was concerned, their own parents didn't know them as well as he did.

"All right, Dominique." He sighed, leaning back in his chair. "What's going on?"

Cole would have liked to ease into the story rather than just blurting it out, and he couldn't understand why Dominique wanted it that way.

He drew a breath to begin, but Dominique interrupted.

"He's here to help us rescue my parents," she said, smiling at Cole.

"Help?" Jean-Luc repeated. "In what way?"

"I'm not sure," she replied. "He was about to tell me that when you arrived."

Both Dominique and Jean-Luc turned their attention on Cole. Uncomfortable because he wasn't sure if Dominique expected him to tell her friend the whole story or to lie, he idly toyed with the ring on his finger, then raised his hand and rubbed his chin.

The movement caught Jean-Luc's eye and he frowned at the odd piece of jewelry on the man's hand. It had a huge blue stone in it, raised numbers and letters, and strange little figures carved in the band. He'd never seen anything like it before, and the uneasy feeling he'd had a moment ago returned.

Cole noticed where Jean-Luc's gaze rested, and the instant he saw that his college ring had made the journey with him, he was sure he had all the proof he needed. He slipped it off his finger and handed it to Jean-Luc. While the Frenchman studied it, he told his story.

He began with his name and heritage; why he'd come to visit France; Lisette and Jacques Forgét; the costume ball; Danielle's room and where he'd found the diary; the chant; how a cold wind had swept through his room and left him unconscious, and that when he had awakened he discovered he had been sent back in time. He spoke of the portrait of Dominique and her sister; of the rebellion; that Dominique's parents had been served secret warrants and imprisoned; that their neighbors were responsible for that part of it; and that Jean-Luc and Dominique were preparing to free the older Duboises from the Bastille. When he was finished and could see that Jean-Luc was far from believing anything he had said, he nodded at the piece of jewelry Jean-Luc held in his hand.

"It's called a college class ring, something a man or woman buys on graduating from college." He knew the word was foreign to them and he tried to clarify it. "An institute of higher learning. I studied French history and the French language there. Now I teach at Illinois State University." He frowned. "Or I did until this happened." A sense of emptiness washed over him, and he shook it off. "Look at the numbers on the side next to the stone. It's the date I graduated from college; the late 1900s."

When a long silence passed and the tension in the air grew so thick Cole felt as if he were strangling on it, he cleared his throat. "I can't blame you for what you're thinking. If someone came up to me and tried telling me he was from the future, I wouldn't believe him either."

"I'm glad to hear it," Jean-Luc mocked. "Because that's just how I feel." He stared at Cole for a second, then slid the ring across the table at him. "That proves nothing. You could have paid a jeweler to make it." He rose from his chair, took a couple of steps, whirled, and leaned forward with his hands braced on the tabletop. "What are you really after, Nicolas Charboneau? If that's your *real* name."

Cole didn't know why, but Jean-Luc's reaction angered him, and he, too, stood up with his hands resting on the table. "All I want, Monsieur D'Rillon," he shot back, "is to stop Dominique from risking her neck to save her parents, and then to find the witch and have her send me back to where I came from."

A sarcastic smile lifted one side of Jean-Luc's mouth. "Do you expect me to believe a witch has that kind of power? To hurl you forward into time two hundred years?" He jerked away from the table and spun around to pace the floor.

Cole straightened. "Are you saying you don't believe Zora is responsible for Danielle's death?"

Dark eyes focused on Cole. "Of course she is. If Danielle had listened to me, she wouldn't have taken ill and—" It pained Jean-Luc to talk about it, and he looked away.

Cole jabbed a finger in Jean-Luc's direction. "You refuse to believe a witch has the power to transport me through time, yet you damn her for casting a spell on Danielle. How can that be? Either you believe or you don't."

Jean-Luc whirled again, glaring. He started to answer but glanced at Dominique and changed his mind, clamping his teeth together instead. Turning away, he crossed to one of the windows and looked outside.

"I need more proof," he finally admitted, swinging around.

"More?" Cole repeated.

"Yes. If you're from the future as you say, then tell me something that has yet to happen, something I cannot doubt when it does."

Cole thought of the story Lisette had told him, and he looked at Dominique. "When was the last time you saw your fiancé?"

"Last night," she replied.

"Has he expressed his fear?"

Dominique glanced at Jean-Luc and back. "We're all afraid, Nicolas."

"And when was the first time you talked to him about freeing your parents?"

"Last night. He agreed we had no other choice. In fact, we were planning to meet this morning to devise a plan. He should be here shortly."

Cole shook his head. "You'll never see him again, Dominique. Siffre Chevalier is on his way to England by now."

Jean-Luc's sarcastic laughter trailed closely behind Cole's declaration. "Try something else, Monsieur Charboneau," he suggested. "There are only two reasons why Siffre won't come as he said he would, and those are that he is dead or imprisoned along with the rest of the good people in this area. He'd never run. Never!"

Dominique said nothing. She knew that Siffre was loyal to her family and especially to her father. That was why Guilbert Dubois had chosen him to marry his daughter. Yet when she had told him that she and Jean-Luc were planning to rescue her parents, she had noticed his uneasiness. Now that Nicolas had charged her fiancé with cowardice, she was certain that was the reason for Siffre's reluctance to approve of their rescue attempt. Or did she want to believe it because she simply didn't like him?

"Well," she said aloud, drawing both men's attention, "I guess there is only one way to prove it." She looked first at Cole, who had made the accusation, then at Jean-Luc. "We wait."

For the past two hours Dominique had gone from studying the handsome face of the man with whom she had fallen in love as he paced the floor, stared out the window, or sat in one of the wing chairs before the cold hearth tapping his foot, to wondering what life would be like in two hundred years. She was having a great deal of difficulty trying to imagine it. She'd been tempted several times to ask Nicolas, but had just as quickly changed her mind. It would only remind her that he would be going back where he belonged, and that he would be going without her.

Jean-Luc, having flatly refused to accept the preposterous idea that Siffre had run away, hadn't waited more than fifteen minutes before announcing that he would ride to Siffre's estate and fetch him back before the hour was out. Dominique hadn't argued with him, since she had been hoping the trip would convince Jean-Luc that Nicolas was telling the truth, and because she wanted the time alone with him.

A good part of the reason her father had chosen a husband for her was that she had taken too long to find one who suited her every whim. Most of the gentlemen who called on her were fops, in her estimation, and lacked the moral fiber and strength she looked for in a mate. Siffre was no exception. He was intelligent, charming, and wealthy, but in all the years she had known him, she couldn't remember a time when he had taken the initiative on any issue, and she was fairly certain he would have been satisfied to allow someone else to help her parents if she hadn't shamed him into it. Truly, if Jean-Luc returned to the château without her betrothed, it wouldn't surprise her.

"Have you ever been in love, Nicolas Charboneau?" she asked, curious.

Cole turned. Bright warm sunshine filtered into the room through the partially opened French doors, bathing Dominique in a soft, alluring light. "Once," he answered quietly. "I even asked her to marry me. But it didn't work out."

Dominique raised one eyebrow, surprised. "What happened?"

"She decided she was in love with someone else." He smiled at her, but when he saw her frown, the corners of his mouth fell in a straight line. "Where I come from, a man and a woman marry because they love each other, not because it's arranged ahead of time."

"Really?" she challenged. "You mean a commoner could marry an aristocrat? With or without the family's consent?"

He nodded.

"Interesting," she remarked as she set aside her cup of tea. She remained quiet for a moment, then asked, "What was her name?"

"Nancy," he replied.

She frowned again. "Nancy," she repeated. "And do you still love her?"

He laughed. "Not at all."

His comment made Dominique think of Siffre. As a boy he had been a likeable sort. Somewhere between youth and maturity he had changed, and Dominique had grown to despise him. He was self-centered and had little respect for women. In her opinion, Siffre would probably be a lot happier if he never took a wife . . . and Dominique would be a lot happier, too.

Cole had been watching the expression on Dominique's face, and he guessed she was thinking about her fiancé as the frown that drew her eyebrows together hinted of disapproval. "You won't have to marry him, you know," he said matter-of-factly. "I assure you that if he hasn't already fled Paris, he will very soon. And once your father learns of it, you'll be free to choose your own husband."

"A commoner, perhaps?" she suggested with a smile.

He smiled, too. "If you wish."

They enjoyed looking at each other for a long

while, until she grew uncomfortable and he realized he was the reason for it. She was the first to turn her head; then she rose, crossed to the buffet, and poured herself some more tea.

The way she moved, the gentle sway of her hips, her slender waist, her scent, everything about her warmed Cole's blood. It was crazy, he knew that, but he'd fallen for this woman— completely, deeply, and without regret. That was what made it so hard for him. He'd finally found the right woman and fate would take her away.

"If I hadn't stopped you," she said, "would you have taken the horse and gone to Paris?"

"Yes," he answered quietly.

She raised the cup to her lips, smiled, and said, "I'm glad I did."

The remark pleased him. "So am I." He grinned at her for a moment, then asked, "And if the gun had been loaded, would you have shot me?"

Her dark eyes sparkled. "Yes."

He laughed. "I'm glad it wasn't."

"So am I," she agreed. She took another sip of her tea and looked at him again, the twinkle in her eyes fading. "So what will you do now, Nicolas?"

She watched him leave his chair and go to the hearth, where he stood with one foot on the stone slab and his right arm resting on the mantel. He looked so very handsome in the dark shade of blue, and it was an image she hoped to recall each day for the rest of her life.

"I'll wait for Jean-Luc to return, and then I'll

help him figure out a way to get your parents out of the Bastille," he said.

"I mean after that," she admitted. "Will you go home?"

He was quiet for a long while, a troubled frown crimping his suntanned brow. "Yes," he finally answered. "I wish I didn't have to, but I must."

"Why?" she blurted out, not caring how it sounded. "There's no reason why you can't stay here, is there?"

"I don't belong here, Dominique," he replied, finding the words hard to speak. "I belong in Illinois, at the university, with my family and friends."

"Even if I asked you to stay?" She knew it was bold of her, but she couldn't help herself. The thought of losing him, after having just found him, was too much to consider or to accept.

Cole felt as if someone had stabbed him in the heart. How could he make her understand that his presence in the eighteenth century jeopardized the way things were meant to be? By just talking to her, he could be making serious changes in the events that would mold the future. Perhaps he shouldn't even be helping Jean-Luc.

Setting down the cup and saucer and coming to her feet, Dominique crossed to where he stood and touched his arm. "Jean-Luc believes the witch killed my sister even though he doesn't believe you're from the future. And I believe it, too. If Zora did it once, she'll do it again. And

I—" The rest caught in her throat. Tears pooled in the corners of her eyes, and she started to turn away.

Filled with an overwhelming need to hold Dominique in his arms, Cole trapped her hand in his and pulled her to him. Their eyes met, and he gently cupped her face as he lowered his head and pressed his lips to hers. The warmth of her, the sweet fragrance of her hair and skin, the feel of her soft mouth answering his kiss, rocked his emotions and stirred a fire deep within him. Why was this happening to him? Why couldn't he stop the feelings? Why couldn't he have left well enough alone?

A commotion sounded in the foyer and shattered the moment. Embarrassed and fearing that Jean-Luc had returned, Dominique hurried back to the settee, while Cole made a silent promise to stop leading her on. A moment later, Jean-Luc burst into the room, breathless and unaware of what had passed between the two people looking at him.

"He's gone, Dominique," Jean-Luc announced, his voice tired and edged with anger. "Siffre packed up his valuables and rode off last night." He looked at Cole. "It seems you were right, Monsieur Charboneau. I wouldn't have believed it, but you were. However, I'm still not sure I accept your explanation for being here. I think Dominique does, and for that reason alone, I'll go along with whatever you say. If she trusts you, then so do I."

Cole nodded his appreciation. He knew this hadn't been easy for Jean-Luc.

"So what do we do next?" Jean-Luc asked.

Cole started to reply, but Dominique cut him off.

"You and I, Jean-Luc, must get busy working out a plan to free my parents," she said, coming to her feet. "They've been in that horrible place for two days now, and we have no idea when they are scheduled to be executed." She looked at Cole. "I'll have Monsieur Beauprés see that a horse is saddled for you, and I'll ask him to accompany you to Paris. I believe he knows where Zora lives, so you won't have to waste any more time." She nodded her head, blinked back her tears, and started to move away as she said, "Now, if you'll excuse us . . ."

The sudden realization that Dominique was dismissing him as if he were nothing more than a servant caught Cole so completely off guard that he couldn't react. He just stood there, mouth agape, a deep frown pulling his dark eyebrows together.

"Wait!" he exclaimed, stopping the couple near the doorway. He stared at them for several seconds, trying to figure out what had just happened. "What the hell are you doing, Dominique?"

"I'm offering you what you want—the chance to speak with Zora," she replied.

"It's not what I *want*, it's what I *have* to do, Dominique," he argued. "But it can wait. Your parents don't have the same luxury."

"What are you saying?" Jean-Luc questioned, confused by the chilly exchange of words between the pair.

"What I'm saying is that the two of you need me more than you know," he answered, looking from Dominique to Jean-Luc. "Unless, of course, you already happen to have a layout of the Bastille *and* know where to find some guards' uniforms."

Jean-Luc shook his head. "And you do?"

"I'm a French history professor, remember?" Without waiting for his companion to answer, Cole brushed past the couple and headed for the study, where he was sure he would find the paper and quill he needed.

The trio spent the rest of the morning closeted away making notes, drawing diagrams, and listening to each other's ideas. It was Cole who came up with the best but most dangerous plan. Neither Dominique nor Jean-Luc liked it very much, but both had to yield to its feasibility.

"There's only one thing wrong with it," Dominique announced, once the threesome had agreed to give it a try.

"What's that?" Jean-Luc asked.

"You've worked it out so I'm not included," she stated. "They're my parents. I want to be involved."

Jean-Luc had caught on to Cole's subtle elimination of Dominique the second Cole had started to talk, and he hadn't said a word. He had guessed the man had done it for Dominique's own safety, and he liked that. In fact he liked this stranger, this man who claimed to come from the future.

"Dominique," Jean-Luc said, "you've agreed to the plan. How do you propose to be a part of it? Nicolas and I will pass quite easily for soldiers once we have the uniforms, but even if we found one small enough to fit you... well..." He flicked his hand at her, indicating her shapely form.

Dominique's brown eyes darkened. "I didn't mean I want to march into the Bastille shoulder to shoulder with you, but I certainly don't intend to sit here waiting. If something should go wrong, I want to be there. I'd be the only friend you'd have."

"Well, what do you suggest, Dominique?" Jean-Luc asked irritably. "That you stand outside with a musket?"

"Don't be sarcastic," she scolded. "You'll need a wagon or cart of some sort in which to hide my parents once they're free, won't you? I'll be the driver."

"Oh, that's a perfect idea," he countered mockingly. "No one will even notice the beautiful, well-dressed woman at the reins of a stubborn mule."

"No, they won't," she rallied. "Because I won't be a well-dressed woman. I'll be an old hag."

Her suggestion surprised and impressed Jean-Luc. Cole, on the other hand, feared Jean-Luc would give in to her idea. Perhaps she was right in thinking no one would bother an old woman dressed in rags, but Cole didn't want to chance it. She was better off staying at the château.

"What do you think, Nicolas?" Jean-Luc asked, still hesitant to agree.

Looking at Dominique, Cole replied, "I think it's a foolish idea."

"And I don't care what you think," she shot back. "I'm going."

"No, you're not," Cole said. "At the risk of sounding horribly chauvinistic, you're a woman, for heaven's sake."

Dominique's chin came up. "Thank you for noticing. But what has that to do with it?"

Cole's temper began to slip. He gritted his teeth, inhaled deeply, and cocked his head. "Jean-Luc and I can take care of ourselves. And we'll be too busy to look after you. You're staying here."

"No, I'm not," she returned, her dark eyes snapping as she moved to stand before him. "They're *my* parents and it's my duty to—"

"To what?" he cut in. "To get yourself caught and beheaded?" The instant the words crossed his lips, he knew he shouldn't have lost his temper.

Dominique's face paled. "You're hiding something, aren't you?"

"No."

"I think you are," she pressed.

"Like what, Dominique?"

"That I'm supposed to die on the guillotine," she supplied.

"I don't know that. No one knew for certain. I told you the story was too vague after being passed around so many times. It's possible you and Jean-Luc escaped with your parents."

"But you're afraid I was caught and executed," she charged. "That's why you don't me to go with you."

"Yes."

"But you don't know for sure."

"No. But what else could I think?"

A soft smile lifted the corners of her mouth. "That I ran away with a handsome stranger."

"This isn't funny, Dominique," he warned.

"No, it isn't," she agreed, turning away from him and heading for the door. "Everything you've predicted thus far has come true. And I agree that our mission will be dangerous." She paused at the door to look back at him. "But this is something I have to do, with or without your permission. And since you don't know absolutely what will happen to me, I have to take the chance.

"Now, both of you wait here," she instructed, pulling the door open. "I'll find some peasant clothes for us to wear, and while Jean-Luc is obtaining the uniforms you need, you and I, Monsieur Charboneau, will visit your witch." Without waiting for either man to reply, she turned and left the room.

LONG shadows of dusk filled the alleyway where Dominique directed Jean-Luc to guide the donkey-drawn cart in which they rode. At the end of the narrow avenue stood the inn where they planned to meet later, after Cole had visited the witch and Jean-Luc had stolen the uniforms from the tailor's shop Cole had guaranteed was commissioned to make them.

"I'm not sure how long it will take me." Jean-Luc spoke in a hushed voice, since the alleyway was crowded and he had no way of knowing who might be friend or foe. "Anyway, we can't do anything until morning without raising suspicion. There aren't any extra guards around the prison after dark." He pulled the donkey to a halt near the inn's front door and helped Dominique to the cobblestones. They had decided Jean-Luc would take the cart, and Dominique and Cole would walk the two blocks to where Zora lived. "Take good care of her, Nicolas Charboneau," he warned with a nod at Dominique. "Because if you don't, you'll answer to me."

Cole knew from the stern look in the Frenchman's eyes that Jean-Luc meant what he'd said. "Better care than she's ever had," Cole promised. "And may I suggest the same for you? You're needed if we're to pull this off."

Jean-Luc smiled and snapped the reins. "Don't worry about me, my friend. I'll be here long after you're gone."

A moment later his thin frame was swallowed up in the crowded avenue, and Cole turned to escort Dominique inside. They paid for the only available room in the place, then headed out again, fighting their way through the throng of people crushing in all around them.

"Stay close," Cole warned as he laid his hand on Dominique's narrow waist and buffeted the elbows and shoulders of the people they passed.

The conversations surrounding them had an angry tone, and many times the words "aristocrat," "wealthy," and "nobility" were tossed around with rancor. Although their disguises—especially Dominique's frayed clothes, tangled black hair, and dirty face—hid their true identities, Cole vowed to take no chances. Their very lives depended on it.

Bruised and anxious for a safe haven, he pulled Dominique into the recessed entryway of the building where she had indicated they would find Zora. He rapped loudly on the door and waited. When there was no response, he knocked again.

"Damn it, Zora," he growled, "answer the door."

As if his demand had been heard, the latch clicked and a narrow stream of lamplight spilled out as the way opened up just enough for someone to see who had come calling.

"What do you want?" a male voice asked guardedly.

"We wish to speak with Zora," Dominique answered.

A scream from in back of them echoed down the alleyway, and Cole shielded his companion with his body as he challenged, "Either let us enter of your own free will or I'll force our way in."

The dark figure, its face in shadow, moved to one side and opened the door for them. Without a moment's hesitation, Cole guided Dominique into the parlor and hurriedly shut the door behind them.

"Is she here?" Dominique asked the tall, barrel-shaped man in brown breeches and shirt, dark hose, and black shoes. "It's vital that we speak with her."

The man's bald head gleamed in the light. He stared at them for a moment, then asked, "What do you want?"

"Her help," Cole replied. "Tell her there's someone here to see her from the twentieth century."

Without flinching or blinking an eye, the man

waited a second longer before he turned and left the room.

"I think it's wisest if I do the talking, Dominique," Cole whispered. "If she knows you're Danielle's sister, she might not be receptive."

He had barely finished his suggestion when a movement to his right drew his attention, and he turned to see a rather pleasant-looking green-eyed woman staring at him. He wasn't sure what he had expected—a hooked nose, a wart, or pointed black hat, even a broom perhaps—but whatever it was, Zora fell short. In fact, there was nothing extraordinary about her, and for some reason this made him a little nervous.

"Georges tells me you seek my help," she said, her gaze shifting to Dominique, then back to Cole. "To go home again?"

"Yes," Cole answered, wishing Dominique would move out of the light. He feared the witch would recognize her.

"Both of you?" Zora pressed.

Without thinking, Cole replied, "Yes."

Zora seemed to relax as she walked to a comfortable chair by the fireplace and sat down. "How did you come to our time?"

Cole dug into his pocket, then stretched to hand her the scroll he had purposely brought with him. He saw the look in her eyes that told him she recognized the paper and the words written on it. "I found it hidden behind a stone in a fireplace—that, and Danielle Dubois' diary."

Zora's face paled and she glanced at Dominique, who had gone to a window to look outside, her back to the room. "She is dead, no?" Zora asked.

Cole prayed Dominique would remain quiet. "Yes."

Zora's gaze moved again to the young woman at the window. "I have heard the rumors—that she died because of a curse I put on her. It is not true." She frowned. "I am not an evil witch, Mademoiselle Dubois. I did not kill your sister. I saw a woman in love who feared for her family. I sought only to help."

Dominique spun around. "Why should I believe you?"

"Your sister was already sick when she visited me. She had a fever, and the congestion here"—Zora touched her chest—"is what took her life."

"Pneumonia," Cole mumbled. "*Did* she have a fever, Dominique?"

The answer was slow in coming. "Yes."

"Before she came here to see Zora?"

Dominique looked away. "Yes," she whispered.

"She did not ask for a cure, Mademoiselle Dubois, even when I questioned her about it. She only sought to spare her fiancé and you," Zora explained. "She was a loving young woman who willingly sacrificed her own life in the hope of saving those she loved." Zora turned to Cole. "It does not explain your presence, however."

Cole quickly told her the story, and when he had finished, she left her place by the fire and went to the writing desk in the far corner, where she wrote something down.

"Here," she said after a while, and handed him the new parchment. "But you must be careful when you recite the verse. If you are touching anything, anything at all, while you say the words, it will go with you. Do you understand?"

"Yes," he replied. "And thank you." He turned to Dominique. "I'd like it better if we were safely tucked away at the inn," he softly advised, noticing the tears in her eyes.

Dominique glanced at him, then at Zora. She started to say something, then changed her mind and moved to the front door. Without a backward glance, she left the witch's home, Cole following closely behind her.

The room they had rented was clean but small, with no extras: just a bed, a nightstand, a wardrobe, and a chair by the window. A fire hadn't even been started in the tiny hearth, and once Cole had locked the door behind them, he set about rectifying the problem. Within moments warmth chased away the chill in the room and disguised the musty smell.

"Are you hungry?" he asked when he saw that Dominique had taken up a vigil at the window and hadn't bothered to remove her tattered cape.

A shake of her dark head answered him, and he felt a pang of sadness. He knew she was probably thinking about how Danielle wouldn't have had to die if she had only accepted Zora's help. He also knew it was too late to change any of it. Hoping to draw her into a conversation and to get her mind off her sister, he came to stand beside her.

"Are you cold?" he asked.

She shook her head again and reached for the strings on her cape. Before she had slipped the garment from her shoulders, he was there to take it from her. But the moment his hand brushed her neck, she spun around and threw herself into his arms.

Cole's heart pounded as the warmth of her young body singed his own and set his blood on fire. She was so soft, so vulnerable, so alluring that he had to fight his yearning to do more than just hold her. He never would have guessed that he could fall in love with someone in such a short time, but he had. And the reality of the situation made him ache inside. She was from another world and another time, and history wouldn't allow his love to grow and blossom. In a few short hours he would vanish, leaving her behind, and she would act out the steps of her life as fate intended.

"Why did she have to die, Nicolas?" she wept. "Why are my parents being made to suffer? It's so unfair."

"Nothing is ever fair," he soothed, resting his chin on the top of her head as he held her within the circle of his arms. He frowned and closed his eyes, thinking of his own situation. He had stumbled around for years looking for the one woman who would make a difference in his life, only to discover she was beyond his reach. Was that fair? And what about Dominique? What would happen to her? One thing was certain. He didn't intend to let her be executed. He would give up his own life first.

They stood holding on to each other for a long while, silent and pensive. The fire crackled in the hearth. Stars twinkled in the sky just beyond the windowpanes, and the agony they both felt ebbed away. Then, without even realizing it, they were kissing, and as their passion grew, they both knew it was destiny's spell that had brought them together, and that a cruel fate would tear them apart. He couldn't stay, and she couldn't go. Unable to resist and not caring about the risk they were taking, they gave in to their feelings, willing to steal one perfect moment together.

The hot moistness of his lips pressed against her own, his rock-hard body touching hers, and the hand caressing her spine sent waves of sheer delight through every inch of Dominique and warmed her all the way to her bones. The scent of him, his masculinity, the feel of his muscular body nearly enveloping her within his embrace stirred longings inside her that she had never known.

Her fingers moved along the bare curve of his shoulder as she pushed the shirt down his arms and let it fall to the floor. Her mouth found his again and Cole met her advance with equal fervor. In wild abandonment he tugged at the fastenings on her dress and helped her out of her shoes and stockings and underthings before he shed his own and lifted her in his arms. They kissed savagely, fiercely, as he carried her to the bed and fell with her upon the feathery mattress. His hands freely roamed the long silkened length of her back, hips, and thighs. He touched her face, her neck, her breasts, then followed the same path with searing kisses.

"Oh God, Dominique," he breathed against her parted lips as he rolled and braced himself above her. "You are the most beautiful woman I have ever known."

She sighed at the compliment and wrapped her arms around his neck. "And you are the most handsome man I have ever known, Nicolas Charboneau."

Lust darkened their eyes. The smiles vanished from their lips. Their blood ran hot through their veins, and before another second was wasted, he parted her trembling thighs with his knee and touched his mouth to hers as he made his first thrust. She winced, then moved beneath him, matching his long, sleek strides with the fluent grace of her hips. Their passion soared. Their breathing grew rapid, and the muscles across his back gleamed as he moved faster, deeper, carrying them to the summit of their long-awaited rapture. In a burst of all-consuming ecstasy, they reached a heavenly plateau where they lingered for a moment until, their passion spent, they tumbled earthward wrapped within the warm embrace of each other's arms.

"Oh, Dominique," he murmured against her temple as he lay on his side, holding her close to him. "If I were to die right now, I would die a happy man."

A bright smile lifted her mouth. "Will you always feel that way?"

"Always," he promised her. "And when you remember me, will you think of me with kindness?"

"And love," she whispered, kissing his chin.

She snuggled closer, closed her eyes, and sighed. "I wish Zora had a spell that would make time stand still. We could live the rest of our lives just the way we are."

"Me, too," he vowed, grinning. A second later the smile was gone, and a troubled frown darkened his eyes.

A noise from somewhere in the hall outside the door to their room alarmed them and they sat up, remembering that Jean-Luc would be arriving soon. Without a word, they scampered from the bed and hurriedly donned their clothes. Then, all of a sudden, the vision of a startled look on the Frenchman's face clouded Cole's mind and he laughed out loud.

"Would you care to share your amusement?" Dominique asked as she finished buttoning her dress and sat down to pull on her shoes and stockings.

"Oh, I was just imagining Jean-Luc's reaction if he'd arrived five minutes ago," Cole admitted.

"And you find that humorous?" she challenged. "You obviously don't know him very well. If he'd found us in bed, he would have killed you before I could have stopped him."

His smile disappeared. "Really? Why?" A thought struck him and he frowned. "You two aren't—"

"No," she quickly answered. "He loved Danielle. But I was to become a part of his family when he married my sister, and he still thinks of me that way, despite her death. Since my parents' arrest, he's taken it upon himself to protect me." Her eyes glowed as she glanced up at him.

Cole smile broadly. "Well, I certainly don't plan to tell him anything. Do you?"

When he recognized the playfulness behind the slight shrug of her shoulders, Cole narrowed his eyes, grinned, and threw himself at her. Tumbling on the bed, they laughed, shared several kisses, and hugged each other.

"I love you, Dominique Dubois," he pledged, brushing a lock of her dark hair from her brow.

"And I love you, Nicolas Charboneau," she replied.

The creak of a floorboard outside their room sent them both scrambling to their feet. A second later there was a knock on the door, and Cole guardedly turned the knob to make sure their conclusion was correct.

"Did you have any trouble?" Dominique asked as she watched Jean-Luc swing into the room and close the door behind him.

"A little," he admitted, tossing down the cloth sack he'd brought with him. "But the uniforms were right where Nicolas said they would be." He smiled at her, noticed the bright flush of her cheeks, and frowned. Was it his imagination or had something happened in his absence? He looked at Cole, who had turned away to pull the disguises from the bag, and sensed the man did so out of a reluctance to meet his gaze.

"Did you pick ones that will fit?" Cole asked as he held up one of the uniforms and deliberately tried to guide the course of the conversation.

"I didn't have time to be selective," Jean-Luc replied, glancing back at Dominique. "So they'll just have to do."

Dominique could feel her friend's gaze as she concentrated on what Cole was doing. In all the years she'd known him, she'd never been able to hide anything from Jean-Luc, and now it seemed that with just one glance, he had guessed what she was feeling for this stranger from another time. Lifting her eyes, she stared at him for a long moment before a soft smile parted her lips. He frowned again, shifted his attention to Cole, then back to Dominique. When her smile widened, he shook his head and chuckled quietly, obviously having understood her obscure message.

"So what happens now?" Jean-Luc asked, turning to the hearth. The night had grown uncustomarily cool and his fingers were numb. Stretching out his hands toward the fire, he glanced back over his shoulder at Cole.

"We sleep, rise at daybreak, and visit the prison," Cole explained. "As soon as we've freed the Duboises, you will leave Paris. And you won't look back until you're safely out of the country."

Remembering Lisette's account of what had happened, Cole turned his back on the couple before either of them could notice his worried expression. "I'd like to think it will be that easy," he said after a moment. "But it never is. That's why we should have an alternate plan should something go wrong."

"It won't," Dominique stubbornly declared.

"I'd like to believe that, Dominique," Cole said, "but I can't. *We* can't. We have to consider what we'll do if something unforeseen happens."

"Like what?" Jean-Luc questioned.

"Well," Cole began, "we could get separated. In that case we must swear that whoever is with Monsieur and Madame Dubois will see that they're escorted out of the city. Their safety comes first. Agreed?"

"Agreed," Dominique and Jean-Luc chorused.

Cole looked directly at Dominique. "You swear that if Jean-Luc and I run into trouble, you and your parents will leave the city without us?"

She hesitated before nodding and whispering softly, "Yes."

"And you?" he asked, turning to Jean-Luc. "Do you swear to leave me or Dominique behind?"

Jean-Luc took longer to agree and only then because he had concluded that Nicolas Charboneau wouldn't heed his own advice, that if something happened to Dominique, he would lay down his life to save hers.

"Good!" Cole finished with a half-smile. He motioned for the pair to sit down. "Then let's go over our plan one more time so that we're sure we know what to do."

Morning came too early for Cole. He hadn't slept much and it had nothing to do with the fact that he'd tried to sleep while sitting up in a chair. He'd simply been too busy worrying to relax and drift off. But even if he had fallen asleep, the time he had left with Dominique was slipping away much too quickly, and there was nothing he could do to stop it.

No one spoke as they readied themselves for the mission they had planned. They left the inn without being seen by the other guests and hurried to the stable, where Jean-Luc had left the donkey and cart and hidden the muskets. Once they were inside, the two men changed into their guard uniforms and loaded their rifles, while Dominique climbed into the cart and took the reins.

"Swear to me that you'll do exactly as we've agreed upon," Cole said with a frown as he laid his hand on hers.

"I swear," she replied. "And you'll do the same?"

He smiled at her and raised her hand to kiss its palm. "I'll do whatever it takes," he promised.

That wasn't good enough for Dominique. "Take care of him for me, Jean-Luc," she insisted as she snapped the reins.

"As best I can," her friend called after her.

They waited until Dominique had driven away before they stepped into the street and headed for the Bastille.

They had planned to walk in right past the guard, down the long corridor to the cell where Jean-Luc had been told the Duboises were being held, and announce the names of those they had come to take to the guillotine. Once they had marched the group outside, everyone would be loaded into the cart and driven away to safety. It was what they had planned, but Cole worried that something would go wrong despite their precautions . . . and so did Jean-Luc.

The sight of the Bastille, despite the fact that Cole had seen hundreds of sketches of the building, still surprised him. It looked like a medieval castle, with a watchtower on each corner, battlements along the front and sides, and tall narrow windows. It had to be six or seven stories high and a block square. All it lacked was a drawbridge and portcullis, and Cole wasn't even sure of that, since a huge crowd of jeering peasants milling around the courtyard blocked his view of the entrance.

What surprised him even more was the general demeanor of the people waiting outside for the first cartload of prisoners to be hauled to the guillotine. Children played games as if they were in a schoolyard at recess. Several of the women sat on the stone ledge of a nearby fountain, knitting various articles of apparel. The men laughed and talked among themselves as though they had just come out of church on a Sunday morning. The scene appalled Cole, and he came to a staggering halt.

"Are you all right?" Jean-Luc asked, seeing the pained expression on Cole's face.

"I . . . I just didn't realize it would be like this," Cole confessed, moving out of the way of an old woman with a basket full of bread. "I've read everything there is to read about the French Revolution, but somehow it never quite prepared me for the crowds and their callousness."

"Yes, I imagine it is rather a shock," Jean-Luc replied. "At least you won't have to see any more of it after today. You did get the chant from Zora, didn't you?"

"Yes," Cole mumbled.

"When do you intend to use it?"

Cole shrugged. "When the time is right, I suppose."

"And how will you know when that is?"

Cole frowned. Was Jean-Luc trying to tell him something? "I suppose I'll have to use my instincts."

They started off again, but when they drew close to the main entrance, Jean-Luc touched Cole's arm and drew him to a halt. "I suspect you really do know how all of this will turn out," he said, "and it's probably best that you don't tell me. I also sense that whatever happens, you'll put Dominique's safety first. She's fallen in love with you, Nicolas, and I think you feel the same toward her. So whatever has to be done, do it. And know you have my approval and my blessing." He smiled and raised his hand to Cole.

"Thank you," Cole replied, warmly accepting the hand held out to him in friendship. "I only have one regret, and that is that my time here has been limited. I would have liked to get to know you better."

Jean-Luc grinned and started to respond when the heavy metal door of the Bastille swung open and the first rush of prisoners bound for execution were shoved outside. The crowd, which had been waiting quietly in the street, exploded in a flood of jeering taunts and shouts, and Jean-Luc and Cole, after making sure the group didn't include the Duboises, used the confusion to push their way inside behind another pair of guards. Once the heavy door was shut and they were alone in the gloomy corridor with the two men, Cole and Jean-Luc lifted their muskets and knocked the guards unconscious before they had a chance to turn around.

"In here," Jean-Luc instructed as he grabbed one of the two guards and dragged him into an empty cell nearby.

Cole quickly seized the other guard and dumped him alongside his partner, while Jean-Luc searched their pockets. Suddenly he grinned broadly and held up the papers he had been looking for, and motioned for his friend to have a look.

It was an offical document listing the names

of those prisoners who were next in line for the guillotine. On it they found Guilbert and Marie Dubois' names, and Cole knew they had arrived just in time. Their next feat was to find the Duboises' cell before someone discovered the unconscious guards.

"Where do we start?" Jean-Luc asked worriedly, knowing they must hurry.

"This is quite a long list," Cole observed, closing his eyes and picturing the drawing of the Bastille he had studied at the university's library. "I would say they're being held downstairs in one of the larger cells."

Jean-Luc held out a hand. "Lead the way, my friend."

They traveled several corridors, made three turns past endless rows of locked doors, and hurried down a flight of stairs. As they neared their destination, Jean-Luc stepped in Cole's way, bringing them both to a stop. A guard stood outside the last cell.

"Let me do the talking," he suggested. "Every once in a while you have a bit of an English accent, and since we've come this far, we don't want to ruin it. All right?"

Cole nodded.

"You there!" Jean-Luc called out to the guard. "We have come for some of the prisoners." He waved the paper in the air.

The soldier jumped to attention, his musket in both hands as he waited for Jean-Luc to approach and show him the document. When he was satisfied that everything was in order, he took a key from his belt, unlocked the door, and swung it open.

Inside, Jean-Luc and Cole paused at the top of the three steps leading downward into the cold, dank, windowless room. There were twenty people in all, half of whom Jean-Luc recognized, including Dominique's parents. He knew that the cart would not hold them all. Praying for the strength it would take for him to leave some of his fellow aristocrats behind, he cleared his throat, held out the paper in front of him, and began calling out names.

Cole knew, even before Jean-Luc had identified them, who Dominique's parents were. Marie Dubois was tiny, like her daughter, with the same chin and nose. Guilbert Dubois, a tall man compared to the other men in the cell, had gray hair, but his dark brown eyes held the same stubborn gleam that Cole had seen in Dominique's. Cole ached to tell them that their daughter was all right and that he loved her, that within a few minutes they would all be together, but he forced himself to remain silent and to pretend he was there to escort them to the guillotine.

"Come with us," Jean-Luc ordered when he had finished, deliberately avoiding looking at any of the people who stepped forward and out into the corridor. When the last one had left the cell, he turned to the guard and ordered the door sealed as Cole led the group away.

For Jean-Luc, hearing the key turn in the lock was the same as hearing the steel blade of the guillotine being released against those he was leaving behind. Without giving it a second thought, he raised his musket and struck the guard across the back of the head, knocking him to the floor, unconscious. He kicked the body out of the way, unlocked the cell, and pulled the door open again.

"Here!" he called to the prisoners, tossing his musket to the man standing closest to him. "It isn't much, but it's the only chance you have." He collected the guard's rifle and the ring of keys and handed them over as well. "Turn your friends loose. Turn everyone loose!" he shouted as he stepped back into the hall and broke into a run.

Jean-Luc caught up with Cole and the others near the front exit of the Bastille, and before they prepared to go outside, he shook hands with Guilbert Dubois and promised Marie that they would be joining Dominique very soon. It was then that Cole noticed that Jean-Luc was unarmed.

"Where's your musket?" he asked.

An odd smile came over Jean-Luc's face. "I gave it to a friend," he replied as he moved to the doorway of the room where they had dumped the first two guards and retrieved one of their rifles. "I guess I'll have to borrow this one."

There wasn't time for Cole to ask what Jean-Luc had done, and Cole felt he didn't really have to ask; he was already fairly certain of the answer. Smiling back at his companion, Cole took a deep breath and asked if everyone was ready. They nodded, and he opened the door.

The instant Cole ushered the group outside, the crowd burst into a chorus of riotous insults, and a few in his party were even hit with pieces of garbage thrown at them. Cole forced himself to remain indifferent to their treatment, until he saw, much to his horror, that the cart and Dominique were nowhere to be seen. Doing an about-face, he hurried everyone back inside and closed the door.

"Where is she?" Jean-Luc asked.

"I don't know," Cole replied, frowning. "And right now, we can't worry about her. We've got to get these people out of here before someone misses the guards." He closed his eyes and concentrated on the drawing of the Bastille. A moment passed before he straightened with a snap of his fingers. "The guardhouse," he announced, directing the group down the hall. "There's an underground tunnel from here to the guardhouse. If we're lucky, we'll be able to sneak out through there."

Behind them as they ran they could hear the other prisoners being set free and filling the corridors. Cole wished he could take them all with him, but there wasn't time, and now he had to find Dominique. He pulled open a heavy door, motioned everyone down the steep steps, and quickly followed, shutting the door after him. At the bottom the space narrowed sharply, allowing only one person to pass at a time. Rats scurried out of the way, and before long a stench rose to gag everyone.

"What is it?" someone asked.

"The sewer," Jean-Luc replied, and suddenly everyone stopped.

"Is something wrong?" Cole called to his friend.

"What are our chances the guardhouse will be empty?" came the reply.

Cole shrugged. "I don't imagine they're very good."

"Then I have a better idea. It won't be pleasant, but at least I know we can get everyone to safety."

Cole heard a heavy grate being lifted and realized that Jean-Luc's idea practically guaranteed success, since the sewer ran to the outskirts of town. By following it, they wouldn't be seen. One by one Jean-Luc helped their companions down into the darkness. The last two to go were Dominique's parents, and Cole raised a hand to stop them.

"I won't be going with you," he said. "I have to go back. Dominique may be in trouble, and I won't leave without her." He handed his musket to Guilbert Dubois. "We made an oath, Monsieur Dubois—Jean-Luc, Dominique, and I—but I'm going to break it. I don't have anything to lose." He stretched out his hand to Jean-Luc. "Take care of these people, my friend, and maybe someday we will meet again."

The two men stared at each other for a long moment, knowing that day would never come.

Someone below warned them to hurry, and Cole turned to help the couple through the opening. Jean-Luc glanced at his friend one last time, then slipped into the darkness behind the others.

Once Cole had replaced the grate, he bolted for the steps. At the top he opened the door and cautiously moved into the hall. The corridor was empty, but he could hear angry voices up ahead, and he rushed for the prison's main entrance. When he reached it, he dashed outside and into the crowd, frantically looking all around for a glimpse of Dominique.

"There was an old hag in a cart here earlier," he said to the person standing beside him. "Did you see her?"

The man shook his head.

Cole asked someone else. The response was the same. He moved deeper into the crowd.

"I'm looking for an old hag who was seen driving a cart," he said to a pair of women standing near the fountain.

"They took her away," the largest of the two replied.

"Who?" Cole demanded. "Who took her away? Where did they take her?"

"Soldiers," the other woman answered with a venomous laugh. "She thought she could fool us. But she didn't. She was an aristocrat, and they took her inside. They'll cut off her head, and we'll all cheer!" she shouted at Cole's back as he hurried away.

Cole decided that if he had been able to move about the Bastille undetected the first time, it would surely work again. Elbowing his way through the crowd, he reached the entrance and went inside. A throng of soldiers and guards herded a group of prisoners back to their cells, and he quickly surveyed each one in the hope of spotting Dominique. When he failed, he touched the arm of the nearest guard.

"I'm here for Dominique Dubois," he said, hoping to sound bored with it all. "Where has she been taken?"

The man frowned. "Dubois?" he repeated with a shake of his head. "Can't help you. I don't recognize the name."

"She was just brought in . . . dressed in rags and pretending to be an old hag. Warrants were issued for her arrest, were they not?" he added for effect.

"Oh, *her*," the guard exclaimed, pointing off to his left.

"Down there."

Cole thanked the man and started off.

"But I'm not sure she's still there," the guard advised, stopping Cole in his tracks.

"Why not?"

"Her name's been added to those in the next group to be executed this morning. Captain Duval already may have come for her."

"Damn," Cole hissed, turning his back on the guard and heading down the hall.

At the end of the long corridor, Cole saw another guard standing beside the last cell door, and he prayed he would find Dominique inside. If he did, the next challenge he faced was convincing the guard to let him take Dominique with him.

He had just decided not to bother debating the issue—he would simply jump the guard, take his keys and musket, and turn Dominique loose—when the sound of a hammer being cocked echoed down the hall behind him.

"Hold it right there, Englishman," the voice demanded.

Cole came to an abrupt halt and slowly raised his hands as he watched the guard in front of him turn and aim his musket at him. A second later the muzzle of the other soldier's weapon was shoved in his back and he was ordered down the hall.

"You want to see Mademoiselle Dubois?" his captor snarled. "Then we'll oblige you." He nodded at the guard, who in turn unlocked the cell and opened the door. "Move!" he shouted, giving Cole a shove.

Stumbling into the darkened cubicle, Cole instantly felt the loving arms that caught him. Hugging Dominique to him, he turned with her in time to see the door slam shut and to hear the key in the lock. It didn't matter now how he'd given himself away, but the mistake would most certainly cost Dominique her life unless he could figure a way out for her.

"I'm so sorry, Dominique." He sighed, brushing a kiss against her temple. "This isn't how it was supposed to end. I meant for Jean-Luc and your parents to get away—and they have," he promised. "Then I was supposed to rescue you." He raised a hand. "And look what I've done."

"I don't care about me," she said, touching his cheek. "Just as long as Mama and Papa are safe."

"Well, *I* care," he answered angrily. "I love you, Dominique. And now, because of my stupidity—"

A disturbance in the hall jerked Cole around. He could hear the sound of footsteps growing louder and the voices of the men who were coming for them. In another minute it would be too late. He had to think of something. But what? Suddenly it came to him—something Zora had said.

"Dominique, do you love me?" he asked.

"With all my heart."

"Do you trust me?"

She hesitated, confused by the question. "Yes."

"Then hold me."

"What?"

"Just do it," he ordered, reaching for her. "Don't let go. I don't want to lose you along the way."

"Along the way?" she repeated. "Along the way where?"

"I'm taking you home with me, Dominique." He grinned. "And Zora told me how to do it." He glanced at the cell door, heard the key strike the metal plate, and quickly turned back.

"All things wicked, All things pure," he began. "Send them hither, two by two. Kindled fires, Darkness told, Destiny's journey, To behold."

Suddenly, a blast of cold air filled the tiny cell.

"You clumsy fool, hurry up!" Captain Duval growled when it seemed the soldier couldn't find the keyhole that was right in front of him. "We have a schedule to keep." His eyes blackened with rage as he waited impatiently for the door to open. He had just been told that six other prisoners had escaped, that they had walked right out with an escort of two guards, and had then simply disappeared. Now he understood how it had happened, and he wanted this Englishman to be the first to feel the guillotine's blade.

"Oh, give me that," he barked when the guard continued to fumble with the lock.

Knocking the man aside, Captain Duval jammed the key into place and gave it a hard turn. The hinges squealed, and the heavy door swung open. But as the captain moved to go inside, he was hit by a rush of chilling air that swept out and into the corridor, flickering the light of the torches on the wall behind him. Frightened, he stood perfectly still, mouth open and eyes wide, as he watched the swirling mist rise to reveal an empty cell.

For the past two days, Paris had been deluged with an intense rainstorm that had flooded the streets, kept the tourists from visiting the Eiffel Tower, and postponed the annual Bastille Day celebration on the square. Yet, amid the deafening cracks of thunder and bright flashes of light, two dark figures in a close embrace, clothed in costumes of long ago, suddenly appeared silhouetted against the blackened, storm-ridden sky.

Kay McMahon

Never one to pay attention in her high school history class, KAY McMAHON is still amazed that she chose a career with the accent on history. In 1983 she sold her first historical romance novel and since then has written a total of seventeen. She shares credit for her success with George, her husband of twenty-five years. They, along with their children, Greg and Jeni, live in rural northwestern Illinois, and when Kay is not busy at her computer, she and her family love to travel.

Eden's Gate

Bobbi Smith

1

Spring, 1993

"THE story of Eden's Gate Plantation is a sad and mysterious one," Jane Martin, the tour guide, told the group of travelers standing with her on the deck of the *River Queen* as it slowed and prepared to pull into the landing at Eden's Gate. "It was built in the late 1830s by the Hampton family, who'd come here from Virginia, and it prospered until the spring of 1860, when tragedy struck."

"What happened?" a petite, gray-haired, elderly lady asked eagerly as she stared up at the white, three-story, pillared home that had just come into view. Atop a low rise about a half mile back from the river, the elegant house was framed by huge, moss-draped oaks and lush green lawns.

"That was the year Jonas Hampton, the widowed owner of the place, lost his only son, Bradford, in a steamboat explosion. Bradford's body was never found."

"How horrible!"

"It was truly a tragic loss. Bradford Hampton was a man of vision, a man ahead of his times. He was university-educated and had made his grand tour. Instead of coming home a spoiled, arrogant young man, though, he returned convinced that changes had to be made in the Southern way of life. His revolutionary ideas didn't sit well with his contemporaries, and this is where the mystery comes in. There were rumors that his death had not been an accident. There were also rumors that he hadn't really been killed in the explosion, that he'd been seen alive at least once after the day he supposedly died."

"Why would anybody have wanted him dead?" another tourist asked.

"According to the gossip of the times, Bradford Hampton was involved with the Underground Railroad. There was never any definitive proof as far as we've been able to ascertain; but in those days, rumor alone was enough to make the neighboring slave owners nervous. That was right before the war, you know."

"What about those other rumors? What happened to the family, to the plantation?"

"Diaries we've read have chronicled Jonas' grief and his anger at Bradford's death. It seems that after a period of mourning, Jonas suddenly freed his slaves and gave them each a parcel of land in exchange for a promise to work the plantation fields as they'd done before. Before he could do much more, though, the war came, and well . . ."

"So there's no real proof that Bradford Hampton ever came back?"

"None. The guides who'll be taking you through the house will read to you some of the passages from Jonas' diaries, about how he missed his son and longed for him to return. It was all very sad."

"Who owns the house now?"

"After Jonas died, it passed to several other families until it finally fell into a terrible state of disrepair. The local Historical and Restoration Society bought the property about twelve years ago and have now refurbished it to its original glory."

"Thank heaven," another tourist put in, touched by the heartbreaking tale.

"Indeed," Kacie Cameron murmured in agreement as she stood slightly apart from the group.

"Did you have something to add, Ms. Cameron?" Jane Martin asked. Then, addressing her group of tourists, she explained, "In case you haven't met her yet, ladies and gentlemen, this is Kacie Cameron."

"Kacie Cameron of K. C.'s Paradise Boutiques?" one impressed lady asked, as everyone turned around to regard the slender, fair-haired, beautiful young woman.

"That's right. Ms. Cameron is one of the Eden's Gate Historical Society's most ardent supporters," Jane told them enthusiastically. "For those of you unfamiliar with Ms. Cameron's work, let me say that she's a marvelous fashion designer. But you can tell that just by looking at her, can't you?"

Kacie blushed prettily at her praise, while the crowd eyed with interest the dressy-casual, pale-yellow sweater and stretch pants outfit she wore from her own collection.

Jane continued to heap accolades upon Kacie, gushing, "Ms. Cameron has opened boutiques in New York, Chicago, Los Angeles, and Miami, and they're tremendously successful because her styles are so fresh and different. Why, anyone who is anyone on the stage, screen, or in the social world shops at the Paradise Boutiques. She's got fans in all age groups, because there's something for everyone in her shops."

"I remember reading about you in one of my business magazines," one man in the group spoke up. "The article was all about how you've achieved such a great degree of success at such a young age and about how your boutique franchises are right up there with Blockbuster Video and Domino's Pizza in terms of desirability. You're only thirty, aren't you?"

"Yes," Kacie answered, smiling.

"The article mentioned, too, that all the profit from one of your designer lines was going to the plantation fund. Is that true?"

"It's your 'Garden of Eden' lingerie line, isn't it?" Madge Patterson, a cheerful, middle-aged woman from Milwaukee, cut in before Kacie could say anything more. "I've bought several of your nightgowns, and I just love 'em!"

"Yes, it is that line, and thank you. I'm glad you enjoy them."

"Oh, no, my dear. Thank *you*!" Madge replied with a bright smile. "You just can't imagine how exciting it is to get to meet you. Why, my husband here just loves your work!" She laughed, while her husband looked decidedly uncomfortable.

"In addition to her business acumen, Ms. Cameron has studied all the documents available on Eden's Gate and has become a scholar on the family's history and on the home itself." Jane looked to Kacie. "Is there anything you'd like to offer before we leave the boat and go on up to the main house? The ladies from the Society are waiting for us."

"I'd just like to tell everyone that Eden's Gate is probably the most accurately restored plantation in the deep South. From the plaster crown moldings to the wallpaper, every item has been carefully reproduced so the house looks almost exactly as it did in 1860."

"Wonderful. Are you here for just a short visit, Ms. Cameron, or will you be staying for a while?" Jane inquired, knowing that the designer was disembarking at the plantation and would not continue on with the tour of the plantations along the Mississippi.

"Actually, the Society notified me that the long-missing Hampton family Bible has finally been recovered, so I've come to do some more research."

"I hope you discover some exciting new information."

"So do I."

"Shall we go now?"

The walkway had been lowered, so the guide led the group from the ship. As they reached the landing, Madge left her husband, who went with the crowd, and waited excitedly for Kacie.

"Ms. Cameron?"

"Yes?"

"My name's Madge, Madge Patterson, and I was wondering if you'd mind my walking along with you?"

Kacie had hoped to enjoy a quiet stroll, but the other woman's enthusiasm made it hard to refuse. "Of course not, Madge. It's nice to meet you. Please join me. By the way, please call me Kacie."

Madge was thrilled. "Tell me, how did you get to be so involved with Eden's Gate? Are you related to the Hampton family?"

"No, I'm not," Kacie answered, though she'd often wondered if there wasn't some distant, obscure connection somewhere in her family tree. "I first read about the plantation in the newspaper when I was only eighteen. I fell in love with the place just from what little information was in that article. I was so fascinated by the family's story that I began saving as much money as I could so I could come and see the house for myself. As soon as I graduated from high school, I made my first trip here."

"Was it as wonderful as you thought it would be?"

"Absolutely. In fact, it was better. It's breath-taking," Kacie replied, lifting her green-eyed gaze to the mansion in the distance. Once again, as happened every time she returned, a tremendous sense of longing welled up inside her, and she wondered how she could have stayed away this long.

Kacie didn't tell Madge everything about her first trip to Eden's Gate. She didn't tell the woman about her reaction to seeing Bradford Hampton's portrait for the first time. She'd been almost frightened by the power of the feelings that had swept through her at the sight of his handsome features captured for eternity in that painting. Kacie had been filled with a painful sense of loneliness, a devastating sense of loss. It hadn't made sense to her, but there had been no denying it.

Kacie had never before experienced anything so intense or so unsettling. Having always prided herself on being an intelligent person, she'd attempted to reason away her confusion. She'd told herself it was crazy to react that way to a portrait of a dead man, but the gut-wrenching emotions that had churned within her as she'd stared up at the dark-haired Bradford Hampton's compelling features hadn't disappeared. She'd known a nearly uncontrollable desire to reach out and caress his lean, hard cheek. She'd wanted to touch him, to see him smile. She'd wanted to hear him laugh. She'd known it was crazy. She'd told herself it was just a picture, that the man was dead, but all the rationalizing in the world hadn't eased the turmoil in her heart and in her soul.

Kacie had reminded herself that there were a lot of good-looking men alive right now and that she didn't react this way when she saw any of them. Seeing Mel Gibson never evoked this kind of response from her; neither did gazing at the handsome Tom Berenger or seeing Gregory Peck in his younger days when he'd starred in movies like *The Big Country*. She'd thought the strange and powerful feelings would fade with time, but during all of her visits, her reaction to seeing Bradford's portrait had been the same. Kacie knew her feelings bordered on being obsessive, but she figured as long as she wasn't hurting anyone, there was nothing to be unduly concerned about.

"Eden's Gate is lovely." Madge sighed, distracting Kacie from her thoughts.

"It's the most beautiful place in the world," Kacie commented. "I'm so glad to be back."

Eagernesss filled Kacie as she thought once again of the note she'd received a week ago from Doris Hoyle, the Historical Society's director. The missive had informed her that the Hampton family Bible had finally been found in a secret hiding place in a grotto wall and that Kacie was invited to view the Bible at her convenience. Kacie had been planning to take the riverboat tour later in the spring, but after getting the letter, she'd booked her trip right away. Now that she was finally back at the plantation, she wondered how she had ever had the strength to leave it.

As they came to the side path that led off to the Historical Society's offices, Kacie excused herself from Madge's company and went in search of Doris Hoyle. Kacie's spirits were soaring, and for the first time in months she felt truly alive. It seemed she'd done nothing but work lately. After her relationship with her last boyfriend had fizzled out from a lack of interest and enthusiasm on both their parts, Kacie had devoted all her energies to creating her new fashion line for the following winter. She'd had no time for another relationship, and now, as she headed for the office, she was glad she had no binding ties to distract her from her purpose. She was there to learn everything new she could about Eden's Gate and the Hampton family. Kacie hoped her efforts would help her understand more about her fixation with the place and with Bradford in particular.

The director was waiting for her when she entered the office. A dark-haired lady of impeccable manner and dress, Doris Hoyle was the epitome of Southern womanhood. Soft-spoken yet firm in her convictions, Doris had been the driving power behind the restoration of Eden's Gate, and she had deeply appreciated all of Kacie's support—financial and otherwise. Their reunion was a warm one, the camaraderie that existed between them genuine.

"The house has been rented out for a reception tonight at eight o'clock, but the guests are restricted to the main floor, so you shouldn't be disturbed," Doris told Kacie as she escorted her to the main house. "As usual, you're in the back bedroom."

"Thanks, Doris." Kacie smiled. The master suite and Bradford's bedroom were included in the tour, but the other bedrooms were part of the bed-and-breakfast plan and were rented out to guests. Kacie had stayed in the same bedroom on every visit, and she adored it.

"Since it's already so late," the director said, glancing at her watch to discover that it was after five o'clock, "why don't we plan on meeting first thing in the morning? We can have breakfast together and then begin our study of the Bible. How does eight o'clock sound?"

"Eight sounds wonderful. Have you had much of an opportunity to look through it yet?"

"I went through it quickly last week, right after I wrote to you, and I found some very interesting things in it. I think you're going to enjoy looking at it."

"I know I am," Kacie agreed. "Where are you keeping it?"

"It's in Bradford's bedroom under glass for now so that nothing can happen to it. You can take a peek at it tonight if you like."

"Thanks."

"I've made arrangements for an early dinner to be brought to you in your room around six-thirty. You should have a relatively quiet evening as long as none of the guests at the reception gets lost and wanders upstairs where it's off-limits. I'll be around all evening if you need anything else."

Kacie thanked her again as they entered the main house by way of the back entrance and used the rear staircase to reach the second floor. Doris accompanied Kacie to her room and then bade her good night. Alone at last in the spacious, beautifully appointed bedroom with its antique furnishings, imported wallpaper, marble fireplace, and over-long gold velvet drapes, Kacie drew a chair to the window and sat down to look out across the perfectly manicured lawns and flowering gardens.

When dinner arrived, Kacie ate on a small table by the window, enjoying the view as she savored the hot, delicious food the cook had prepared. Knowing that the servants would still be working to ready the house for the reception that night, she decided to wait until later to see the Bible. Kicking off her shoes, she shed her clothes and changed into a comfortable pair of shorts and the one-of-a-kind T-shirt she'd designed for herself in honor of Eden's Gate. She stretched out on the comfortable canopy bed, meaning to rest for a little while.

Kacie hadn't thought she'd fall asleep, and she wasn't sure exactly what woke her, but she came awake suddenly and sat up in the bed to discover that it was already after ten. Annoyed with herself for having wasted precious time by sleeping, she jumped out of bed, anxious for her first look at the Hampton family Bible.

She checked her appearance in the full-length mirror, then quickly ran a brush through her sleep-tousled blond hair to make herself look presentable just in case she ran into anyone in the hall. Dismissing shoes as unimportant, she hurried barefoot from her room down the dimly lit hallway to Bradford Hampton's bedroom.

Kacie could hear the music and the revelry going on at the reception below, but paid little attention to them. Parties held no interest for her when she was about to get her hands on the book she'd been hoping to read for years now.

Entering the bedroom, Kacie flipped the wall switch, and the period lamps, now wired for electricity, lit up the room with a warm golden glow. She closed the door behind her and paused for a moment to let her gaze sweep the room. The dark furniture was massive and heavy, and spoke of a purely masculine presence. Her gaze fell upon the wide four-poster bed that had belonged to Bradford Hampton, and she felt an unexpected flush of heat rush through her. Wistfully, she wished things had been different, that he hadn't died so violently, that he'd married and had children and lived a long and happy life. His death had been such a waste. Men like Bradford Hampton were hard to come by.

With an effort, Kacie tore her eyes and thoughts away from the room's first occupant. She spied the Bible on the dresser and hurried to see it. Removing the protective glass case, she opened the Bible almost reverently.

Kacie's concentration was fierce as she leafed slowly through the thick, leather-bound book. Reality faded as she became entranced by the family birth and death records in the front. They covered every Hampton for generations, but ended with the entry for Bradford's birth and that of his mother's death a few years later. Kacie stared down at the page with Bradford's name written on it, thinking how odd it was that Jonas Hampton had never entered the date of his son's death, April sixth, in the book. She wondered if Jonas had held out hope that somehow, one day, his son would return to him.

Kacie flipped carefully through more pages and then turned to the back of the Bible, hoping to find something more there. She was disappointed, though, for there were no further references to Bradford anywhere. She was about to close the book when she noticed that there was a carefully made slit in the back binding. Kacie touched the tear as if she hoped to heal it, and was surprised to discover a lump beneath it. Curious to see what it was, she gently slipped her fingers inside and, with utmost caution, drew out a sheet of paper.

Kacie's hands were shaking as she unfolded the brittle paper, and her eyes widened in excitement as she stared down at the map she'd discovered. A chill ran down her spine, and her heart actually skipped a beat as she studied it. There was no mistaking the handwriting. She'd studied Bradford's letters and papers often enough to be able to recognize his powerful male script. Her thoughts were flying. What had she found? It was a map of some sort, and she wondered if this had anything to do with the Underground Railroad. The rumors had said he was involved, but no real proof had ever been found. There were notes written at the bottom of the paper, but they were so faded she could only barely make them out. All she could really decipher on the fragile, yellowed sheet was the name signed at the bottom.

"Brad," Kacie whispered.

Suddenly as she said his name out loud, a terrible light-headedness came over her. Wave after wave of dizziness crashed through Kacie until she thought her knees might buckle. She braced herself against the dresser, one palm on the open Bible, as she fought to regain her equilibrium. It didn't help. Her senses intensified to an almost painful perception. The faint, delicate perfume of the magnolia blossoms just outside the bedroom window became cloying and suffocating. The music from downstairs that had been only a faint melody moments before assumed a throbbing, haunting pitch. The room seemed to whirl and tilt before her.

Half-dazed, Kacie told herself that if she could just sit down, she'd be all right. In desperation, still clutching the map, she stumbled toward the bed. Grasping one of the bedposts for support, she sank down on the mattress, wondering what was wrong with her and hoping the dizziness would quickly pass.

Kacie heard the door open. With great effort, for her head was still spinning, she looked up to see who it was. There, standing in the bedroom doorway, was none other than Bradford Hampton.

2

BRADFORD Hampton? It couldn't be. . . . Kacie blinked, thinking he would disappear. When she opened her eyes and he was still standing there staring at her with an amused yet puzzled look on his face, she blinked again. She opened only one eye this time and found that he hadn't moved. Her less than trustworthy senses were telling her that a tall, broad-shouldered, darkly handsome man who looked exactly like Bradford Hampton was standing right in front of her, a mere six feet away.

Kacie couldn't help herself. She smiled. She knew it couldn't really be Bradford, but whoever he was, he was a gorgeous hunk of a man. If she had to be rescued from her momentary dizziness, it might as well be by a good-looking Prince Charming like this guy. He was certainly dressed for the part of a romantic hero in his fancy suit with its brocade vest that looked like something straight out of *Gone With the Wind*. Kacie hadn't known that the reception tonight was a costume party, but it didn't matter. This man made the clothes; the clothes didn't make him. He could have come to her rescue in grubby jeans and a sweatshirt, and she would have smiled the same ridiculous smile.

"I didn't know it was a costume party tonight, but you know you really shouldn't be in here," Kacie confided, thinking he was a guest who'd wandered away from the reception downstairs.

"Oh?" He sounded surprised. "And why is that?" His voice was deep and mellow, and sent shivers of awareness up her spine.

"Because the second floor is off-limits to party guests," she explained, wondering why he hadn't been told.

"Well, since I'm not a party guest, I guess it's safe for me to be here. What about you? Should you be in here?" As he spoke, Brad took a step forward into his room, closing the door behind him.

"Oh, yes. I have permission," Kacie answered with authority.

"Really?" Brad couldn't quite believe what was happening. There in the middle of his bed sat the most beautiful woman he'd ever seen, and she was practically naked! His gaze was hot as it raked over her. He had no idea who she was, but he intended to find out. "And just who was it who gave you permission to wander around my house dressed . . . or . . . er, should I say undressed like that?"

"Ms. Hoyle did, but—"

"Who?" Brad's tone sharpened, for he knew no one by that name, and he was growing suspicious.

"The director." Kacie's smile faltered, then vanished, and her eyes suddenly narrowed as she realized what the man had said a moment before. "Did you say 'your house'?"

"That's right, my house. I'm Brad Hampton, in case you didn't know, and this is my house and that's my bed you're sitting on."

He sounded so convincing that Kacie couldn't help laughing out loud. "Yeah, right, you're Bradford Hampton and I'm Madonna."

"I'm afraid you bear little or no resemblance to the Madonna," Brad answered tightly, not understanding why she thought his identity was particularly funny.

"Not *the* Madonna," she corrected. "Madonna." At his blank expression, she went on, "Never mind. Look, I have to admit you do look a lot like Bradford Hampton in the portrait downstairs in the study, but whoever you are, don't you think you're taking this whole costume thing just a bit too far?" Good-looking though he was, this guy was beginning to sound pretty weird, and Kacie thought it might be best if she got the heck out of there. She rose to her feet.

"At least, madam, I have my *costume* on," Brad countered, his heated regard sweeping from the thrust of her full breasts against the tight shirt she was wearing to her long, shapely legs and bare feet.

"Yeah, right. Look, I'm feeling better now, so why don't you just go on back to your party. I won't tell anyone you were up here." Realizing she'd left the map lying on the bed, she quickly retrieved it and started to move past him.

"That's very kind of you," he said in a wry tone, "but not so fast. I want to know who you are and what you're doing here." His demand was made in the imperious tone of a man completely confident of his position.

Kacie sighed in exasperation. "Not that it's any of your business," she countered with equal arrogance, "but my name is Kacie Cameron, and I'm here because I was looking for and hoping to find something like this." She indicated the map that, peculiarly, she suddenly noticed wasn't so brittle or fragile anymore. She frowned as she continued, "Now, Brad, why don't you head on back downstairs and tell Ms. Hoyle that I need to see her right away. She's going to be very interested in the information I just found—"

"What the hell!" Brad reacted to the sight of his map in her hands without thinking. Storming forward, he snared Kacie by the upper arm and grabbed the document that could mean life or death to so many.

"What do you think you're doing! Be careful! That's old and it might . . ." Kacie protested frantically, trying to break away from his steely grip. She didn't know who this guy was, but it seemed to her his elevator didn't go all the way up.

"I want answers and I want them now!" Brad snarled, glaring down at her. "Who are you working for? How much do they know?"

"The only thing I know for sure is that you're crazy. Let me go!"

Using a trick she'd learned at a police-held self-defense training class, Kacie stomped hard on his booted foot while violently jerking her arm. He gave a yelp of pain and loosened his grip on her just enough so she could break loose and make her escape. She darted for the door.

Brad stood there, his foot aching, unable to believe what was happening. Whoever this woman was, she was a wildcat! He started after her, but stopped cold in his tracks when he saw the writing on the back of her shirt. He could only stare at her back as she threw open the door and charged out into the hall. Befuddled, he paused where he was, trying to understand: *"The heavenly South will rise again . . . Happy 160th birthday, Eden's Gate, 1832–1992."*

Kacie ran out into the hallway. The sounds of music and laughter swelled around her, reminding her of the celebration going on below. She didn't want to go down the front steps and risk ruining the party, for the society earned a lot of money from such festivities, so she raced down the hall in the direction of the back staircase.

Kacie didn't feel she was in any real danger. She figured Doris was somewhere nearby and all she had to do was find her and let her know what a weirdo the Bradford Hampton impostor was. When Kacie heard Brad emerge from the room behind her, she quickened her pace. Rushing on, she turned the corner at the end of the hall, thinking she was almost home free. To her great and utter dismay, she came face to face with an elderly gentleman on his way up the stairs. He was obviously a part of the reception, too, for he was dressed in a period costume much like Brad's.

"Excuse me, sir." Kacie decided to brazen it out. She started down the steps, trying to move around him, but to her surprise the man didn't budge. He just stood there, blocking her way, staring at her with an openly shocked expression.

"My dear young woman, where are your clothes?" the silver-haired man asked as he stared at her legs.

"I'm wearing my clothes," Kacie snapped, more than a little irritated. The way this old geezer was gawking at her, she could almost believe he'd never seen a girl in shorts and a top before. "Now, if you'll excuse me . . ."

"I can't let you go downstairs looking like that, my dear," he told her, refusing to get out of her way.

"Excuse me?" she countered, her hands on

her hips, her eyes flashing at his condescending tone. "What do you mean *you* can't let me go downstairs?"

"It wouldn't be proper," he explained. Then, at the sound of footsteps in the hall, he looked up and smiled. "Ah, Brad, my boy, would you mind telling me just what's going on here?"

"Father . . ." Brad was relieved to see him. He'd paused in his bedroom only long enough to fold the map and put it in his jacket pocket before coming after Kacie and he'd feared she might have eluded him. "I'm glad you caught her."

"Caught her?" Jonas glanced from his son's very serious expression to the defiant, nearly naked young woman standing before him. "What are you talking about? Who are you, young lady?"

"I'm Kacie Cameron, a paying guest here, and I demand to see the director at once!"

"A paying guest?" Jonas looked up at his son and frowned. "Bradford, what is the meaning of all this?"

"We'd better talk about it in my room. Bring her back upstairs."

Though her path was blocked going down, Kacie knew she still had a chance to get past Brad. Deciding to play submissive for a minute in the hope that the men would let their guards down, she turned quietly and made her way back to the second-floor hall. She knew a moment of success when Brad didn't take hold of her again, and she walked past him with great dignity, her head held high.

Brad stayed right with Kacie as she moved coolly down the hallway. Hellion though she was, his curiosity was piqued. He knew he wouldn't rest until he found out who she was and what she'd been doing in his room. If her intent had been to find the map, and she'd obviously done that, then why had she stayed and risked being found? And why had she been sitting on his bed so scantily clad? Had she stayed with the intention of seducing him in the hope of getting even more information? The idea seemed farfetched considering there was a house full of people below, and it was doubtful that he would have returned to his room any time soon that night. Brad scowled. He didn't know what her story was, but he certainly meant to find out, especially since she'd nearly crippled him. His foot was still sore, and he was glad she hadn't been wearing shoes. If she had, the damage undoubtedly would have been much worse.

Brad cast Kacie a sidelong glance and noticed how grim her expression was. He wondered if she was cold since she was wearing so little, and thought it might be a good idea to offer her a blanket once they were in the room. He knew it might prove difficult for him to have a serious conversation with her looking as she did now. She certainly was a lovely woman, though. It was too bad she was so treacherous.

Kacie was ready. They were going to walk right past the door to the master bedroom suite on their way to Brad's room. With any luck at all, she could run in there and make it out onto the balcony where she could yell for help. Surely one of the men the Society usually hired to park cars at the parties would hear her cry and come to her aid. With fierce determination, she didn't let any emotion show on her face as they neared the doorway. Then, in a flash, she bolted through the open door. She slammed it shut behind her and ran full speed toward the balcony doors.

"Damn it!" Brad rarely swore, but this mystery woman was driving him to distraction. He fumbled with the doorknob, then finally sent the door crashing open. Leaving his father to follow, Brad gave chase.

Kacie was certain she was going to get away. She ran for the French doors, threw them wide, and darted outside. But her cry for help died on her lips as she stopped dead and stared at the view from the balcony. There was no paved driveway below, parked bumper-to-bumper with cars. Instead, there was a shell-lined drive full of horse-drawn carriages!

Kacie stared about her in bewilderment. Carriages? Horses? What was happening here? She heard the men coming after her and started to run along the balcony, hoping to reach the back bedroom where her things were.

Since she knew the house by heart, Kacie found the room without any trouble. As she burst through the French doors of her bedroom, she discovered that it was completely different from when she'd left it less than a half-hour before. The furniture was gone, and only a settee and a few tables remained. There was no trace of her luggage or clothing. The room was devoid of any trace of her presence.

"What ... But where ... ?" Kacie stared around her in complete and utter confusion.

"I don't know what kind of game you're playing, young lady," Brad declared as he caught up with her, "but I mean to find out right now." Taking her by the shoulders, he swung her around to face him.

After the chase she'd led him on, Brad was surprised when she offered no resistance. He gazed down at her in the low light and was startled by the look of abject panic on her pale, strained features.

"Who are you?" Kacie whispered hoarsely, still unable to believe the unbelievable.

"I told you who I am. I'm Bradford Hampton, and I want some answers from you. Who sent you?"

"Nobody sent me. I came down here because the director notified me that the Bible had been found—"

"Found?"

"We'd been looking for it and ..."

"You'd been looking for our family Bible?" Jonas spoke up as he joined them. "Why?"

"Because it had been missing since before the turn of the century, and we were hoping it would give us some more information about Bradford's activities."

"And just what did you hope to learn about

my activities?" Brad demanded tightly.

"You . . . no . . . not you . . . Bradford Hampton. The real Bradford Hampton . . ."

"I assure you, miss, this *is* the real Bradford Hampton," Jonas said carefully, wondering what kind of terrible delusions this woman was suffering from. For all that she was a pretty young thing, her state of undress and obvious mental confusion convinced him that she was not right in the head. He didn't know who she was or where she'd come from, but they had to do something with her and fast. They had a house full of guests! "Perhaps Miss Cameron needs to see a doctor? Perhaps some medication to calm her down would help?"

"Look," she bit out sarcastically, wondering about these two loonies, "I don't need any calming down. When I find my overnight case, I'll take a couple of aspirins for the headache you're giving me. Right now, all I want to do is locate Doris Hoyle. She told me she'd be here all night. I'm sure she can straighten everything out to your satisfaction."

Brad exchanged a worried look with his father. "Miss Cameron, why don't we go back to my room? It'll be more comfortable there, and we can talk."

"Look, buddy, we can talk just fine right here. All I want to know is what's going on around here? Where is everybody? What happened to all the cars?"

"Cars?" Brad and his father looked perplexed.

"Yes, cars, and where are all my things? Who

hid them? If you think this is some kind of joke, I'm not laughing."

"No one hid your things, miss." Jonas tried to sound conciliatory, for the woman was obviously deeply disturbed.

"Of course they did," she argued. "When I left this room less than half an hour ago, all my clothes and—"

"Miss Cameron, you couldn't have left this room a half-hour ago. This is my mother's sitting room. Since she died eight years ago, no one comes in here."

A wave of dizziness threatened Kacie again, and she was almost glad for Brad's strong hands holding her. "What are you talking about?" she asked, feeling more and more lightheaded.

"I'm talking about your delusions . . . or your lies, whichever they are. I've never seen you before in my life, and yet I find you in my room, nearly naked, stealing some of my personal papers."

"Stealing? I had permission! Besides, I wasn't going to keep it. I just wanted to study it," she protested weakly.

"I'm sure you did. Who's paying you?"

"Paying me? What *are* you talking about?"

"I think it's time you stopped answering my questions with questions of your own. This *is* 1860, and even though you are a woman, you were caught stealing—"

"What did you say?" Kacie stared at him, her eyes widening with a crazy mixture of emotions.

Suddenly the horses and carriages outside, the men's period clothing, and the changes in the furnishings swirled maddeningly, tauntingly, through Kacie's consciousness. Everything sharpened to a crystal clarity, and she knew! Her head began to pound as she forced herself to ask again, "What year did you say this was?"

"It's 1860."

The dizziness intensified. There was a loud ringing in her ears, and her legs suddenly seemed incapable of supporting her. As a blessed peace claimed her, Kacie murmured the words she'd said so many times before in jest.

"What?" Brad asked in surprise as she mumbled something. He was even more shocked when, without warning, she collapsed into his arms. "She fainted," he told his father incredulously.

"What did she say?" Jonas asked, thinking there might be a clue in her words.

Brad looked bewildered as he answered. "It didn't make any sense. She said, 'Beam me up, Scotty.' "

3

"BEAM me up, Scotty?" Jonas repeated. "Who's Scotty?"

"I have no idea, but I think you'd better find Warren and send him up to my bedroom," Brad told his father as, carrying Kacie, he started out onto the balcony on his way back to his own room.

Jonas hurried from the sitting room to seek out Dr. Warren Coleman, their longtime family friend and physician. Jonas knew Warren could be counted on to handle the situation with discretion and a minimum of questions.

When Brad reached his bedroom, he gently lay Kacie on his bed, then quickly drew a blanket over her. He remained standing there, studying her perfect features and wondering at her part in all this. She'd mentioned only two people— a woman named Doris Hoyle, whom she called the director, and someone named Scotty. He'd never heard either of those names before and that worried him. He thought he knew all the people involved in trying to destroy the Underground Railroad, but obviously he didn't.

As Brad considered his options in dealing with Kacie, he thought again of the writing on her shirt. He'd never known anyone to wear clothes with writing on them, except for the poorer folks who made their garments out of flour sacks and the like. The writing on her shirt had definitely not been labeling from a flour sack, though. *"The heavenly South will rise again."* What did that mean? And the reference to 1992. That was over a hundred and thirty years in the future. He thought of her reaction when they'd told her what year it was, and he frowned.

There was a soft knock at the door, and Brad opened it to find Dr. Coleman standing there.

"Brad? Your father said you needed me." Warren Coleman was a gray-haired, kindly-looking old man, whose knowledge of medicine and life went unchallenged. He glanced from the tall, handsome young man he'd delivered thirty-two years ago to the young woman who lay unconscious on the bed.

"Please, come in." Brad held the door as the doctor strode toward the bed.

"What happened?" he asked as he gazed down at the beauty.

"She fainted."

Warren's eyes met Brad's, and when he saw his closed, guarded expression, he knew better than to ask anything more. He threw back the blanket and was startled by the clothing she had on. He conducted his examination without comment as Brad looked on from across the room. When he'd finished, he covered Kacie again and turned to Brad.

"There's nothing wrong with her as far as I can see."

Just as he spoke, Kacie gave a low moan and began to stir. "My head . . ." Feeling completely exhausted, her head throbbing, Kacie opened her eyes to find a strange man hovering over her. "Who are you?"

"I'm Dr. Coleman. It seems you fainted."

"I guess I did." Kacie managed a weak smile, thinking everything that had happened had been a bad dream. "I'm sorry if I caused any trouble."

"No trouble, my dear. It's always a pleasure to come to the aid of a beautiful young woman."

"Is Doris here? I'd like to talk to her, and I really ought to get back to my own room. . . ."

"Doris? No, there's no Doris here, but Brad is," he answered, motioning for Brad to come forward.

Kacie's eyes grew round as Brad stepped into her line of vision. "I don't believe this! I wasn't dreaming . . . You really are here. . . ."

"Of course," the doctor soothed. "He's been here the whole time. He's been very concerned about you."

"I'm sure he has. Listen, Doc, I have to get out of here. . . ."

She started to sit up, but Dr. Coleman would have none of it. He pressed her back down on the bed.

"I'm afraid you're not going anywhere, young lady. You're very weak, and until we know exactly what caused that fainting spell, the best thing for you is to stay in bed."

"You don't understand. I don't have time for any bed rest. I have to figure out what's going on here."

Warren looked to Brad in confusion.

"She's been very upset, even to the point of being a little irrational. You see how she's dressed. She was wandering the halls that way," Brad explained.

"Perhaps a dose of laudanum would help?"

"No . . ." Kacie tried to put in her two cents' worth, but the men ignored her as if she didn't even exist.

"Please," Brad agreed. "Maybe if she gets some rest, she'll be more her old self."

The doctor said no more as he prepared a dose of the potent medicine.

"If you think I'm going to take any medicine, you've got another think coming!" Kacie declared with open hostility.

"It's for your own good," Brad told her, moving to sit on the bed beside her.

When Kacie would have bolted, Brad caught her and pinned her against his chest. Squirm though she might, he held her easily with one arm. Gripping her chin with his free hand, Brad kept her still so the doctor could give her the medicine.

"Doctor, you've got to listen to me!" Kacie tried to fight Brad, but he was too strong. To her fury, she was forced to choke down the hated laudanum.

"Now, now, my dear. I trust Brad knows what's best. Just rest for tonight, and I'm sure by tomorrow morning you'll feel much better."

"You don't understand," she continued to argue as Brad released her. "There's nothing wrong with me."

The physician gave Brad a sympathetic look, and Brad stood up to speak with him before he left the room.

"She must have hit her head. I'll keep a close watch on her tonight."

"Good idea, my boy. You can't be too careful with this kind of thing." Though Dr. Coleman was curious to know who she was and what she was doing in Brad's bed, he did not ask. "She'll sleep for a little while with that dose, but I can't say for how long."

"Thanks."

Knowing there was nothing more he could do, the physician quietly left the room. Brad turned back to where Kacie was sitting up, trying to get out of bed.

"What do you want from me?" Kacie asked slowly, amazed that a peaceful languor was stealing over her already. She wanted to leave, and she wasn't afraid to fight this man who was calling himself Brad, but for some reason she just couldn't get up the energy to keep moving.

"The only thing I want from you is answers, and I'm not letting you go until I get them," Brad answered as he stopped before her. "Now tell me, who sent you and how much do they know?"

"Sent me? Don't you get it? I wasn't *sent* here, not the way you mean."

Brad stared at her, perplexed. "And just what is it you think I mean?"

"You think I'm here to steal your map or something, but I'm not. I don't even know why I'm here . . . I don't even know how I got here, but I'm here. . . ."

She gave a faint chuckle as she gazed up at him. This Brad Hampton was one very attractive man with his dark hair, dark eyes, and firm jaw. His shoulders were broad; his waist was trim. He was absolutely, positively gorgeous—as gorgeous as the portrait downstairs. At the thought of the man in the portrait, Kacie sighed. She'd been in love with the Brad in the painting for years, and though the man standing before her was just a wild fantasy her poor little brain was cooking up, for now she was going to pretend he was real and just enjoy it.

"You don't really exist, you know," Kacie murmured, feeling quite lethargic as the medicine took stronger hold of her senses. She lay back on the bed, suddenly too tired to keep struggling. Comfortable against the pillows, she added more to herself than to him, "I can't believe I'm talking to a dead man. You're a ghost. . . ."

Brad stiffened, thinking her words were a threat from whoever had hired her to spy on him. "I assure you, Miss Cameron, I'm very much alive, and I intend to do everything in my power to stay this way."

"Nope. You're not alive. It's 1993, and you've been dead for over a hundred and thirty-two years. You died in the spring of 1860," Kacie told him sorrowfully. She drifted farther and farther down into forgetfulness, murmuring, "I just wish I coulda stopped it. . . ."

"What!" Brad was honestly beginning to believe she was insane.

"I'm just dreaming, is all." She gave another soft laugh. "As crazy as it is, I have to admit that this is probably the best dream I've ever had. I've wanted to talk to you forever. You're just so handsome." She sighed again as she felt herself falling asleep. "If you were real, I'd be the envy of everyone at home. . . ."

Brad didn't know what to do or say. Stunned, he stood staring down at a sleeping Kacie. His mind raced. She thought she was from the future—from the year 1993? She had to be crazy! But even as he almost believed that, he couldn't help wondering how she'd come to be in his house and in his bed.

Brad reviewed in his mind everything she'd said. She'd talked about wanting to learn more about his activities, about wanting to study his map—the map that revealed the stations on the Underground Railroad. No one else even knew he had the map, yet this woman had made her way into his home, had gone straight into his bedroom, and had located the hidden map without anyone catching her. That was virtually impossible. There were servants everywhere, and yet not one had seen her enter. She'd told him, too, that he was going to die this spring. The thought sent a chill of caution through him, but he shook it off, dismissing it as totally ridiculous.

Needing time to think, not to mention a stiff shot of bourbon, Brad rang for a maid. When she arrived, he instructed her to stay in the room with Kacie and not to leave under any circumstances. He saw the curious look on her face, but offered no explanations. With one last glance at his mysterious sleeping beauty, Brad left the room.

Brad rejoined the party and danced with several of the single young ladies in attendance. Pretty though they were, Brad found his thoughts never strayed from the beautiful young woman upstairs in his bed. Again and again he asked himself who Kacie could be and why she was here. He found himself paying particular attention to all the guests at the party, thinking the people she'd mentioned might be there, but he found he knew everyone in attendance. There was nothing amiss.

An hour later, after having made the rounds of the ballroom, Brad couldn't stay away from Kacie any longer. Haunted by the mystery of her appearance, he returned to his bedroom and, after dismissing the maid, settled in a chair near the bed to keep watch.

The candlelight bathed the room in a soft glow. The slumbering Kacie looked even lovelier in the gentle light, and Brad found himself fascinated by her. Question after question besieged him as he remained by her side. Who was she? How had she come to be there and why? What did she want from him? There were no answers to his questions, though, and so Brad remained by her bedside through the long, dark hours of the night, waiting and watching and wondering.

Jonas stood in his study with a small group of men from the neighboring plantations.

"I tell you, Jonas, this is not just a case of a few runaways! I've lost three slaves in the last two months!" complained Daniel Lawrence, a big, dark-haired, mean-looking man, as he tossed down a straight shot of Jonas' best bourbon. "This is an organized effort! It's probably one of those damned agitating emancipators from the North down here stirring up trouble!"

"How can you be so sure?" Jonas asked. "We haven't had a problem here at Eden's Gate."

"I'm sure because the runaways couldn't have disappeared so completely without help. Used to be that the hounds could track them down in a day or two. Now it's almost as if they've disappeared off the face of the earth."

"Daniel's right," Frank Riley, another neighbor, agreed. "I've lost two myself. Whoever's running this operation knows what he's doing."

"What do you plan to do?" Jonas asked, not greatly surprised to hear that their slaves were fleeing. For years, he'd known and disliked these men. They were the kind who took pride in being brutal to their slaves.

"We've got a few leads, but nothing substantial yet," Daniel answered. "When we find out what's going on and who's behind it, we're going to take matters into our own hands."

"Is there anything Brad or I can do to help?" Jonas offered.

"We'll let you know."

It was after two in the morning when the last guest had departed. Jonas' thoughts were troubled as he made his way upstairs to retire. He knocked quietly at Brad's bedroom door and was pleased when his son quickly came out into the hall.

"How is she? Warren told me he gave her some laudanum to quiet her."

"She's still sleeping. I'm going to sit up all night with her, just in case she wakes up."

"You'll be all right?"

"I'll be fine."

Jonas nodded, then told him about the conversation he'd had earlier in the study. "Daniel and Frank were angry tonight. It seems they've had quite a few runaways lately. They seem to think there are outsiders at work here, helping them escape. They said when they find out who's behind it all, they're going to put an end to it in their own way."

Brad smiled thinly. "I'm sure they'll try if they get the chance."

"Brad, you know I've never tried to interfere or stop you from doing what you believed was right, but I know how vicious those men can be. This isn't a game. They're deadly serious. Are you sure you want to continue?"

"I'm positive," Brad answered firmly. He was convinced slavery was wrong, and he was willing to put himself at risk to do what he could to stop it.

"Then be careful, my son," Jonas warned him, their eyes meeting in understanding.

"I know," he agreed grimly, the memory of Kacie's reference to his death hovering around the edges of his mind. "It's hard to say how much they know, but there's too much at stake not to take them seriously. And then there is the girl."

"Did she say anything else?"

"Only that she thinks the year is 1993."

"She *what*?" Jonas had never heard anything so outrageous in his life.

"She thinks she's from the future. Of course, she'd already taken the laudanum when she said it, so she was probably just hallucinating."

"Yes, it must have been the medicine talking."

"I'm sure it was," Brad agreed.

"What do you intend to do with her?"

"I'm going to keep her here until I find out who she is."

Jonas agreed with his decision. They had to take every precaution. "If the occasion should arise where someone asks, we'll tell them she's one of your mother's relatives visiting from up North."

"I almost wish she were," he said, hating the thought that she might be a spy and dismissing as ridiculous the idea that she might be who she said she was.

Somewhat reassured that his son would take care, Jonas said good night and went to his room.

Brad returned to his bedside vigil to find Kacie still sleeping soundly. He thought that asleep she appeared the picture of innocence. From the tumbled mass of her golden curls to her faintly flushed cheeks and delicate, perfect complexion, she was a beauty beyond compare. But it wasn't only her loveliness that drew him to her. There was something else about her, something he couldn't quite put a name to. He wanted her to be as innocent as she looked. He wanted to delve into her reasons for being here and find a pure motive. He wanted to believe that if she had been sent here to spy on him, it was because someone was using her to get to him. He wanted to . . .

Unable to stop himself, Brad reached out and gently touched her cheek. His caress was light against her silken flesh, and he was shocked by the feelings that shot through him with just that simple touch. He withdrew his hand as if he'd been burned.

"Brad . . ." Kacie whispered his name in her sleep.

It was a soft, sweet murmur, as gentle as a summer breeze, and a heat of sensual awareness shot through him. He wanted to take her in his arms and hold her close. He wanted to . . .

Brad backed away from the bed. Exerting his iron-willed self-control, he sat back down in the chair. As the minutes, then the hours passed, Brad kept watch and wondered what he was going to do with her in the morning.

"Well, Daniel, what do you think? Is Brad involved?"

Daniel looked thoughtful as he contemplated the question that had been nagging him for days now. He and Frank were sitting together in the privacy of his library, having just returned from the party at Eden's Gate. The servants had all retired for the night, so they knew they could talk freely.

"I'm still not sure."

"But the slave we caught was screaming 'I'll never reach the Promised Land . . . I'll never see Eden' right before he died."

"Too bad he died. We might have been able to get a real answer out of him if he'd hung on a little longer. I had to make an example out of him for the others, though. I've already lost three slaves; I'm not going to lose any more. If scaring them that way works, I'll do it." Daniel felt no remorse at having whipped the runaway to death.

"Do you think he was praying when he was talking about Eden or do you think he was talking about some connection with the Underground Railroad? He kept saying if he could get to Eden, the Lord would save him. I can't help thinking he meant Eden's Gate."

"I wish I could be certain, but I'm not... yet. We both know there's been talk about Brad Hampton's views on things, and his mother was from up North, even though she's been dead all these years. Still..."

"What do you want to do?"

"Give it a little more time. We've got to be sure before we do anything, and I've got a plan that just might work...."

KACIE came awake, but didn't open her eyes. She lay perfectly still, trying to remember all the details of the wild dream she'd had. In her fantasy, Bradford Hampton had been alive and well. A smile crept over her face as sleep-drugged recollections of her conversation with Bradford came to her. In her heart, Kacie almost wished it had been real, but in her mind she knew it was impossible. It had been just a dream.

Stretching lazily, she finally faced the fact that she should get up. She opened her eyes and, with a jolt, realized it was still night and that she was in a strange bed. Kacie turned quickly, intending to hurl herself from the bed, and it was then that she saw Brad, standing at the open French doors with his back to her, gazing out into the darkness of the night.

Stopping in mid-motion, Kacie muttered, "Oh, boy." It really had happened. She really was with Brad in 1860. But how? And why? The questions tormented her, but she had no answers.

Brad heard her moving and turned. For the last several hours as he'd waited for her to awaken, he'd been debating how to treat her. Finally, he'd decided to be cautious until he'd figured out why she was in his house and what she was planning to do. But in spite of all his good intentions, as he looked at her now and saw how beautiful she was, he found himself smiling at her. Her golden hair was loose and tumbling about her shoulders in a mass of untamed curls. Her eyes were still heavy-lidded and her cheeks were sleep-flushed. She looked sensual, completely and utterly desirable, and Brad cursed his body's strong reaction to her.

He had known many beautiful women in his life, but none of them had ever had such a powerful effect on him. With an effort, he gave himself a fierce mental shake. He reminded himself to concentrate on the reason she was there, not on how beautiful she was.

"Good morning," Brad greeted her, his smile never fading.

"Is it?"

"It's dark now, but it's after five already. The

sun should be up in just a few minutes," he explained.

"Have you been in here all night?" Kacie didn't know why the thought of Brad watching her while she slept made her feel shy, but it did.

He nodded. "I was worried about you and thought it would be best if I stayed with you. How do you feel this morning?"

"I'm fine." She rose and moved to stand by him at the window, looking out across the gardens to fertile fields beyond where the field hands were already hard at work. If she'd harbored any doubts about what year it was, they disappeared as she stared out at the activities going on outside. She was back in 1860; 1993 had vanished.

Faced with the undeniable but wild truth, Kacie tried to figure out how to deal with it. Girding herself, she decided to handle it as she did everything in her life—head-on.

It was obvious that Brad still had doubts about her, and rightly so. So the first thing she knew she had to do was convince him that she was no threat and that he could trust her. Kacie knew it wouldn't be easy, but she was determined.

"Brad? Are you really involved with the Underground Railroad?" she asked boldly, without preamble.

He was shocked. "What?"

"In the research I was doing, there were rumors that you had been, but no one has ever been able to prove it."

"Perhaps they couldn't prove it because it wasn't true," he answered evasively.

"Then why was that map hidden in the Bible, and why was it so important to you? It looked to me like a record of the stations. If you aren't involved, why did you have it? And was your grotto really where messages were relayed?"

"Where did you hear all this?" Brad demanded. There were only three people who knew that the grotto was the message drop. If she was a spy as he suspected, why was she telling him what she knew? And if she wasn't a spy . . . "What do you want? Why are you here?"

His hands on her shoulders, he turned her to face him. Beneath his hands he could feel how terribly fragile she was, and he reminded himself that she was just a flesh-and-blood woman. His dark eyes searched her expression for some clue to her motivation, but he saw no guile there, no deceit.

Kacie met his gaze without fear. "I don't know why I'm here, but I am," she answered softly, very aware of the heat of his hands on her and of his big body so near hers. She felt the urge to reach up and press her lips to his. Her heart told her that this was Brad, the man she'd dreamed of; the man she'd been waiting for all of her life; the man she loved. She wanted to cast aside her fears and doubts and live for the moment, but the knowledge that Brad had died in 1860 was still with her.

At the thought of this vital, handsome man dying, Kacie made her decision. She didn't know how much time she had, but she was going to save him, to somehow find a way to keep him from boarding that ill-fated steamboat. "Brad? What did you say the date was?"

"It's 1860," he replied, feeling an unbidden desire to draw her to him and hold her close. He dropped his hands away from her shoulders as he focused his thoughts on how she'd come to be there in the first place.

"I know, but what day?"

"March third." ·

"Good."

"Oh? Why?"

"I was just wondering, that's all." Relief swept through her. There was still time. The explosion wasn't going to happen for over another month. She had until April sixth to convince him of her sincerity.

The eastern sky was brightening now as pale pink-and-gold streaks etched their way across the canopy of darkness. Kacie stared at the dawn of the new day, her first day with Brad, and offered up a silent prayer that somehow she would succeed in helping him.

Wanting to act as normal as possible by his standards and not hers, she asked, "Are there any clothes around that I might borrow while I'm here with you? I know you find my things a little strange, and I don't want to embarrass you by wearing them."

"I'll have one of the servants check," he answered, surprised by her request.

"I was wondering, too, since I am dressed like this, if breakfast could be brought up here to the room?"

"Of course. Would you like to freshen up first?"

"Sounds wonderful."

"Feel free to use the water closet." He gestured her toward the small room. Eden's Gate was one of the most modern homes on the river, boasting inside facilities and running water from a storage tank on the roof.

"Thanks."

Kacie tended to her personal needs, while Brad rang for a servant and gave her his instructions. That done, he waited for Kacie to rejoin him, his thoughts centered on what she'd said the night before as she'd fallen asleep. He knew he had to solve the mystery of her unexplained appearance in his life.

When Kacie emerged from the bathroom a short time later, she found that they were alone. Brad was waiting for her, a pensive look on his face. Plates of biscuits, hot eggs, and grits were already on the small table that had been brought into the bedroom for them to use. It was set for two, and at the center of the table was a bud vase with a single, exquisite blossom in it. Enchanted, she bent to the flower and cupped the fragrant, delicate bloom in her hands.

"This blossom is lovely," she told him.

"It's from my mother's garden. Flowers were her passion," he explained as he drew out her chair for her.

Kacie sat down, giving him a smile of thanks for his courtesy, and then met his dark-eyed regard squarely as he took the seat opposite her. "And gaining freedom for everyone is yours."

His expression sharpened at her reference to his secret activities. "And what about you, Kacie? What do you care about?"

Her heart lurched at the intensity of his gaze. She hadn't meant to let their conversation get so serious so fast, but she had no idea how much time she would actually have with him. She had to do what she could while she had the opportunity. Unable to stop herself, she reached across the table to touch his hand. "You, Brad. I care about you."

The touch of her hand was electrifying, and he was stunned by the power of his reaction to that single, simple gesture. "Why, Kacie? You don't even know me."

"I know you, Brad. I know you're a fair and honest man. You're the kind of man who believes in righting injustice wherever it exists. You're a visionary."

Her fervor in singing his praises amazed him. "Who are you?"

"I'm your friend, Brad. I know you're finding this all a little difficult to believe, because I am, too. But I believe I'm here to help you. I'm here to keep you safe."

He gave a short laugh as he turned her hand over so it was resting palm up in his hand. He gently touched her palm, marveling at its softness. "You're going to keep me safe?" he repeated incredulously, remembering how delicate she'd felt when he'd taken her by the shoulders earlier. "It's a man's job to protect a woman, not the other way around."

Kacie's breath caught in her throat at his sensual ploy. "Sometimes it can work both ways," she countered, finding his chauvinism endearing.

She fell silent as their gazes met and locked. It seemed as if he were judging her, searching for truth in her eyes. After a long moment, she forced herself to pull her hand away from his mesmerizing hold.

"Shall we eat?" Brad finally said.

Kacie was glad to be distracted and she helped herself to the assortment of hot, delicious food set before them. They ate in relative silence. When she finished the last bite of the fluffy, flaky biscuit she'd spread thickly with golden butter, she could no longer restrain herself from asking, "What do you intend to do with me?"

It was a question that Brad had been asking himself. He was troubled. She was a stranger to him, yet he found that he almost instinctively believed and trusted in her. That bothered him, for trusting someone he didn't know could very well prove disastrous. "You may have free run of the plantation. Just don't try to leave."

"You don't have to worry. I have no intention of leaving. I'm going to stay right here so I can . . ." She almost slipped and told him about the explosion, but quickly decided this was not the time.

"So you can what?" Brad was surprised by her answer, but before he could get any more out of her, there was a knock at the door. "Come in."

A maid entered the room, followed by a male servant carrying a big trunk. "This was in the attic, Mr. Brad. It has some of your mother's things in it."

"Thanks, Clara." Brad directed the servant to leave the trunk by the bed. Frustrated because he couldn't continue their conversation in front of Clara, he got up from the table to open the trunk once the male servant had gone.

"We packed away some of my mother's things. There might be something here you can wear."

"You're offering me your mother's clothes?" Kacie was breathless and wide-eyed with wonder. She'd been a student of fashion all her life, and she was thrilled to think that she was going to get a chance to wear clothing that up until now she'd seen only in pictures or museums.

"Clara will help you with whatever you need." Brad started from the room, but Kacie's call stopped him.

"Brad?"

"Yes?" He glanced back to where she stood looking so wonderfully provocative in her short pants and tight shirt. He wondered distractedly why he'd had the clothes brought down to her. Honor, he reminded himself. Honor. Still, her legs were incredible and . . .

"Thank you."

"You're welcome."

With that, Brad was gone, and Kacie was left to do something that she'd only dreamed of until now. She was going to try on antique clothes. Of course, they weren't antiques now, but one day they would be.

Kacie almost laughed with delight as she delved into the trunk. She felt like a child at play, and thought that maybe she really was in paradise.

It took some time and effort, but with Clara's help Kacie managed to don the correct undergarments, a suitable day gown, and a few accessories. The dress she chose was a high-necked, long-sleeved creation that fit her perfectly. Kacie had had her doubts about wearing the clothes at first, for she'd imagined that most Southern ladies were built like Scarlett O'Hara, but it turned out that she and Andrea Hampton, Brad's mother, were about the same size. Kacie had felt comfortable and free in her modern clothes, but in this hoop-skirted garment, she felt positively, magnificently feminine. The skirts swirled about her as she walked and she loved the feel of them.

Twirling before the full-length mirror in the room, Kacie smiled at her reflection. The deep-turquoise dress looked as if it had been made just for her. Clara found a brush in the trunk and untangled Kacie's hair, then styled it up, away from her face. The style brought emphasis to her eyes and to the graceful line of her neck. Kacie was impressed, for she looked every bit the polished Southern belle. She found herself hoping that Brad would think her pretty.

After Clara had gone, Kacie took one last look in the mirror and, satisfied that Brad would find no flaw in her appearance, she went eagerly in search of him. As she descended the staircase, she heard the faint murmur of men's voices coming from the study, and knocked lightly on the door.

"May I join you?" Kacie asked as she opened the door and entered the room at Jonas' invitation.

Brad had been seated opposite his father at the desk, but at the sound of Kacie's voice they both rose. Brad's eyes widened in pleasant surprise at the sight of her in appropriate clothing. He would have thought it impossible, but the full-skirted turquoise gown had transformed her into an even greater beauty. He couldn't stop himself from crossing the room to her.

"You look wonderful," he said, his dark eyes aglow with open male approval.

"Thank you." Kacie smiled up at him. Glancing at Jonas, she said, "Good morning, Mr. Hampton."

"Good morning, Miss Cameron, and please call me Jonas."

"I'm Kacie."

Lovely though she was, both men remained suspicious. She knew far too much about Brad's activities for them to let their guards down.

"I have a few things I have to do around Eden's Gate today. So I'll be gone for quite a while," Brad told her, intending to leave her safely in the house with his father.

"May I go with you? I'd love to tour the grounds and see how the plantation works," she said. She wanted to spend as much time with him as possible.

Having her with him would make it easier for him to keep track of her, so Brad readily agreed. "Fine. Father, we'll be back in time for dinner."

Brad led Kacie from the house, carrying a luncheon basket the cook had prepared, and as they entered his carriage he placed the basket in the back. They drove down the shell-lined path that wound its way through the lush gardens. It was a warm, perfect day. The sun was shining, and the air was perfumed with the scent of flowers and blossoming trees.

Kacie was very much aware of Brad beside her, and she found herself thinking of Adam and Eve and wondering if their Eden had been so perfect. The garden the Historical Society had re-created in the future was lovely, but it was far from the real thing. Kacie caught sight of the bush that had borne the blossom that had been on their breakfast table, and she asked Brad to stop so that she could admire it. They stepped down from the carriage, and Brad watched her, entranced.

"This one belongs here," she told him, cradling one of the treasured blossoms in her hand.

"Why's that?" Brad asked, thinking that she, not the flower, belonged there in the garden surrounded by nature's splendor, for she was far more beautiful than any blossom.

"Because it's glorious. Your home was aptly named, you know. I can think of nowhere on Earth more perfect . . . more of a paradise." At the mention of paradise, Kacie thought of her boutiques and of the business that had been her whole life. Sadness filled her as she realized that it all might be lost to her forever, that she might never see her family and friends again. But then she looked at Brad and her unhappiness vanished. She had no answer as to why she was there, but she made up her mind from that moment onward to take each day as a gift and not question the destiny that had brought her here, to him.

"My mother chose the name Eden's Gate," he was saying.

"I know. She named it after her family's home in Virginia."

Again she startled him with her knowledge, and caution tempered the feeling of enchantment that had held him. "You seem to know so much about me, while I know very little about you."

"What do you want to know?"

"Everything." His reply escaped him before he even realized he'd said it.

"I'm thirty years old."

His eyebrows rose at her revelation. He would never have guessed her to be that old. "You're an old maid," he said with a chuckle.

"I'm single because I choose to be," Kacie countered with a defiant lift of her chin. Still, even as she defended herself, she remembered how she'd felt as all of her friends had married and started families and she'd remained alone. "Besides, thirty isn't old. You're thirty-two."

"But I'm a man."

"So? Maturity is what counts, not age," she told him with dignity.

"If you say so." Brad was grinning and his eyes were sparkling as he urged her to continue, "Please, go on. I really am interested."

Kacie couldn't help smiling at him. She hadn't known of his sense of humor, and it pleased her. "I live by myself in Chicago, and I drive only American-made cars."

"Drive? You mean carriages?"

Kacie was still smiling as they got back into the carriage and started off down the path once more. "Sort of. I own a Mustang GT. It's red and very fast." Kacie imagined Brad driving her car, his big, strong hands sure and steady on the steering wheel, and knew he'd look wonderful in it.

"So you ride a Western roan?"

"You could say that," she answered wryly, knowing it would be fun to talk to him about cars and their names. She wondered what he'd think about Vipers, Broncos, Cougars, and Thunderbirds, or about being able to drive sixty-five miles an hour, but she didn't want to disturb the temporary truce they seemed to have declared. "I make my living by designing clothes, and I'm happy to say that I'm fairly successful, which allows me to make trips to Eden's Gate several times a year. What more do you want to know?"

"Did you design what you were wearing when you arrived?" he asked, thinking it strange that she could make a living as a seamstress if the clothes she'd been wearing earlier were samples of her wares. Still, he couldn't complain about the way she'd looked. He remembered all too clearly how the pants she'd worn had hugged her hips and how shapely her slender legs had been.

"I designed the T-shirt," she told him, suddenly wondering what he would look like wearing one, the soft cotton hugging his wide, strong chest. The more she thought about it, the more she decided he'd look even better without a shirt of any kind.

Brad nodded, and then knowing he had to have the answer to the question that had been worrying him since he'd left her in the bedroom that morning, he broached the subject. "Earlier, you said you were going to stay right here so you could do something, but you never said what. What are you planning, Kacie? What is it you think you're going to do?"

Kacie's smile faltered, as did her light-hearted mood. She didn't want to ruin the beauty of this moment. This was her dream come true. She was here, alone with Brad in the garden just as she'd imagined so many times before. Yet, Kacie knew if she deliberately avoided answering him, his distrust of her would grow. "I know you don't believe what I've been telling you, but I want to stay to convince you that you're in danger." She lifted her worried gaze to his.

He saw how concerned she seemed to be, and he wanted to take her in his arms and tell her everything would be all right, but he didn't. He held back, knowing he had to have answers to his questions before he could even think of touching her. "How can you know I'm in danger, if you're not involved in some way?"

"Does it matter? All that matters is that I *am* here. Can't you just trust me and believe that I'm here to help you and protect you?"

The sincerity in her eyes truly touched his soul, and again the instinctive feeling that he should trust her filled him. He almost allowed himself to believe, but then reality returned. He told himself that he had found her in his bedroom with the map in her hands. She'd told him things that were impossible for her to know, yet she remained with him and her presence meant more than all the logic and reality in the world. She hadn't tried to escape or contact anyone with the vital information she knew. She said she wanted to protect him. He smiled at the thought, for he seriously doubted she'd be much help if it came down to a battle. Deciding to humor her for now, he replied, "You're not very big and certainly not very strong, but feel free to protect me all you want."

At his answer, Kacie realized she'd been holding her breath as she awaited his reply. She almost sighed in relief, but her tone was deadly serious when she spoke again. "Brad, if you really believe me, then whatever you do, don't get on any steamboats next month."

"I'll make it a point not to."

They fell silent, each assessing what the other had said. His response had been too lightly given for Kacie's complete peace of mind, but at least she had the satisfaction of knowing that she'd warned him and that she still had enough time to try to convince him further—she hoped.

As they continued their drive, Brad reached out and gently took her arm. He drew her to his side and, looping her arm through his, brought her hand to rest on his forearm and covered it with his own, holding the reins with his other hand. It still filled him with a sense of wonder that she thought she could defend him, and a great surge of protectiveness swelled within him. She was so delicate and feminine. He was the one who should be protecting her.

The unexpected intimacy of Brad's actions startled Kacie. She cast him a sidelong glance as they moved along, but found that his attention seemed to be completely focused on the path ahead. Without a word, she allowed herself to be swept along with him, and she found herself leaning into him, savoring his nearness and the new depth of meaning his gesture gave to their relationship.

As they rode farther away from the house, Kacie suddenly recognized the narrow, secluded path that led to the grotto.

"That's the grotto path, isn't it? It looks a little different, but not too much."

Brad hoped that eventually she would stop surprising him, but it hadn't happened yet. "Yes, the grotto's there."

"I have to see it. Can we please take a look? The

grotto was ... is my favorite place here. There were times when I would sit for hours, just thinking about everything that had happened. Remembering ..." She wanted to say "Remembering what I'd read about you and your father" but she stopped herself. Brad reined in the horses and they got out of the carriage. Kacie started down the path, and Brad followed.

Reaching the entrance, Kacie went inside. The small, manmade cave was cool, dark, and peaceful. It pleased her to discover that the Society's restoration was accurate. A crucifix and two candles stood on the small altar at the front, and two kneelers had been placed before it. When she'd visited it, she'd thought it a sad place, filled with tragic emotions from the past. But now the grotto felt serene and quietly blessed, and she couldn't resist taking the opportunity to pray for help to save Brad's life.

Brad stayed at the opening of the cave to watch her as she knelt down, and he was touched by the genuine nature of her reverence. Still, he was careful not to glance at the place where he kept his important messages hidden. After a moment of quiet reflection, Kacie rose and walked up to the altar. She reached out and touched several of the stones in the wall.

"Is this where the secret chamber is?" she asked, remembering where the director had told her it was located. She was amazed at how perfectly it was hidden.

He was again stunned by her revelation. "How did you know that? No one knows about that chamber but my father and me."

"I know, because that's where the director told me the Bible was finally found. They'd been looking for it for years."

She knew she'd shocked him again, so she went to stand beside him in the sunlight.

"Brad, please, trust me." Kacie put a reassuring hand on his arm, and she could feel the tension in him. "I would never do anything to hurt you."

Brad gazed down at her, spellbound. He could see only honesty and openness in her eyes. In the distance, a songbird called out its soft melody, and a gentle breeze stirred the leaves on the trees arching overhead, dappling the ground with a kaleidoscope of sunbeams. The warmth of the day wrapped them in an intimate embrace, and the moment seemed magical. They were alone in a world where time and reality were suspended. There was only the two of them, together.

If this was a dream, Kacie decided she was going to live it to the fullest. She took a tentative step closer to Brad, and as his strong arms enfolded her and brought her against him, it seemed her soul cried out with a joy so intense that it was almost painful. The contact was electric, and she knew as his lips sought hers that this was where she belonged—in Brad's arms.

Brad told himself it was crazy, but then the whole situation was crazy. He thought about the repercussions of what he was doing, but suddenly they didn't seem to matter. Nothing mattered except holding Kacie and kissing her. As his mouth moved over hers, all rational thought fled, and there was only Kacie—and the magic of her kiss.

Kacie clung to Brad's broad shoulders, savoring the heady thrill of his lips on hers. How many times had she imagined herself in his arms? She didn't know why this was happening, and she didn't care. She only wanted to enjoy him. His embrace was bliss, and she knew beyond a shadow of a doubt in that moment so sweet that she loved him and that her love was strong enough to endure anything.

5

BRAD and Kacie broke apart, each stunned by what had passed between them.

"I had to travel over one hundred thirty years back in time to find you," Kacie told him, her emerald eyes aglow with happiness, "but you were worth it. I've been looking for you all my life."

Brad lifted a hand as if to caress her cheek, but then changed his mind and let his hand drop.

The feelings surging through him were far too powerful to ignore, yet far too dangerous to act upon recklessly. He needed time to think.

Kacie read the uncertainty in his expression and understood. She'd had years to discover her love for him. He'd known her less than twenty-four hours. She smiled and broke the tension by asking, "Were we going to the stables next? I did want to see your horses. I've heard the bloodlines are superb."

Brad was glad to have a reason to move off down the path away from the intimacy of the grotto. Over the next several hours, after having shared their picnic lunch, he showed Kacie the plantation at work. He told her with pride of his plans to expand his stables and raise the finest horses in the state. He also told her he intended to free all the slaves when he took over the plantation and that he would give them each a parcel of land of their own to work in return for their staying on at Eden's Gate as laborers.

Kacie's admiration for Brad grew even more as he explained his firm belief that free men worked harder than "owned" men, that giving a man an incentive to do well paid dividends, whereas punishing him with whippings and brutality did not. Kacie found that Brad's dream of the future held opportunity and justice for everyone. This affirmation of his true character deepened her love for him. He was everything she'd imagined he would be.

It was late afternoon when they returned to the house. Brad went to discuss the business of the day with his father, while Kacie retreated upstairs to freshen up for dinner. While she'd been gone, the maid had moved the trunk of clothes and Kacie's few things into a guest bedroom just down the hall from Brad's room. The maid showed her to the new room now, and after drawing her bath and laying out a gown suitable to wear to dinner, she left Kacie in peace to soak and enjoy the quiet of the moment.

Kacie sighed as she rested in the hot, perfumed bath water. It had been an incredible day. The memory of Brad's kiss alone was enough to bring a smile to her lips. Being with him had been wonderful, and she wanted never to be parted from him.

But the bliss of the moment turned to horror as the real future broke into her thoughts. Not only was war on the horizon, but unless there was some way she could stop it, Brad would be killed next month. Panic jolted through her, and it took all of her willpower to curb it. She told herself that she would find a way to save him, but the fear that she would be whisked back to her own time before she got the chance cast a dark, threatening shadow on her happiness.

Her heart was suddenly as chilled as the bathwater she was sitting in, so Kacie climbed from the tub and began to dress for dinner. She donned the clothes the maid had set out and was pleased with the fit of the long-sleeved, high-necked emerald gown. She brushed her hair and left the room to find Brad.

She was descending the staircase when she saw him in the parlor talking to his father. Her heartbeat quickened as she paused halfway down the steps to watch him. Brad was the most devastatingly handsome man she'd ever seen. He had obviously taken the time to change for dinner, too, and he looked more wonderful than ever in his black pants and white shirt. She longed to run to him, to throw her arms around him and kiss him, but as much as she wanted to, she knew she couldn't. Ladies in 1860 just didn't do that kind of thing.

"Brad?" She called his name softly as she came to the parlor door.

"Kacie." His smile was warm and inviting. "Come in."

As she entered the room, Brad thought she was absolutely lovely. The green of the dress highlighted her sparkling eyes and fair complexion, and he could barely take his eyes off her. While he'd been talking with his father, Brad had tried to convince himself that her kiss hadn't really been as incredible as he'd thought, but seeing Kacie now after only a short time apart, he knew he was wrong. The kiss had been perfect, just as she was. If only there wasn't that remaining doubt about her . . .

"Shall we dine?" Jonas spoke up, breaking the sensual reverie that existed between the two young people.

The men escorted her into the dining room, and Brad seated her at his right at the table.

The meal was a sumptuous repast, and Kacie took great care to keep her conversation light yet interesting. She wanted to avoid anything that might be construed as controversial.

Jonas enjoyed the banter and realized with some surprise that this mysterious woman who called herself Kacie Cameron was well-read and intelligent. Brad had asked him earlier to put his suspicions about her aside and let him handle the situation, and Jonas had agreed. Though he still did not trust her completely, by the end of the evening he had to admit he did like her.

Brad walked Kacie to her room that night. "I hope you find the room comfortable."

"It's fine, thank you," she answered, very much aware of him beside her. They stopped outside her bedroom door, and as she opened it, she turned to him. "Thank you for today. I enjoyed being with you."

He stared down at her in the muted light, entranced by the strength of the attraction between them. "I enjoyed being with you, too." He said the words before he'd realized it. Then, puzzled by their whole situation, he couldn't stop himself from asking, "Who are you, Kacie? Why have you come into my life?"

Kacie, too, was caught up in the intimacy of the moment. She lifted her gaze to his as she answered, "To love you. . . ." Her voice was a whisper as she raised her hands to frame his face. The moment was Elysian, and she drew him down to her, unable to resist the temptation to kiss him once more. "Only to love you."

In the deserted quiet of the hall, their lips met and paradise was theirs. Brad wrapped his arms around her and held her close as his mouth moved over hers. He sought and found the bliss that had been his earlier at the grotto, and the power of it sent desire pounding through him.

Kacie didn't know whether to laugh or cry. This was ecstasy! She'd found her heaven! Yet even as she exulted, she realized that at any second she could be torn from Brad's arms forever. Anguish filled her. She wanted to be with him. She wanted to love him. Did she dare risk it? Kacie knew the answer even as she asked herself the question. She would take her happiness while she could. She would willingly surrender to the desire that promised her sweet fulfillment. Returning Brad's kiss with even more fervor, she pressed herself tightly against him and reveled in the contact.

Brad felt her willingness, and as much as he was enjoying every moment of holding her close, he knew he had to stop. There was too much at stake for him to give in to his own passion. Desire Kacie though he did, he had to be cautious. He ended the kiss and held her from him. He could see the confusion in her eyes, but knew he had to end it before things got out of hand.

"Good night, Kacie," he said softly, kissing her gently.

"Brad . . ." She sighed his name.

"I'll see you in the morning," he told her, ignoring his own desire that urged him to throw caution to the wind and make love to her.

When Kacie had gone into her room and closed the door, Brad retreated to his own bedroom. The night passed slowly for him as sleep proved elusive. His thoughts were of Kacie, and try as he might, he couldn't seem to put the glory of holding her out of his mind.

Kacie's own emotions were in turmoil, and she was up all night, too, trying to figure out what to do. Her heart told her she loved Brad and that she should take her happiness where she found it, no matter how crazy it seemed. But the painful truth of knowing that at any moment she could be torn from this place and year and returned to her real life in 1993 filled her with fear. She spent the night weighing her love for him against her fear of losing him forever, and by dawn she knew there could be no hiding from the truth of her feelings. She loved Brad, and she would celebrate that love for as long as this twisted quirk of fate allowed.

The days that followed passed in a whirlwind of activity. Kacie and Brad spent as much time together as they could, laughing and growing in their understanding of each other. Simple touches, soft smiles, and gentle kisses all took on a deeper meaning. Without spoken words, each seemed to understand the ultimate outcome of their carefully controlled desire.

They tried to ride together every day, and Kacie found that she loved riding down by the river. She enjoyed watching the Mississippi flow by and often imagined that the occasional steamboat they saw churning its way up or downstream was the *River Queen* on a tour. It was there one afternoon that they reined in their horses for a rest.

"Do you want to sit on the bank for a while?" Brad suggested.

"That would be lovely."

Ever the gentleman, he dismounted and hurried over to help her down. Kacie appreciated his help, and she rested her hands on his broad shoulders for balance as his hands found her waist to aid her in her descent. Her body brushed full-length against him as she slid to the ground, and the contact with his hard body left her breathless and glowing. The days she spent with Brad were the happiest she'd ever known.

"Thank you," she said as she gazed up at him, her eyes shining with love.

"My pleasure," Brad answered, and he meant it. He thoroughly enjoyed having Kacie in his arms.

"Do you want to sit under the trees?" she suggested as she moved regretfully away from him.

"Fine." He followed her to what was becoming their favorite place. It was a secluded, grassy spot that offered them a panoramic view of the river.

They sat there together, sharing soft kisses and watching the river flow by on its way to the sea.

"The river's timeless, you know. There's really no end to it and no beginning," Kacie told him thoughtfully. "Just like what I feel for you."

"And just what is it you feel for me?"

"You know I love you, Brad. I always have and I always will, no matter what happens."

"Nothing's going to happen," he reassured her after seeing the shadow of worry that shone momentarily in her eyes.

"I wish I were as certain as you are. The trouble is, I know what might happen. . . ."

"Kacie, we've never really talked about this . . ." He paused as if searching for the right words. "But do you really believe you were sent here from the future?"

"I know I was. One minute I was standing in your bedroom in the year 1993 and suddenly it was just like Scotty beamed me—"

"Scotty? You said that name before. Who's this Scotty?"

Kacie couldn't help laughing now that she remembered sighing Scotty's name when she fainted that very first night. "Scotty's a character in *Star Trek.*" At his confused expression, she quickly explained, "In my time, we have television and movies. They're pictures that move and talk."

"Right, and what else do you have a hundred and some odd years from now?"

"Well, that Western roan I told you about is really a car. That's a carriage with a motor instead of horses. And then there are airplanes and the space shuttle. You know we've even put men on the moon."

"That's impossible," he denied.

"So is my being here, but I'm here. The most important thing I think you'd like to know is that in my time, everyone is free. There is no slavery in the United States in 1993."

"I think I would like your times," he agreed, still refusing to completely believe that what she was saying was absolutely true, but having more and more trouble denying it. "What other inventions are there?"

"There's air conditioning that keeps houses cool in the summer, and paved expressways where cars can travel coast-to-coast quickly. There's electricity that gives us light indoors with the flick of a switch, and microwave ovens that cook dinner in less than five minutes."

"It sounds fascinating. I think I might like to visit your time and see all these things."

"I know you'd like my Mustang," she told him with a smile. "If I ever have to go back, I'll take you with me."

He slipped an arm around her shoulders as he drew her against him. "I hope you never go, Kacie, but if you do, don't go without me."

His words touched her deeply, and she turned to him and kissed him passionately.

"I don't ever want to leave you, Brad."

Their lips met again as if to seal that vow between them.

As the month of March ended and April began, Kacie's concern over the explosion grew. Although Brad had not been off the plantation in all that time, knowing that the critical moment was only a few days away filled her with dread.

She loved Brad with all her heart and soul, and was desperate to keep him safe. She knew that if she could just keep him with her until the seventh, everything would be fine.

On the afternoon of the fifth, while Kacie and Brad were having lunch, a messenger delivered a letter to Brad requesting his presence at an important business meeting. When he said he'd be back that evening, she didn't worry, but she did miss him terribly. The hours passed slowly for Kacie. She felt alone and lost without him.

As darkness fell and Brad still did not return, Kacie's imagination ran rampant. She dined alone with Jonas, her appetite gone as worry consumed her. When at last she heard him come in the front door, she was tremendously relieved. There was no hiding her pleasure at seeing him as he came to stand in the dining-room doorway to greet them.

"You're back," she breathed, her face alight with happiness.

"It took longer than I thought it would," he explained, his gaze on Kacie. He hadn't realized how much he enjoyed being with her until he'd been forced to leave her today. He'd been as eager as a schoolboy to return to her and had nearly run his horse into the ground on the way back.

"Is everything taken care of?" Jonas inquired from where he sat at the head of the table.

"It's all worked out," he answered, his expression growing shuttered at the mention of the meeting. He strode into the room and settled in at the table, pouring himself a cup of coffee from the silver service.

"Good. Are you hungry? Do you want some dinner?" Jonas asked him.

"Coffee's fine," he answered, drinking the hot, strong brew.

They fell into conversation, discussing what had happened that afternoon while he'd been gone, but while they talked of mundane things, his thoughts were far from ordinary. His meeting had been with his contacts in the Underground Railroad, and the news had not been good. Word was out that a raid was planned on several of the stations north of Eden's Gate. No one knew how the identity of the people on the Railroad had been discovered, and right now, no one cared. The important thing was getting word to them so they could be ready.

The possibility that Kacie might have been involved nagged at Brad, but having kept such a close watch on her for the last month, he refused to believe it. As he gazed at her now, he saw only beauty and innocence. His body stirred at the thought of holding her and kissing her, and he excused himself from the table. He couldn't afford a distraction.

Brad's departure was so abrupt that Kacie was hurt by it. She turned her attention back to the meal and finished dining with Jonas, acting as though nothing was bothering her.

Brad paced his bedroom. He needed to concentrate on the trip he had to make, but try as he might, he couldn't banish Kacie from his thoughts. He could think only of the honeyed taste of her lips, the sweetness of her body pressed against his. He knew this was not the time, but all the logic in the world did not ease the need in him. He loved her. It was as simple and basic and right as that. He'd tried to deny it, had tried to tell himself it was a purely physical attraction between them, but leaving her today had convinced him. He did love her.

The memory of her warning not to travel by steamer slipped into Brad's thoughts as he stood in the middle of his room debating his next move. He could make the trip upriver in half a day by boat, but as insane as it sounded, he knew he would travel by horseback in the morning. He didn't question the sense of it. He would just do it.

His thoughts moving back to the woman he loved, Brad knew he could stay away from her no longer. When he left at dawn, he would be gone for several days. He wanted to take the memory of her love with him. Tonight, he would go to her. Tonight, they would be together.

Brad left his bedroom by way of the balcony. He used the outdoor steps to reach the gardens, for there was something there he wanted to give to her. A moment later, he was back upstairs, standing outside of her still-empty bedroom.

Her room was dark as Kacie entered, and she paused just inside the door to light the lamp on the dresser. A soft, muted glow illuminated the room, and she turned to start getting ready for bed. It was then that she saw it—the single, delicate blossom on her pillow. Kacie's breath caught in her throat. She glanced up and saw Brad standing outside the open French doors at the rail of the balcony, his eyes upon her. Kacie's heart sang. She didn't say a word as she picked up the flower and moved to the doors.

"Brad . . ."

Their gazes locked, his dark, intense, and questioning, hers open, loving, and shining with invitation.

"Kacie . . ." Her name was a groan on his lips as he crossed the short distance between them in two strides and swept her into his embrace. He'd wanted her for so long, and tonight he would have her. His mouth sought hers in a blazing kiss as he crushed her against his chest.

Kacie let the blossom drop as she wrapped her arms around Brad and returned his embrace full measure. She'd loved him forever and would no longer deny her need to be one with him.

They came together passionately, each starved for a taste of the other's love. When Brad lifted Kacie into his arms to carry her to the bed, she looped her arms around his neck and kissed him. He lay her upon the softness, then followed her down, his big body covering hers in a heated brand.

Kacie gloried in the sensuousness of his body on hers, and she reached for him hungrily, craving this closeness with him, reveling in the wonder of it. Brad was there with her, loving her. As he caressed her, she responded openly, knowing this was what she'd always wanted.

Driven by desire, Brad unfastened the bodice of Kacie's gown. He parted the fabric and slipped her chemise lower to bare her breasts to his heated kisses. Kacie was mindless with pleasure as Brad's intimate touch sent shivers of excitement through her.

"Love me, Brad," she told him huskily as she began to move restlessly, invitingly beneath him.

Eager to be rid of all barriers between them, Brad drew slightly away from her as he helped her to undress. She felt a bit shy before him, but the warmth of his gaze soon eased her nervousness.

"You're beautiful," he declared, his dark gaze wandering over her slender figure. From the lush fullness of her breasts to the gentle curves of her hips, she was delectable.

"So are you," Kacie responded, unbuttoning his shirt and pushing it from his shoulders to bare his hard-muscled chest to her caress.

They lay back together, exploring each other and arousing each other to a fiery pitch. His hands were never still, skimming over her satiny flesh, cupping and molding, teasing and pleasuring her until she was aching for more.

"Love me, Brad . . . please . . ." she whispered, her mouth seeking and finding his in a passionate exchange.

When at last he stripped away the rest of his clothes and came to her, Kacie opened to him like a flower to the warmth of the sun, and when he moved to possess her, she welcomed him eagerly. Brad kissed her as he began to move, pressing deep within her past the proof of her innocence. Made one by the act of love, they knew paradise. With tender touches and soft words of love, they luxuriated in the rare glory of their joining. Then, unable to hold back any longer, Brad moved in the timeless rhythm of love and possession.

It was all new to Kacie. Though she'd had many boyfriends who would have been more than willing to take her virginity, she'd never wanted to be with any of them. Brad, however, was different, and Kacie knew this was what she'd been saving herself for. She loved him and wanted to give all of herself to him.

They moved together, surging to new heights of passion, each kiss and caress taking them higher and higher until ecstasy burst upon them. Their legs entwined, their bodies still one, they lay in each other's arms enjoying passion's peaceful afterglow.

"I love you, Kacie," Brad professed in a husky voice.

"I love you, too," Kacie responded, kissing him desperately. She was thrilled by his declaration, but the fear of losing him was always with her. Having known the beauty of his love now, she shivered at the thought that at any minute it could all end.

Brad felt her shiver. "What's wrong?"

"I'm afraid," she whispered, her eyes clouded with worry as she tightened her arms around him.

"There's nothing to be afraid of, Kacie."

"You don't understand, Brad." There was real anguish in her voice.

"Yes, I do, love." He reached down and lifted her chin so their eyes met. "I love you, Kacie. As long as we have each other, nothing can come between us."

Kacie wanted to believe that. She wanted to believe with all her heart. "But there are things that could happen, things that could tear us apart."

He interrupted her with a soft kiss. "No, love. As long as we love each other and have faith, everything will be all right. You trust me, don't you?"

"With my life."

"As I trust you with mine. We'll be fine, Kacie. Nothing will separate us. Nothing."

"I hope you're right," she whispered.

They lay quietly together. The languor of love stole over them, and Brad drifted off to sleep first.

The turmoil of her emotions kept Kacie awake. She was filled with love for Brad, yet terrified of losing that love. As she nestled beside him, she swore that she would do everything in her power to save his life. If she accomplished at least that much, it would all have been worth it.

6

"WHATEVER you do, son, be careful," Jonas warned. It was an hour before dawn, and Brad had just told him that he was leaving to deliver the warning about the raid to the next two stations. "Will you be back tonight?"

"No. I'm going by horseback. I won't be back until tomorrow."

Jonas was puzzled. "Why ride? You could be back tonight if you went by steamer."

Brad wasn't sure how to explain his decision so that it would make sense to his father. He knew it was crazy, but he trusted Kacie. "Kacie seems to think that something terrible will happen if I go by boat."

"You believe Kacie? Something just might happen if you follow her advice! She could be setting you up! You'll be riding alone—"

"Kacie's not setting me up," he denied firmly, no doubt in his mind.

"How can you be so sure?"

"I've fallen in love with her."

"You're in love with her? But what about that wild tale of hers about being from the future?"

For a moment, Brad's expression reflected the confusion he felt over her claims, but then the truth of his love shone through. "I don't know where she came from, and I don't care. All I know is that I want her with me always. When I get back from this trip, I plan to ask her to marry me."

"You do?" There was no denying that Jonas was stunned.

"I love her, and I trust her."

"You two are very different, you know," he cautioned.

"So were you and Mother," Brad countered with a grin. "She was a Yankee, too."

They stood together in silence, their gazes meeting in understanding. Jonas knew his son's mind was made up, so he went to him and put an arm around his shoulders. "I want only your happiness."

"My future's with Kacie. I want to spend the rest of my life with her."

Anxious to leave so that he could return that much sooner, Brad left for the stables. He wanted to be well on his way by sunup. As he rode off toward his rendezvous, his thoughts were with Kacie and the love they would share once he returned.

In the darkness, Arlin Gates, the man hired by Daniel Lawrence to keep an eye on Bradford

Hampton, watched and waited. His lonely vigil was rewarded when he saw Brad ride away from Eden's Gate just before dawn. Knowing the man who'd hired him would be pleased, he followed Brad.

Kacie awoke slowly. The glory of Brad's love-making the night before still filled her. Expecting to find Brad slumbering peacefully beside her, she smiled as she rolled over to face him. It surprised Kacie to discover that he had left her, and the realization jarred her fully awake. After a moment's reflection, though, she thought she understood why Brad had gone. It certainly wouldn't have been proper for him to have spent the entire night in her bed. Her happiness returned, and she got up and dressed quickly, eager to see Brad again. She wanted to make sure that last night had really happened, that it had not been a wonderful dream.

A short time later, Kacie was standing in the dining room at the foot of the table, facing Jonas where he sat at the head. Her expression mirrored her terror. She couldn't find Brad anywhere, and it was the sixth of April. Frightened, she asked, "Where's Brad?"

"He had to leave early this morning to take care of some business in town."

"Will he be back today?"

"No, he thought it would be late tomorrow before he could return."

Brad was traveling and this was the day of the fateful explosion! Kacie was in a panic. She was afraid to ask, but she had to know. "How did he travel?"

Jonas heard the very real concern in her voice. "He told me about your warning, and that's why he went on horseback, Kacie. It's a short trip by steamer, but almost a full-day one by road."

"Thank God," she murmured in tremendous relief at the news.

"Kacie," Jonas began slowly, completely confused, "I don't understand any of this."

"I love Brad, Jonas. That's the only thing any of us needs to understand," she told him. "I love him more than you can imagine, but I'm afraid for him, too."

"Why would you be afraid for him?" he demanded, trying to get to the truth of her background.

"I will not betray you and Brad, Jonas. You have to believe that. And you have to believe that Brad's never betrayed any confidences to me. It's just that I have a feeling I know what he's doing, and sometimes he can be too brave and too self-sacrificing for his own good. When he believes he's right, there's no stopping him, and I just want to keep him safe. I don't want anything to happen to him."

"But how can you know any of this if Brad hasn't told you?"

Kacie's gaze met his and he found no guile or deceit there.

"You have to trust me. Brad does."

For a moment, time was suspended as Jonas

chose whether to believe in his son's judgment of this woman or to cling to his own doubts and fears. Finally, the pleading look in her eyes convinced him. He would trust her.

"He'll be back tomorrow, and I'm sure he'll be on horseback."

Brad rode at a steady, ground-eating pace. He had an uneasy feeling about the trip and took extra caution as he traveled. He sensed that someone was following him, but he never caught a glimpse of anyone and finally decided it was his concern for secrecy that was making him suspect the worst. These were dangerous times, and his foes were deadly, cunning people who would stop at nothing to put an end to the Railroad.

It was late afternoon, almost dark, when Brad reached the small upriver town where he was to meet his contact. He entered the bar where messages were passed and sat down to wait. The place was relatively quiet, and had he had the time, Brad would have waited until there was a crowd, for it was easier to blend in that way. Today, however, it was important that he not delay. No one knew exactly when the raid was to take place, and he had to warn his compatriots right away.

Shortly after he'd entered the bar, while he was waiting to give the news to his contact, Brad noticed a man enter. There seemed nothing out of the ordinary or suspicious about him, so at first Brad paid him little attention. When

Brad's contact arrived, he quietly passed on the warning to the man, who was known to him as "Saint," identifying himself as he always did by his own code name, "Adam." Brad waited a few minutes after Saint had departed, then paid his bill and left, too. He knew it was late, but he had one more stop to make that couldn't wait.

Arlin had been silently observing everything, and he knew his boss was going to be pleased with what he'd discovered. Lawrence's hunch had been right: Brad Hampton was involved with the Underground Railroad. Rather than head back right away with the news, Arlin decided to trail after Hampton just a little longer to see if he could find out where the next stop was. Lawrence had told him there would be a big bonus if he brought back any other information he could use.

Brad saw Arlin come out of the tavern shortly after him. He thought the man was acting a bit strangely. Deciding to be cautious, Brad chose not to continue on to his next rendezvous. Instead, he walked down toward the river, just to see what would happen. It did not surprise him when the man came after him on foot.

Brad trusted his instincts, and at this moment his instincts were warning him of danger. Stepping into a deserted alley, he waited until the man had come even with him and then surprised him by grabbing his arm and yanking him around to face him.

"I want to talk to you," Brad seethed, his grip on Arlin threatening.

"Me? Why do you want to talk to me?"

"I want to know who you are and why you're following me."

"I wasn't following you—"

"I know better," Brad told him with undisguised menace, giving him a shake.

Arlin paled as he realized this man knew he was lying. He didn't know how Hampton had spotted him, but this wasn't the time to worry about it. He had to get away. Reaching down with the smoothness of one used to fighting with knives, Arlin drew his knife out of his boot and slashed at Brad, cutting his upper arm.

Brad was livid, and his temper erupted. They grappled until Brad finally managed to overpower Arlin and knock the knife out of his hand.

"Who sent you after me?" Brad snarled, slamming Arlin up against the side of a building.

Momentarily defeated, Arlin answered, "Lawrence sent me . . . Daniel Lawrence."

"I should have known. And what about Cameron? How is Kacie Cameron involved in this?" Brad had to know, he had to find out.

"Whoever this Casey Cameron is, he ain't involved," Arlin answered quickly. "Lawrence hired me and told me to watch you and report back to him."

Brad's relief was immense at the discovery that Kacie was as innocent as he'd hoped. In that instant, Brad let his guard down, and Arlin knew it.

Though not a brave man, Arlin was a survivor. He made his move the moment Brad wasn't expecting it, jerking free and diving to grab his knife. He pounced on Brad as he turned to do battle and managed to pin him to the ground. He grinned down into Brad's face, showing uneven, blackened teeth.

"Once I tell Lawrence what I know, you're dead, Hampton, and so is your family. Hell, I might as well save them the trouble and end your miserable life right now!" Arlin was ready to cut his throat in a single wicked motion, but Brad wasn't about to give up the battle.

With all the strength he could muster, Brad threw Arlin off. They struggled together, rolling over and over on the ground, fighting for supremacy. As they grappled, Arlin managed to get on top. He raised his arm to stab Brad, but Brad reacted instinctively and grabbed his arm in a viselike grip. Brad forced Arlin's arm downward with all his might, twisting it as he did so the knife was pointing away from him.

In the face of Brad's unrelenting pressure, Arlin's strength failed him. His arm buckled, and his knife drove deep into his own flesh. He collapsed and lay still, wounded on his side. Brad's own bleeding arm was aching and he was exhausted by the fight. He pushed Arlin's limp body away from him, got to his feet, and staggered over to lean against one of the buildings.

Arlin's agony was unbearable. The stab wound was like a burning flame in his flesh, but he was not about to give up. As Brad leaned against the building, his back to him, Arlin lurched to his feet and with what strength he had left, he hit

Brad from behind. Brad fell, dazed, as Arlin fled on foot, heading for the riverfront, desperate to escape back to Lawrence so he could tell him what he'd learned.

An older steamer, heavily ladened with merchandise, had already raised its gangplank and was pulling out on its way downriver as Arlin reached the levee. In one last frantic effort, he leaped onboard. In the darkness, no one saw him.

Brad had been momentarily stunned by the man's unexpected assault, but he recovered quickly. He ran after Arlin and made an even more desperate leap to the boat's deck. It was close, but Brad managed to get a tenuous hold on the railing. He hung there precariously for a moment while he struggled to catch his breath. Though his arm hurt, Brad finally hauled himself onboard. He, too, went unnoticed in the night.

Once he'd regained his footing on deck, Brad looked around. The deck was stacked high with crates and merchandise, making it a jumbled maze. Ignoring his throbbing arm, he began to search for Arlin. It took over an hour, but he finally found him, barely conscious, in a remote corner near the livestock pen. He bent over him and took him in his arms.

"You may have stopped me," Arlin gasped, "but you won't stop the raid."

"The hell I won't," Brad vowed. "You're going to die if you don't get help soon. Give me the exact date of the raid and I'll do everything I can to save you."

A flicker of hope shone on Arlin's face. "The ninth," he whispered, then went limp in Brad's arms, his head lolling to one side. He was dead.

Distraught over the man's death, Brad moved away to the rail and leaned heavily on it. He was deeply troubled by Arlin's death, but at least now he knew exactly when the raid would take place. He thought of Kacie then, and of what Arlin had told him. Hearing that Kacie hadn't betrayed him had filled him with joy. Everything she'd said had been the truth.

The steamer gave a mournful whistle, and the realization hit Brad. He was on a steamboat in the middle of the Mississippi! His hands gripped the rail. If Kacie had told him the truth about so many things, had she also told him the truth about the steamboat explosion? His stomach lurched sickeningly as he realized the date. It was the sixth. He was on a steamer. Suddenly he heard an ominous rumble and felt the ship tremble.

Kacie was beside herself with worry all day. Though Jonas assured her that Brad had made the trip on horseback, she knew she wouldn't rest until the sixth of April had ended and he was back safely in her arms. Hour after hour she wandered the halls of Eden's Gate trying to distract herself, but everywhere she looked there were memories of Brad. Nothing worked. She prayed that his love for her was true and his trust unshakable.

Night fell, and Kacie's fears grew. There were

only a few hours left of the terrible day, yet she had never known time to pass so slowly. Each minute seemed an eternity.

At Jonas' insistent invitation, Kacie joined him for dinner. Her attempt at pretending normalcy was an abject failure. Her conversation lagged, and despite her best effort to eat, she tasted nothing of the food placed before her.

"If you don't mind, I think I'll say good night," she said.

"I'd really enjoy it if you'd stay and keep me company for a while." It was as close as Jonas could come to admitting that he, too, was concerned about Brad.

She read the unspoken worry in his expression and realized he was just as upset as she was. "Of course."

As they went into the parlor to have their coffee, Kacie glanced at the clock. It was almost nine. Just as they took their seats on the sofa, they heard a distant yet terrible roar that shattered the tense quiet of the night.

"Oh, God . . ." She came to her feet. The delicate china cup she'd been holding slipped from her fingers, and she jumped as it shattered on the floor. The horrible thought that the steamer had just exploded and that she hadn't changed anything assailed her. Brad had said he was going to ride. He had told his father he wouldn't take the steamer, yet there was still the chance . . . Heartsick with fear, she gathered up her skirts and ran from the room.

Jonas followed her and they raced down to

the river landing. Over the tops of the trees, the glow of the burning steamer turned the upriver night sky a harsh orange-red. People were dying and there was little they could do.

"Wait at the house!" Jonas ordered Kacie. "I'll take some men with me and we'll see if we can help."

"I want to come with you!" she protested.

"No, you'll only slow us down! Now do as I say! I'll be back as soon as I can!" He barked out orders to the men who had joined them at the landing to watch the spectacle, and within a few minutes they were riding across country toward the disaster.

Kacie's nerves were stretched taut as she watched them ride off. She felt helpless and very, very frightened. What if she hadn't changed anything? What if, in spite of all her warnings, Brad had boarded that steamer and died?

Kacie bit back a sob at the thought and with tears blinding her, stumbled back up the walk. She didn't even consider going back to the big house. Instead, she went straight to the grotto. She lit the candles and knelt on the kneeler. She clasped her shaking hands tightly before her, and her eyes closed as she prayed fervently to God for His help. The thought of never holding Brad or kissing him or talking with him again was just too much for her to bear.

"Please, don't let Brad be dead! Please, if You didn't want me to save him, why did You send be back here? Oh, God, please . . ." Tears fell as she pleaded unceasingly for his safety. "I love

Brad with all my heart, God, but I'll give him up forever if he's alive and well . . ."

Kacie remained on her knees, praying desperately through the long, dark night. She tried to tell herself that Brad had not been on the steamer. She tried to convince herself that he would return to her happy and healthy the next day, but always the ugly memories of history as she'd learned it intruded and destroyed what little solace she'd had with those thoughts.

Hours passed and she heard nothing. Still, she did not abandon her vigil. Brad was out there somewhere, and she would not leave the grotto until he was back with her. Over and over, she recited every prayer she knew.

Her maid sought her out to see if she was all right, and Kacie bid her to bring her the Bible. When she did, Kacie clutched it to her as she continued to beseech God with her unending pleas for help. She had been touching the Holy Book when she'd first come to Brad, and she hoped with all her heart that this time it would return him to her.

Dawn came, the rays of the morning sun cutting through the darkness in the grotto. Kacie took little notice. Her entire being was focused on Brad. Not knowing her love's fate filled her with a devastating agony. He had to be alive! He had to!

Kacie was concentrating so hard on her prayers that she didn't hear the footsteps approaching.

"Kacie?"

Only when Jonas said her name was she jarred

back to an awareness of her surroundings, and she trembled as she lifted her fearful gaze to him.

"Jonas . . . Brad, is he . . . was he . . . ?" she asked in a strangled voice.

"I'm here, Kacie . . . I'm right here . . ." Brad stepped from behind his father. His face was battered and bruised and his clothing was torn, but he was alive.

"Brad! Oh, thank God!" Kacie cried as she launched herself into his arms. Her heart sang with joy as she clung to him. He was alive! Alive!

Jonas saw the depth of their love and understood.

"Why were you on the steamer? What happened?" she asked frantically as she held him close.

"It doesn't matter, sweetheart. All that matters is that you were right. If you hadn't warned me about the explosion, I wouldn't have known to jump from the ship when I heard the rumbling of the engine, and I'd be dead now. Thanks to you, my work can continue and more lives than you know will be saved." As he spoke, he drew the map from his pocket and slipped it into the Bible, still in Kacie's hands. "I love you, Kacie. I want us to be together always." Brad did not know what forces had brought her to him, but he knew he wanted never to be separated from her. She was his life.

"Oh, Brad . . . I love you . . ."

His hand covered hers on the Bible as he drew

her to him and kissed her, their lips meeting in a sweet celebration of their future. A dizzying, whirlwind of emotion enfolded them as they embraced. They clung together, one in heart, mind, and soul. Somewhere, as if from far away, they heard Jonas calling their names.

The kiss ended, yet Brad and Kacie did not move apart. Wrapped in each other's arms, they remained standing together until the light-headed sensation that had gripped them passed. For an instant, they had both thought it was their passion and desperation that had filled them with such an unusual feeling, but then they looked up. Jonas was gone, and Kacie could hear the sounds of modern-day living nearby.

"Dear God . . ." she murmured. The Bible was still clutched in her hand, and she moved out of Brad's embrace to look outside. She saw the gardener at work using a power tool and turned back to Brad, not knowing whether to be happy or scared.

"What is it? Where's my father?" Brad asked, seeing the strange look on her face and going to stand beside her and look out.

"It's 1993, Brad. You've come back with me." She was awestruck by the realization.

"Kacie?" Brad glanced down at her, remembering everything she'd told him about being from the future. He'd doubted her, and now . . .

"I don't know how or why, Brad. I just know we're here." She took his hand in hers as she stood on tiptoe to kiss him again.

"I have to go back," he insisted. "There are

things I have to do. People are counting on me."

She lifted one hand to caress his cheek. "We have no control over this time travel. Don't you think I would have returned home in the beginning if I'd had the chance?"

"Then all my work was for nothing."

"No, no, love. It's better that you're here, safe with me. Your father continued your work, but then the war came."

"War?" Brad tensed, struggling to understand and accept what she was saying.

"The North and South fought, and though the South lost the war, in the long run, my darling, you won."

"I don't understand." He frowned.

"Remember when I told you that everyone was free in my day? Well, slavery was abolished. Your work did mean something," she assured him. "Come with me." She took his hand and drew him out of the grotto and into the garden.

Brad took a step away from her and stared around in surprise. In the distance, a car was coming up the now-paved driveway, and he was fascinated as he watched its progress. A roar high overhead startled him, and he looked up in total amazement.

Kacie was nervous as she watched him. She wasn't sure just how he was going to react to being brought forward to her time, and her heart was pounding with a mixture of fear and hope. When he turned to her after a moment, she waited expectantly for him to speak.

"I was right to believe in you," he said softly, his smile gentle and loving. "Show me the way, love. I'll follow wherever you lead."

Kacie smiled back at him and took his hand once more. "You showed me your world. Now I'll show you mine."

As Kacie led Brad into the sunlight, she gave thanks for the glory of the new day, for the future she knew would be theirs, and for the trust of the man who held her hand in his.

Bobbi Smith

BOBBI SMITH is a firm believer in the power of love. Love, she feels, does indeed make the world go round. It is the perfection of human nature and our true reason for being. Love offers us a reason to get out of bed in the morning. Love gives us the strength to keep on going against the most insurmountable odds. Love alone provides the nourishment for the soul. It cheers the sick and lonely and brings smiles and tears to those who give and receive it. Love cannot be analyzed, for often it is far from logical. It is the most wondrous gift we can give someone, the most priceless present to receive. And yet, though it costs nothing, it cannot be bought at any price. Love cannot be touched or captured, locked up or hoarded and saved. Love must be shared or it dies. Love is pure, selfless, and everlasting. Love is timeless, transcending all barriers, touching our hearts even across vast distances and untold years. Love does indeed conquer all. To be loved is to live happily ever after, and that is Bobbi Smith's wish for you.

Avon Romances—
the best in exceptional authors and unforgettable novels!

LORD OF MY HEART Jo Beverley
76784-8/$4.50 US/$5.50 Can

BLUE MOON BAYOU Katherine Compton
76412-1/$4.50 US/$5.50 Can

SILVER FLAME Hannah Howell
76504-7/$4.50 US/$5.50 Can

TAMING KATE Eugenia Riley
76475-X/$4.50 US/$5.50 Can

THE LION'S DAUGHTER Loretta Chase
76647-7/$4.50 US/$5.50 Can

CAPTAIN OF MY HEART Danelle Harmon
76676-0/$4.50 US/$5.50 Can

BELOVED INTRUDER Joan Van Nuys
76476-8/$4.50 US/$5.50 Can

SURRENDER TO THE FURY Cara Miles
76452-0/$4.50 US/$5.50 Can

Coming Soon

SCARLET KISSES Patricia Camden
76825-9/$4.50 US/$5.50 Can

WILDSTAR Nicole Jordan
76622-1/$4.50 US/$5.50 Can

Buy these books at your local bookstore or use this coupon for ordering:

Mail to: Avon Books, Dept BP, Box 767, Rte 2, Dresden, TN 38225   B
Please send me the book(s) I have checked above.
☐ My check or money order—no cash or CODs please—for $_____ is enclosed
(please add $1.50 to cover postage and handling for each book ordered—Canadian
residents add 7% GST).
☐ Charge my VISA/MC Acct#_____ Exp Date _____
Phone No _____ Minimum credit card order is $6.00 (please add postage
and handling charge of $2.00 plus 50 cents per title after the first two books to a maximum
of six dollars—Canadian residents add 7% GST). For faster service, call 1-800-762-0779.
Residents of Tennessee, please call 1-800-633-1607. Prices and numbers are subject to
change without notice. Please allow six to eight weeks for delivery.

Name_____
Address _____
City _____ State/Zip _____
                                                          ROM 0992

America Loves Lindsey!

The Timeless Romances of #1 Bestselling Author

Johanna Lindsey

PRISONER OF MY DESIRE 75627-7 $5.99 US $6.99 Can
Spirited Rowena Belleme *must* produce an heir, and the magnificent Warrick deChaville is the perfect choice to sire her child—though it means imprisoning the handsome knight.

ONCE A PRINCESS 75625-0 $5.95 US/$6.95 Can
From a far off land, a bold and brazen prince came to America to claim his promised bride. But the spirited vixen spurned his affections while inflaming his royal blood with passion's fire.

GENTLE ROGUE 75302-2/$5.50 US/$6.50 Can
On the high seas, the irrepressible rake Captain James Malory is bested by a high-spirited beauty whose love of freedom and adventure rivaled his own.

WARRIOR'S WOMAN 75301-4/$4.95 US/$5.95 Can

MAN OF MY DREAMS 75626-9/$5.99 US/$6.99 Can

Coming Soon

ANGEL 75628-5/$5.99 US/$6.99 Can

Buy these books at your local bookstore or use this coupon for ordering:

Mail to: Avon Books, Dept BP, Box 767, Rte 2, Dresden, TN 38225   B
Please send me the book(s) I have checked above.
☐ My check or money order—no cash or CODs please—for $_____ is enclosed
(please add $1.50 to cover postage and handling for each book ordered—Canadian
residents add 7% GST).
☐ Charge my VISA/MC Acct#_____Exp Date_____
Phone No_____Minimum credit card order is $6.00 (please add postage
and handling charge of $2.00 plus 50 cents per title after the first two books to a maximum
of six dollars—Canadian residents add 7% GST). For faster service, call 1-800-762-0779.
Residents of Tennessee, please call 1-800-633-1607. Prices and numbers are subject to
change without notice. Please allow six to eight weeks for delivery.

Name_____

Address_____

City_____ State/Zip_____

JLA 0892